How to Ruin a Wedding

SOPHIE ANDREWS

Edited by Libby Rosonet

Accuracy Read by Despina Karras

Cover Design by Ellis Leigh of Kinship Press

Digital ISBN 978-1-957580-43-2

Paperback ISBN 978-1-957580-44-9

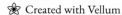 Created with Vellum

Content Note

How to Ruin a Wedding is a romantic comedy inspired by the very unromantic comedy, My Best Friend's Wedding. While this is a romance with a happily ever after, it does contain a few mentions of domestic abuse, alcoholism, and paraplegia due to a car accident.

For Julia Roberts- thanks for showing all the girls with big mouths and bigger laughs, we're totally beautiful.

One

People might think I'm a good person, but I'm not.

The truth is I'm a liar.

When my cousin, grinning happily with a sheen of sweat on her forehead, caught my arm after the crowd dispersed from the dance floor following the screaming rendition of "Don't Stop Believin'" to ask what I thought about DJ Gunner, I gave her a thumbs up.

But that's a lie.

The middle-aged *Jersey Shore* knock-off was terrible, with his LED shutter glasses and constant "Lemme hear it!" and "Shake it! Shake it!" He even brought blow-up props, a few guitars and saxophones that only my Uncle Joe touched, playing his own rock concert beneath the flashing neon lights displaying the initials of the bride and groom. And the playlist? "Electric Slide" and "YMCA"? Come on.

I tossed back the last of my champagne, watching Dad spin Mom around in her wheelchair. Nothing like an open bar to bring out the best in people on the dance floor, including my parents.

But the food was good. Not a lie.

Tyler, my best friend and trusty plus-one, stuffed the last of his roasted potatoes in his mouth and draped a lazy arm around the back of my chair as the next song slowed down. "Feel like dancing?"

"To 'Sweet Caroline'? Could this wedding be any whiter?"

He smirked and leaned in, his breath hot on my bare shoulder when he sang "Bah bah bah" on cue during the chorus. "And, yes, this is a very white wedding," he said, referring to my family—my very Irish, very white family—in varying degrees of pale and porcelain.

"Oh, Jaysus, Mary, and Joseph." I quirked my lips to the side to mimic Nellie, my great-grandmother who had come over from Ireland with my great-grandfather, Sean.

"Hey!" At the table next to ours, Uncle Pat, two drinks beyond two sheets to the wind, leaned over the back of his chair. "You sound just like Granny."

I inched closer to Tyler, away from the fog of whiskey.

"My god, you look just like her too."

"Thanks," I said with a nod, like I hadn't heard it before. I'd inherited my great-grandmother's dark wavy hair, blue-gray eyes, and pointed nose, and I had been told on more than one occasion I had the same "ferocious" spirit.

"You know," Uncle Pat said, pointing at me with the index finger of his hand that was curled around a glass of Jameson, "I think it was Nellie who was the fighter. More so than Sean. She hated the English. *Hated* them."

When he paused for a sip of whiskey, Tyler trailed his fingers down my arm, squeezing my hand. He'd been around long enough to know the story and how Uncle Pat could ramble. "Come on," he whispered in my ear, "before he starts about the war."

I stood with Tyler's hand in mine, and Uncle Pat tipped his head back, blinking up at my best friend, who had come to every major family event with me for the last decade. "Do I know you?"

Tyler patted my uncle's shoulder. "Yeah, I'm Tyler Rodriguez, you've met me a few times. Congratulations on your daughter's—"

"What's the difference between an Irish wedding and an Irish funeral?" Uncle Pat asked, rubbing at his red nose.

"I don't know." Tyler shrugged, although I was pretty sure he'd heard that one already.

"There's one less drunk," Uncle Pat and I both said at the same time.

"Good one." Tyler played along good-naturedly. "But I'm gonna take your niece out for a spin." He twirled me to the dance floor with a flourish, and I gave into a laugh. He was a show-off, but I was used to it by now and strung my arms around his neck as his hands circled my waist.

We had danced together so many times like this that his fingertips automatically found my spine, and I pressed my body against his. I never tired of feeling his jaw against my cheek or the low rumble of his voice as he hummed the melody of the song in my ear. I glanced up at him. That was one of his best qualities, his height. I could wear heels, and he was still taller than me. I asked, "Are you having a good time?"

He slanted his gaze down with a teasing smile. "You know how much I love Mahoney weddings. Good drinks, good jokes."

I rested my chin on his shoulder. "They should be cutting the cake soon so we can sneak out after."

"You want to leave?"

"You don't?" I jerked my head back, the curls of my up-do bouncing with the movement. Now that Ellen and Austin were married, my bridesmaid duties were officially over, and I could really use a Dairy Queen blizzard.

This wasn't our first wedding together, probably not even

the tenth. Tyler and I had always been each other's dates, usually giggling at some inappropriate joke in the corner, and then hightailing out the back door for some fast food.

"I don't know," he said. "We don't have to. Your uncles haven't even argued over who gets the mic first to sing."

I eyed him, trying to understand why he wouldn't follow our normal routine, but his gaze had already drifted around the ballroom. "Okay," I agreed after a moment. "We'll stay."

He swayed us in a slow circle so I could see the trio of pink clustered by the bar. The other bridesmaids were Ellen's three best friends, all dainty little things. The pictures of us lined up would be ridiculous with me, at almost six feet, a head taller than the rest.

"What are their names again?" Tyler asked.

"The other girls?"

"Yeah."

"The blonde with tattoos is Jess C. The platinum blonde is Jess T. And Sarah is the short-haired blonde one."

Tyler sniffed a laugh in my ear. He may have had a glow-up during college, but he never lost his sniffling chuckle. If a rat could laugh it would sound like him. I loved his dumb laugh.

"Sarah's the maid of honor, right?"

I rolled my eyes at *that* tone. "Yes."

It's not like I wasn't used to the man Tyler had become. We'd grown up next-door to each other, playing tag and riding scooters as kids. In high school, we'd sat together at lunch while I'd completed my AP homework, and he had taken apart and then put back together some new gadget. Our prom photo held a place of prominence in my bedroom, right next to the one in our caps and gowns. We'd visited each other in college as often as we could. It's where he'd put on a solid fifteen pounds of muscle and started to understand women actually liked men who were future software engineers. Then when he'd gotten the IT job that paid him to

4

travel all over the country, he'd promptly learned how to play catch up on all the hook-ups he'd missed when he was younger, charming women with his dimples and just-this-side-of-cocky smile.

I knew the whole playbook, had dissected it with him during our late nights together. I laughed along like a best friend would, giving advice when necessary. But all the while, I've been silently waiting, biding my time until Tyler ran out of steam and realized I had been there all along.

When Neil Diamond's song ended, Tyler stepped back, dropped his hand to mine, our pinkies folding around each other as they often tended to do, and asked, "You want another drink?"

"Nah, I'm good."

He strolled off to the bar, perching himself next to Sarah, and I made my way back to the now empty table. I traced the condensation on my water glass with the tip of my index finger, trying not to notice the way Tyler—all golden tanned and angular features—leaned on his elbow with his legs crossed at the ankles as if he was so cool and casual, he'd fall over if it weren't for the bar. He fixed his thick square glasses and skimmed a hand through his hair, pushing it away from his temples.

That was the thing about him. He was effortless. The very attributes that'd made him uncool when we were kids—his smarts, his height, his glasses, his mess of curly hair—made him a hot commodity now.

DJ Gunner held a blow-up boom box on his shoulder and announced the bride and groom were cutting the cake as my mom rolled up next to me, her cheeks flushed from exertion.

"Where's Dad?" I asked, scooching my mother's water glass closer to the edge of the table so she could lift it up, drinking from a straw.

"You know him," she said, carefully placing the glass back

down. He was no doubt standing outside of some emergency exit door, polishing off a cigarette only to pretend he hadn't.

"He's got to quit."

She lifted one shoulder, grazing the ends of her sandy hair, which I had blow-dried and curled this morning. "I know but..."

She didn't have to finish the sentence. Mom had told me a few years ago that she wouldn't begrudge him his one vice after all he did for her. And who was I to argue?

"Ellen is beautiful, isn't she?" Mom said but before I could answer she went on, "It was a good idea to add the illusion neckline otherwise..." She tucked her forearms against her chest, miming Ellen's triple Ds spilling out of what was originally a strapless sweetheart gown.

I agreed, glancing down at my own chest, filling out the bodice of my dress, and straightened the necklace Ellen had gifted all the bridesmaids to wear. At least the matching bridesmaid dresses I had convinced Ellen to choose were comfortable. The wide straps allowed all of us to wear a regular bra, while the cinched waist and chiffon provided a forgiving silhouette.

"This color though," Mom said, the corner of her mouth pulling down.

I held my hand up. "I know."

Even though I managed the day-to-day business of her wedding gown boutique, Michelle's Belles, Mom was still very vocal about her opinions.

"She wanted us all to match," I explained. "The other girls can pull it off. I'm the odd one out."

Mom reached up, running her knuckle down my cheek. "Still gorgeous though, Pepto-Bismol dress or not."

"Who needs Pepto-Bismol?" my dad asked, arriving at the table.

"No one, John." My mom patted his hand with the side of her fist as she sent me a secretive wink.

"Calling all the single laaaaadies!" Gunner spun a glow stick above his head and pumped the volume all the way up as a few women started to the middle of the dance floor.

Dad tossed a piece of gum in his mouth then poked my shoulder. "You gonna go up to catch the bouquet?"

"Nope."

"Ah, go on." Mom angled her wheelchair at me, purposefully knocking into my chair. When I refused to get up, Mom motioned to Aunt Kate to help her.

Great Grandma Nellie had eleven children, including Thomas, my dad's father, who had six kids with his wife, Geraldine. The Mahoneys were a big family, both in number and in physical size. I didn't stand a chance against Aunt Kate pulling the back of my chair away from the table while Mom laughed. I stuck my tongue out at my parents and aunt and stalked to the floor.

Dad clapped, ever the cheerleader. "Go get 'em, Till!"

"I think you know the rules," Gunner bellowed into the microphone, aiming the glow stick at the crowd of women in front of him. "But I'll review them anyway. No tackling and no biting. Everything else...is fair game."

Someone booed from the side, and I stepped away from the giggling pack of women to skirt my gaze around, searching for Tyler. I found him up toward the DJ booth with his phone out. I was about to throw my middle finger up at him but noticed his attention wasn't directed at me.

It was on Sarah as she stretched theatrically, earning a chuckle from Tyler. I nonchalantly stepped away from the crowd as Ellen turned her back and counted to three before tossing the bouquet of pink roses over her head. Peals of laughter rang out, and I dutifully applauded a victorious

Sarah, even if I couldn't quite screw my face into a smile as she ran right to Tyler to accept a high five.

I whirled around, finding my way to the table dotted with the bowls of candy favors. Perusing the Starbursts, M&Ms, jelly beans, and ring pops, I settled on filling my little baggie up with M&Ms and grabbed a ring pop for the road. I stuck it in my mouth right as Tyler appeared next to me.

"Hey," he said, practically vibrating with energy.

"Hi."

He leaned in close, smelling faintly of the same cologne he'd been wearing since high school but more of the vodka cranberries he'd been drinking. "So, I was thinking..."

I raised an eyebrow, the ring pop bulging in my cheek, already guessing what he was about to say.

"You could take my keys and drive home. Sarah and I are kinda..." He wagged his head to the side in what he probably thought was innocence. "I could hitch a ride with her."

Even though I expected it, getting ditched never got any easier. I tucked my index finger in the plastic ring and pulled it from my mouth with an audible pop, holding it between us. He didn't hesitate to shove it in his mouth, and I folded my arms. "You're proposing, as the guy who brought me to this wedding, for *me* to drive your car home while *you* go hook up with *another* bridesmaid?"

He handed the ring pop back to me. "Well, when you put it like that..." He grinned, his twin dimples making him appear so much younger than our twenty-seven years. Like the little boy I grew up with. "Yes, that's exactly what I'm proposing."

To him, it was a game. To me, it was never-ending disappointment.

With his knees slightly bent and one hand on the table next to me, he was like a runner in the blocks. He wasn't asking; he was telling. He was basically already gone.

I grunted. "Fine."

"Yeah?" When I nodded, he pressed on. "Are you sure?"

"Yes," I said because he didn't ask me for an honest answer. He asked to be polite. I held my hand out, palm up for his keys, which he deposited with a kiss to my cheek.

"You sure you're fine?"

"I'm fine." Lie from the lying liar.

"Okay." He jogged backward toward Sarah. "I'll text you later."

I slumped back against the wall as Tyler met Sarah by the door, his arm slipping around her shoulders.

"Hey, cuz." Ellen hip-checked me, full of joy and smiles.

She wasn't quite as tall as me but had enough force to push me over a few inches. Not that I was real steady to begin with. Not when Tyler played with Sarah's pink strap on her shoulder.

Ellen followed my line of sight. "Is that Tyler?"

I nodded.

"With Sarah. My Sarah?"

I nodded again.

"I know you said he's a player, but I didn't think Sarah would move on so quickly from—"

Ellen's chatter became white noise as Tyler led Sarah to the exit, his hand on the small of her back, and my own skin echoed with the remembrance of his hand on a cool October night during our first year at school. On fall break from Notre Dame, I had driven the six hours to Carnegie Mellon. Even though we'd only been away from each other for a few weeks, I had been homesick for him. When I'd arrived at his dorm, he had swept me up in a tight hug and twirled me around, gushing over how much he had missed me.

That night, he had taken me to an off-campus party thrown by a friend of a friend, where we'd drunk warm beer with some theatre majors. We'd left after a few hours, his hand on my back, and walked back to his dorm, then had snuggled together on his single bed. I'd fallen asleep in the cradle of his arm and chest, and in the morning, when we had woken up, he had searched my eyes for an eternity, all our years of friendship coalescing in that one *moment* between us.

It was the first time it had felt like Tyler wasn't only my best friend.

He'd combed his fingers through my hair and leaned down brushing his lips gently against mine until his dorm room door had burst open. His roommate had been there with a pretty girl, informing Tyler she'd needed help with her computer.

Tyler had smiled at me with a wink and had jumped out of bed. He'd tossed on a hoodie and had followed his roommate and the girl out to the hallway. "I'll be right back," he'd told me.

And when he'd returned twenty minutes later with the girl in tow, I'd pretended it was fine—that I was fine—ignoring the hurt of seeing him walk away then and now.

Because I, Tilly Mahoney, am a liar.

And I'm in love with my best friend.

Two

Since I was running late, I threw on the first thing I spotted in my closet, a plum-colored cotton sundress. After plopping a floppy hat over my misbehaving hair, I was out the door, texting Tyler.

There's an accident. Stuck in traffic. Be there ASAP.

Lie.

We hadn't talked to each other in a few weeks. I hadn't seen him in much longer, not since Ellen's wedding, so as soon as he'd texted to meet up for brunch, I'd immediately agreed. But as usual, I'd closed the store last night and then binged a series about the Roman Empire before falling asleep on the living room couch. I didn't even have time to shower before the upstairs neighbors woke me up by tap dancing or dropping soup cans or whatever the hell it was they did up there.

When I opened the door to the restaurant, Tyler waved from his seat in the back. He stood up to hug me, and I noticed he was tanner than usual. "Where've you been?"

"Work in Cupertino, and then we took some time off down in San Diego."

I registered three place settings at the table at the same time he said the word *we*. "We? Who is we?"

"Yeah, I wanted to tell—"

"Hey!"

I squinted over my shoulder at the voice, tinkling and warm. Verbal sunshine. "Sarah?"

Ellen's maid of honor opened her arms for a hug, forcing me to her with strength belied by her petite stature. "So happy to see you again! I'm so glad you're here. We have so much to talk about."

I ground my molars, curving my lips in an approximation of a smile. Brunch was a sacred time for Tyler and me, especially since we didn't get to see each other all that often. We'd never invited anyone else, nevermind a girl Tyler had hooked up with. I couldn't believe she was here, and that fact alone had my hackles raised. I didn't know Sarah all that well, except for her oversimplification of the English Language. *So...*

"What's going on?" I asked.

"Come on. Come sit," Sarah said, letting go of me to motion to the seat next to her. Tyler grinned and lounged back in his chair across from Sarah.

I didn't like this—whatever it was—and every muscle in my body contracted in anticipation.

"I love your dress." Sarah waved her hand down the length of me. "And the hat. Very Stevie Nicks."

Now, I was an excellent liar. I did it daily, for little reasons like being late for brunch, and big reasons like pretending I wasn't in love with my best friend. I was so good at lying, I had a sense when other people were too.

But I couldn't tell if Sarah was lying or not. Seeing as how my style was not like hers, I couldn't imagine she loved what I was wearing. She reminded me of the girls who wore athleisure wear all the time, as if they didn't spend two hours curling their hair and putting on eyelashes. Whereas, I really did wake up like this.

"What have you been up to, Till?" Tyler asked, flipping the single sheet menu from the front to the back like he didn't know what he was going to get, which was always the same. Eggs Benedict and a Bloody Mary with the works—a stick of chorizo, hard-boiled egg, and a couple of shrimp.

"Nothing. The usual. Work." I glanced around, waiting for someone to pop out from behind the fake palm tree in the corner like one of those shows where someone does something wrong, and they tape the interaction to see what other people do. "But what about you? What's going on?"

Sarah reached across the table to hold onto Tyler's hand, like they were an item. Like they were in love. "Since we met at the wedding, everything's been a dream."

Weird. Seemed like the beginning of a nightmare to me.

"I've been traveling a lot with work, you know," Tyler said to me as if it was enough of an explanation, but when I shook my head slowly, Sarah took over.

"We've talked, like, every day since the wedding. Honestly, I've never felt so...like, it's...perfect."

"Perfect," I repeated as the waiter arrived to take our orders. I ordered a mimosa, heavy on the champagne.

"Sarah met me in California, and we drove down the coast," Tyler told me even as his eyes remained on the woman in front of him. "It felt right."

"To drive down the coast?" I asked, trying not to drown in their lovesickness. Tyler never became attached like this, but the way he gazed at Sarah like she might sprout rainbows out of her ass at any moment had me downing my mimosa as soon as it was placed in front of me.

"Everything felt right," Tyler said with his sniffling laugh.

My attention toggled between them during their silent

conversation. Tyler and *I* had silent conversations. How could he be having one with someone else?

"We told our parents," Sarah said, and a pain bubbled in my stomach. Maybe from drinking too fast.

"But I wanted to tell you first before we went public," Tyler finished, and I touched my fingers to my breastbone, where my insides knotted beneath it. Maybe it was indigestion.

Sarah held her left hand in the air, her slim fingers with a pale pink manicure faced out toward me. One giant pear-shaped diamond sat on top an encrusted band on her finger, *the* finger. "I'm going to be Mrs. Rodriguez!"

My mind came to a sudden and complete stop like a record scratch.

There weren't many things in my life that were constant except interest on my college loans and Tyler. So this... This was the last thing I expected.

"Wow, uh... Huh. Kind of fast, isn't it?" I stuttered after an eternity.

Sarah raised one shoulder in a cute little shrug. "When you know you know, I guess."

I hated her.

Hated everything about her. From her perfect asymmetrical pixie cut to her pouty lips.

"Wait. Wait, wait, wait." I squeezed my eyes closed in thought, racking my brain for the few conversations I'd had with her while participating in wedding festivities. "I thought you had a boyfriend."

"We broke up right before the wedding."

"Ellen's wedding? That was three months ago," I said to be sure I wasn't living in some sort of time warp. "I don't mean to sound rude—" I absolutely did "—but this is quite the rebound."

Sarah laughed. She actually laughed. "I know, right?"

Tyler merely sat there staring at his fiancée—his fiancée!—until she wiggled his hand, and he snapped awake from his trance.

He removed his hand from Sarah's grasp and pushed the salt and pepper shakers away to hold both my hands, and my throat tightened. I knew everything about Tyler, the exact golden brown of his skin and how he always had a farmer's tan in the summer. I knew his right ear was slightly pointier than the left, and he secretly listened to Miley Cyrus in the car. He'd held me at the hospital in those dark days after my mom's accident. After we got the news of her paralysis, he'd driven me around all day, listened to my fears, let me cry on his shoulder, and then he'd sweetly kissed me on the lips before tucking me in my childhood bed.

My life had always been inextricably linked to Tyler's. And now he was going to marry someone else who he barely knew?

No.

Absolutely not.

"Till, I want you to be the Best Man. I mean, Best Woman."

My eyes blurred at Tyler's words, and I swallowed hard, my throat tracked with pebbles which hadn't been there before.

His thumb coasted over the back of my hand. "You're the one person in the whole world who knows me best. There isn't anyone else I want standing beside me when I get married."

I cleared my throat. "Not even Ricky?"

Ricky was Tyler's closest cousin and friend, besides me, of course. He always hit on me whenever we were together, but he was harmless in a goofball sort of way.

"Not even Ricky." Tyler smiled, his cheeks indenting, and I had a hard time blinking back tears.

I thought back to all the time we had spent together in the

treehouse in his backyard as kids. How he'd come all the way to Dublin to help me pack up my things after I'd decided I needed to leave my study-abroad program and quit school. I remembered how this past New Year's Eve, he'd wrapped his arm around the front of my shoulders, pulled me back against his chest and nuzzled my ear, whispering, "You're my favorite person ever created."

I couldn't stand up next to him at his wedding as he promised his forever to someone else.

No fucking way.

"What about your brothers?" I suggested in an attempt to save face.

His smiled waned. "You know they're busy with their families, besides I'm not as close to them as I am to you," he said, his voice low and pleading. "There is nobody else."

I found myself nodding like a bobble head, and he stood, reaching across the table to kiss my cheek while Sarah clapped. "Aww, this is so great! I'm so happy!"

"*So* happy." I gestured to the server with a lift of my empty glass. I'd need a few more. "When's the big day?"

"I've always wanted a fall wedding, so I was thinking September 26th. Not too hot, not too cold. Just right."

I hid my relief behind a sip of water. That was more than enough time for them to realize what a bad idea it was to get married. For Tyler to recognize Sarah wasn't the one for him.

"A year and a half, that's plenty of time to plan," I said, fingering the utensils in front of me, feeling the weight of the knife in my hand.

"I meant this September," Sarah corrected as Tyler sat forward in his chair with his elbows on the table, his smile blindingly happy.

I hid my grimace. September was three months away. They would be married in a matter of weeks. Unless...

A terrible, awful idea sprouted in my brain.

I wouldn't let it get that far. Goldilocks had messed with the wrong goddamn bear, and I was going to ruin this wedding. Forget the chair and porridge. I'd tear down the whole house before I let someone claim what was mine.

Three

Brunch lasted forever with Sarah describing, in excruciating detail, how Tyler proposed with a stick-on tattoo he'd bought for fifty cents from a machine in the lobby of a diner off the coast. And then how he'd taken her to a jewelry store in the Gaslamp district in San Diego to let her pick out whatever ring she wanted. She said she had cried so much that she'd chosen the tear-drop diamond to represent her happy tears.

To top it all off, Tyler even let Sarah eat off his plate.

He *never* shared his food. In fact, he usually ate off *my* plate.

As soon as I shoved my French toast down my throat, I feigned being late for work. But that was a lie. Michelle's was closed on Sundays. How, after all this time, Tyler still didn't know that fact was beyond me.

Maybe it was all the wedding talk clouding his brain.

Gag.

I drove straight to my parents' house, letting myself inside since they still hadn't returned home from church yet. Being the good lapsed Catholic girl I was, a tiny twinge of guilt poked at me as I passed the small wooden crucifix hanging above the kitchen doorway. My parents had dutifully put me in Catholic school and made sure I'd attended church every Sunday until I was old enough to drive myself. That's when I'd started making up excuses to either not go or lie and say I'd go to mass on my own and then would head to brunch with Tyler. It's when our love of brunch had begun.

I was pretty sure my parents knew I hadn't attended mass, but they'd never mentioned anything about it. In fact, for a while, they had stopped going too.

Until my mom's accident. Then as soon as she was able, my father had religiously wheeled my mother into the back row of Our Lady Help of Christians church. My parents had turned toward religion when the world had tilted on a different axis, while I'd turned away completely, had lost my naiveté, and hardened my heart a little bit more than I'd like to admit.

Or, really, a lot more than I'd like to admit.

I made myself at home, kicking off my shoes in the living room before curling up on their overstuffed chaise lounge, and flipping on the television. The Hallmark Channel was on, as usual. My parents were obsessed.

I watched the movie for a while, about a happy-go-lucky woman who entered her dog in a show, where she met the judge, who happened to be a tall, dark, and handsome man. But then I couldn't stop thinking of my own tall, dark, and handsome man.

I couldn't believe he was getting married.

"Tilly?" Mom's voice echoed through the house a few moments before my dad waved from the space between the kitchen and living room.

"What're you doing here?" he asked.

I sat up, taking in my dad's church attire of khakis and a polo shirt, which wasn't any different from his everyday work attire, teaching high school social studies. He smiled at me, his

SOPHIE ANDREWS

long face weathered with stress and age. When I didn't answer, he pointed his thumb to the kitchen. "I'm going to make turkey sandwiches for lunch. Want one?"

I shook my head and stood up as Mom wheeled further into the room. "Hi, honey. I was going to—"

"Tyler's getting married," I blurted before thinking better of it.

Both of my parents paused at my words and then simultaneously cooed. "Oh, how wonderful!" and "Really? Good for him."

I trudged between them to plop down at the kitchen table, hiding the searing effect their words left on my skin. Pretending to fix my long hair around my face, I hid until the redness I knew was there faded from my cheeks, neck, and ears.

"Who is it?" Mom asked, settling in the open space next to me.

"Sarah, Ellen's maid of honor."

"Oh, the little one with the pixie cut? She's adorable!"

I clenched my jaw and nodded because I couldn't disagree.

Dad went about assembling all of the supplies for sandwiches and set to work. "You just found out?"

"Yeah." I set my elbow on the table, my chin on my palm. "We went out this morning, and he brought her along. He wants me to be the Best Man."

"Aw." Mom reached for my other hand, stilling my fingers from playing with the floral table mat. "That's so sweet."

My mother didn't have much dexterity left, but she curled her index finger around the side of my hand. The first time she'd performed this tiny movement after her accident, I'd been so grateful for the small, wonderful action.

When I got the phone calls six years ago about my mom being in the hospital, everything changed.

I would never say it out loud and rarely acknowledged it

20

even to myself, but sometimes I resented it. I resented everything—the world, my situation, the inability to have the full strength of my mother's arms around me right now. It was a reminder of how much my mother had lost, and how much I'd given up.

I wouldn't do anything differently, not quitting school and moving home, and certainly not taking care of my mom when she'd needed it most. I didn't deserve pats on the back or accolades; I'd done what any daughter of an amazing mother like mine would do. But if there was one thing I wanted, it was to feel as if I wasn't on pause anymore. As if that frozen patch of January ice hadn't forever altered the trajectory of not only my mother's life, but of mine too.

"You okay?" Mom asked, her forehead wrinkling with concern. "You don't seem very happy."

"I'm tired, that's all." Lie.

She moved her hand up to my shoulder, brushing my hair behind it. "Is Sarah nice?"

I let out a tiny snort. "If you like staring into the sun."

"What's that supposed to mean?"

"You know, she's *so* happy, bursting with joy."

Mom smiled. "Well, she is getting married."

Not if I had anything to do with it.

"You excited that Tyler asked you to be his Best Man? Are you going to wear a tux or dress?"

Of course my mother would think about the fashion. "I'm not sure. We didn't get that far," I said, specifically skipping over the first question. "But you know I like a good jumpsuit."

She nodded. "So, when's the big day?"

"September 26th."

My mother lifted her arm, doing an approximation of a wave. "Plenty of time."

"This September."

She let her hand fall. It plunked on the table. "Not even Jesus could pull off a miracle like that."

"But he did like a good wedding, huh?" I said, thinking I'd need the savior on my side to derail this wedding. Was that blasphemous?

Most likely.

Dad set a plate in front of Mom along with her adapted fork. "We got married six months after I proposed."

"Yeah, but that was a hundred years ago. Things are different now. Venues are booked up a year or more in advance. Is she buying her dress off the rack? And September is the new June. My goodness..." Mom blinked rapidly. She lived for weddings and had owned Michelle's Belles for about ten years now. After working as a seamstress in other shops for most of her life, she had finally saved enough money to open her own bridal salon, but only a few years into it, she'd become paralyzed and unable to perform the physical labor it took to run the boutique. So I'd stepped in.

"Till, you sure you don't want something to eat?"

"No, I'm good, Dad." I rose from my chair. "I just wanted to stop and say hi. Haven't seen you in a couple of days."

"You could stay. We got a new puzzle." Dad motioned to the thousand-piece jigsaw box, depicting different front doors. "Or, I got the new History Channel show DVR'd about the subterranean cities."

"John, the new Hallmark movie is on tonight. It's supposed to be the one with the cute guy I like. What's his name?"

I shook my head in amusement. "Cute guy? Narrows it down."

"He was in the Christmas one with the cat, and he was a firefighter."

Dad furrowed his brow, really thinking about it. "*The Nine Lives of Christmas*?"

"I can't believe you know the names of the movies, Dad."

"What can I say? I like when people get to live happily ever after."

"Don't we all," Mom agreed, tucking into her homemade pasta salad.

Did it make me a terrible person to break up my best friend's wedding? Probably. But after everything I'd given up, didn't I deserve my own happily ever after?

"I gotta go." I kissed both of my parents' cheeks before heading out the back door.

Following the accident, my parents had sold my childhood home to buy this rancher and renovated it with appliances and furniture modified for my mother's needs. It added to their ever-growing bills, but my dad, the ultimate optimist, had told me he liked this house better anyway. Less grass to cut. Less rooms to clean.

My parents had met shortly after my mom moved to Philadelphia to work for a custom bridal gown designer, and they'd married as soon as Dad had finished college. They had eventually settled in Doylestown and lived happily ever after with me, their one, perfect child until it wasn't perfect anymore. Though you'd never know it with the way those two still made moony eyes at each other. My parents were idyllic examples of loving each other for better or for worse, and I had always wanted what they had, a beautiful and supportive love.

Still did.

Unfortunately, the guy I wanted it with had lost his brain.

Back at my apartment, I opened my laptop and got to work, searching for anything about Sarah Kelly.

With two first names, who could trust her?

At first, all I found were the basics: her graduating class from high school, where she taught as a fitness instructor, and some feature in the local newspaper about being a personal trainer. But then I got into the good stuff. Unflattering social

23

media photos from college and all the videos of bad dancing. Did Tyler know how bad of a dancer she was? At least I could keep time.

Then I uncovered the *really* good stuff about her ex-boyfriend. His name was Zack Olsen, and he appeared to be a real mountain man type from the few out of focus pictures of him. They had been together for over a year, and even though he wasn't in very many photos with her, she often tagged him in her posts. The most interesting part was that they still followed each other. They had only broken up three months ago, so he very well could still have feelings for her. He might have even wanted her back.

There was only one way to find out, and after a deep dive on him too, I hovered the cursor over the contact link on the Olsen Heating & Plumbing website to make an appointment.

As far as I could tell, I had two options.

I could exit out of the internet browser, forget about this whole thing, and let Tyler get married while I suffered in silence.

Or, I could click on the link, send an e-mail, requesting Zack to come over and check a leak. Instead of remaining silent, I could convince him to be on my team to break up Tyler and Sarah.

But if I chose option two, there would be no turning back. I'd officially be plotting to destroy my best friend's wedding.

With a deep breath, I closed my eyes and clicked.

Four

I still hadn't decided what lie I'd tell Zack by the time he buzzed, and in a rush, I disconnected a few things from inside the toilet tank before answering the door. The man in front of me stood about my height with worn dirty jeans, boots, and a dark gray Olsen Heating & Plumbing T-shirt that had seen better days. "Hey, I'm Zack. You have a plumbing problem?"

"Hi, yes, come in. I'm Tilly." I opened the door wider, allowing him room to walk past me.

"What can I help you with today?"

"I, uh, have an issue with my toilet." I tipped my chin to the door at the back corner of the apartment, and he headed that way, giving me a moment to assess his stocky build, the stain on the leg of his jeans, and the clump of his feet. He'd be a difficult one to get on my team.

"What's been going on?" he asked, setting his toolbox on the floor in my tiny bathroom.

"I don't know. It's not flushing."

Slanted brows and heavy lids partially hid his eyes, but with his wavy auburn hair and beard more red than brown, I thought maybe I knew him from somewhere. And not just my cyber stalking. He crossed his thick freckled forearms one over the other across his chest. "What did your landlord say?"

"She told me to call a plumber."

Zack tilted his head, studying me for a moment, and I toyed with the mother of pearl pendant necklace Nellie had given me. I didn't like that he seemed to see right through my lie.

He lifted one big shoulder, apparently not caring one way or the other, and I wondered why Sarah had broken up with him. Aside from the hard exterior, he was rather attractive. Under the big beard, those lips were objectively kissable. The muscles didn't hurt either. He was a little short for my tastes though. But aside from his looks, maybe he had a terrible personality.

Compared to Tyler, with his perfectly disheveled hair, bespoke clothes, and charmingly nerdy personality, what did these two men have in common that Sarah would go from dating a ginger mountain man to marrying my tight pants-wearing, arthouse cinema-loving best friend?

"Everything all right?" Zack asked, and I shook myself out of my reverie, my cheeks heating from being caught staring so blatantly.

"Sorry, you look familiar." *From photos with your ex-girlfriend*, I didn't add.

He rubbed his palm over his mouth and beard, holding onto it for a moment before letting go, and it hit me.

"Oh my god, of course! You were in the shop with your sister."

His brow arched ever so slightly. "Hm?"

"I manage Michelle's Belles, the wedding gown shop. You came in with your sister when she tried on her wedding gown. I remember now," I added more to myself than him, thinking back to about a year ago. We so rarely had men in our store, especially not ones like Zack Olsen. He had parked himself on one of the maroon chairs, one ankle crossed over the other knee, petting his beard while he waited. And waited and waited. "We had trouble getting the back laced up." I smiled at the recollection of him sitting so patiently. "It took me and another girl to get it tied up right, but you didn't complain. At all."

"Oh. Uh, yeah," he mumbled then bent down to one knee, checking something behind the toilet.

"What's your sister's name again?"

"Chloe."

I snapped my fingers. "Right. She wore an ivory mermaid with a tulle skirt and floral lace applique. How was the wedding? It was about six months ago, right?"

Zack peered over his shoulder at me. "Yeah, December 19th. How'd you remember?"

"I've got a brain for details and wedding gowns."

I'd always had a good memory. It's what made me a good storyteller, Nellie used to say. Or a better liar, I supposed.

"She was beautiful in her gown," I said, and that wasn't a lie.

It's amazing what brides tell salespeople when they're in a dressing room together. When I'd helped Chloe, she had relayed the story of how her dad was in and out of her life, and her mom had recently died from complications of alcoholism, so her brother was walking her down the aisle. At the time, Chloe was just out of college, fresh-faced and radiant, gushing over how she'd been with her fiancé since high school. She was in love and excited for her brother to see her dress.

His reaction, even though I had witnessed it so long ago, was still as clear in my head as if it happened yesterday. When she'd finally appeared from the dressing room, he had teared up, dragging a knuckle over one of his eyes, and I'd moved away from their private moment to give them space.

"Yeah," Zack agreed, yanking me back to the present as he stood to bury his hands in the toilet tank.

"I have a confession to make." I tried not to fidget with my necklace by folding my arms. "I know you, or I should say *of you*, for a different reason."

He paid me no mind as he put back together whatever I had pulled apart.

"My best friend, Tyler, is marrying your ex-girlfriend, Sarah."

He stilled for only a moment before continuing his work.

"They met at my cousin's wedding in March."

He stopped then and straightened, washing his hands in my sink. "At Ellen Mahoney's wedding?"

I nodded. "So you know?"

He placed the top of the tank back on and pushed the handle down, flushing. "Good as new. It was an easy fix. I don't know why your landlord didn't do it. Or you," he said with a bite of sarcasm. "The internet is an amazing thing sometimes."

"Amazing," I deadpanned, but I was not to be deterred. "I was in the wedding with Sarah. She had told me you guys were dating, so I was surprised to hear you broke up."

Instead of answering immediately, he cracked his knuckles. With his brusque presence, he must've been used to intimidating people. Fortunately—or maybe unfortunately—for him, I wasn't one of those people.

After a few seconds of brooding, he gave in with a grumbled, "Yeah, me too. We were supposed to go to the wedding together."

"Really? What happened?" When he squinted at me, I held up my hands in defense. "I can't believe everything that's happened, you know?" I tried to sound as well-intentioned as possible. "It's all really fast."

Evidently, he hadn't expected an inquisition, and his eyes

widened. They were a lovely color once you could finally see them, a mottled-green like the Atlantic Ocean.

"Was it a bad break-up?"

He did the beard petting thing again. "You always so personal with strangers coming into your home?"

I strolled out into the kitchen and filled up two mason jars of water. "Only you." I offered him one of the them. "I'm curious if we might have the same...emotions about these upcoming nuptials."

He accepted the glass from me, and I noticed even his fingers had a few tiny freckles on them.

"Emotions?"

"Baggage, okay?" I gave in with a sigh and leaned heavily against the counter. I didn't enjoy how the truth was spilling out of me. Who knew how hypnotic beard petting could be? "I don't want Tyler and Sarah getting married, and from the way you still follow and like her posts on social media, I have an inkling you don't want them to either."

His eyes didn't leave mine as he took a gulp of water then set the glass down. "We were together for a year. I didn't want to break up."

"Are you still in love with her?"

A beat passed. "Why don't *you* want them getting married?"

"Because I love Tyler," I said matter-of-factly.

He stared at me in what was probably disbelief. "You're a trip."

"I wanted you to come here so I could meet you, talk to you."

"You made it up?" He angled his head toward the bathroom. When I nodded, he rested one hand on the counter, the other on his hip, and shook his head. "What did you think you were going to accomplish?"

"I wanted to see if you would help me."

"With what?"

"Breaking up the wedding?"

"What?" He huffed and tugged on his ear, perhaps making sure he heard me correctly. "You want to break up their wedding? Are you crazy?"

I wagged my head side to side. Debatable.

"You were together for a year," I said, rushing out my argument before he ran out of my house screaming. "I saw all the pictures you guys posted of each other, at the beach and those ones of you camping in the rain. You loved her. You must have, to sleep in a tent in the rain. You still do, right? You want her back."

I didn't give him time to answer. "You think *I'm* crazy, but don't *you* think it's at all nuts that they're getting married after only a couple of weeks? I've known Tyler my whole life. He would never suddenly up and get married. Clearly, he's not thinking rationally."

Zack pointedly tilted his head. Like when someone says they can't find something, and it's right in front of them.

Yes, I knew it was ironic for me to accuse someone else of being irrational when I was the one attempting to ruin my best friend's wedding. But desperate times called for desperate measures.

He chewed his bottom lip for a few seconds before telling me, "Sarah was always spontaneous like that. It was one of the reasons she broke up with me. I didn't know how to live spur-of-the-moment. I wasn't romantic, she said."

Now we were getting somewhere. "So it was a bad break-up?"

"If you consider a sudden and screaming break-up bad then yes. I was giving her time to cool off. I figured we'd get over it, but then..."

"Do you want her back?"

"She's getting married," he said slowly, as if I needed time to interpret his words. "To another man."

"But what if I could help you? What if I could teach you to be more romantic and spur-of-the-moment and whatever else she said she wanted you to be? Weddings are my business, I can read brides like I can read the clock on my wall, and Sarah won't marry Tyler."

She wasn't right for him. Not with her annoyingly chipper personality, *Women's Health* cover body, and apparent disloyalty since she'd moved on from one guy to another with barely a blink. But I wasn't about to bad mouth the girl to the guy who wanted her back.

"I can show Tyler that Sarah isn't right for him while we work together to make her see you *are* right for her."

He shifted his feet as if weighing whether or not to walk out of my place that very second. "And what do you get out of this?"

"Tyler."

"He's an asshole," Zack said, his feet firmly planted.

"He is not! He's wonderful."

"Sure. Sounded real wonderful when I called Sarah a few days after we broke up and heard him in the background telling her to hang up. Like a possessive dick."

I frowned. Tyler had never been that way with me.

"Look, I'm not okay with them going through with this wedding, and I will do everything in my power to stop it. It's up to you if you want to help me or not." Spinning around, I grabbed one of my business cards from my antique desk and scrawled my cell phone number on the back and handed it to him.

He read both sides, then lifted his focus, scrutinizing me and my home.

"What?" I asked, a little impatiently.

"You don't seem the type to work at a wedding dress store?"

I jerked my head back, curious at what exactly this guy saw in me. "Why?"

"I don't know. You seem..." His gaze coasted around again, to the wall hanging of the Celtic Tree of Life, the old black and white photos, the potted and hanging plants, and loads of candles.

"Well," I said, "you can't stop there. I seem what?"

His eyes traveled down the length of me. I hadn't dried my hair after my shower so it naturally curled and waved around my shoulders, and I was dressed for work in tailored black pants and tank top. My mother insisted everyone wear a uniform color of black.

"You're whole—" he waved his hand around "—everything is...I don't know."

I suppressed a smile at his discomfort and bent forward as if I could pull the words out of him. "I'm what?"

"You're kind of witchy," he murmured.

I gasped in delight and pressed my hand to my heart. "Thank you."

He raised his bushy brows in surprise then gave into a tiny half-smile, only to wipe it away almost immediately. "I'm sorry."

"Don't be. It might be the best compliment someone's ever given me." My cell phone buzzed, and I silenced it without checking the number. "So, now that we're friends and all, any chance this visit could be on the house?"

"We're not friends." He picked up his toolbox. "And I'll invoice you."

I walked with him to the door, holding it open. "Sorry for ambushing you."

"No, you're not." He placed his hand around the door, right above mine. "You're a terrible liar."

Now I was insulted.

"Gonna think about my offer?"

He made a show of putting my card in his pocket. "Nope."

"Now who's the liar?"

He ignored me and closed the door behind him. Once he was gone, I retrieved my phone from my desk. An unknown number had left a voicemail.

"Hey, Tilly, it's Sarah. I got your number from Tyler. I have a favor to ask. I'm so bad at, like, being a planner, and since you have so much experience with running your mom's boutique, and Tyler says you're a total wedding genius, I was hoping you'd help me. You know, get your opinion with the flowers, the cake, and whatever? And obviously the dress. I'd love you forever. Call me back! Thanks, doll!"

Message received, universe.

If I had Grinch hair, it would curl in evil glee as I called her back. "Hey, Sarah. I'd love to help plan your wedding."

Five

In the last week, Sarah and I had communicated every day. The girl needed constant reassurance and emotional petting. I had helped her with a schedule for all the things she needed to accomplish before the wedding, and even though I was still coming up with my own plan of attack, I'd given up on Zack's help. That's why I was shocked to find a message from an unknown number that could only be him when I checked my phone on a snack break. **I can't believe I'm saying this but I'm in.**

A second message immediately followed. **This is Zack BTW.**

With a laugh, I tossed my peanut butter cracker on the counter and replied, **Want to meet up to strategize?**

I waited anxiously for the bubble to pop up, feeling like I should be twirling a mustache while I devised a scheme to tie a damsel to the railroad tracks.

When he did, a punch of giddiness swept over me. **This feels a little Dr. Evil-ish doesn't it?**

Obviously, I wasn't a saint for wanting to break up my best friend and his fiancée, but having a sidekick made this mission feel a little less impossible...and wrong. I texted him back. **I can't be Dr. Evil. I don't have a bald cat.**

Good.

His short response had me chuckling as I typed out my request. **Can you meet tonight?**

A minute passed, and I got nervous he might back out, before he finally answered. **I'm going to go for a hike tonight. Meet me at Foothills Park at 6?**

I frowned. **Hiking?**

I wasn't much for climbing mountains or any other form of exercise that wasn't Pilates, which I could do in the comfort of my own home with no one watching. But he didn't respond, and I didn't want to blow my chance with him. **Fine.**

Zack was my only back-up. I couldn't lose him now, so I sucked it up, threw on sneakers when I got home from work, and headed out to Foothills Park. I figured it wouldn't be hard to spot his coppery hair, but when I didn't see him, I sat on a small boulder, contemplating my next move with Tyler and Sarah.

This coming weekend, Sarah's parents were hosting an engagement party, and I was slated to help her find her wedding dress next week. Truth be told, I was an excellent salesperson. I could sweet talk and upsell brides for everything. Beaded tiaras, scalloped veils, two pairs of shoes—one for the ceremony and one for the reception? Yes, girl.

I sold it all. Were these extra expenses necessary? No, but neither was a wedding after three months. So, if I could sell a two-tiered cathedral length floral and crystalized veil to a bride with a small beach wedding, I could certainly talk Sarah out of marrying Tyler.

The rumble of a truck brought my attention to where it parked a few yards away from me. The door with the Olsen Heating & Plumbing logo opened, and Zack stepped out, dressed like he'd come straight from work.

I pushed off the boulder. "Hey."

He offered a tip of his chin in my direction as he shut the door and ambled around the other side of the truck.

"How's it going?" I asked, closing the distance between us.

"All right." He nabbed a duffle bag from the passenger side and didn't say anything else to me as he took hold of the back of his shirt and pulled it over his head.

I averted my eyes at the sight of his brawny chest and casually leaned my back against the other side of his truck, trying to forget about the lion inked in black on his left pec and shoulder. Yet just as I did, something unzipped behind me. Using every ounce of my self-control, I kept my head from turning to confirm what I knew, that he was taking off his jeans.

I cleared my throat. "So, uh, you hike a lot?"

"Sometimes."

Pretty sure boots clunked on the ground. "It's hot out. You really want to do this?"

A mix of a snort and a huff sounded before the passenger door closed again. He stalked back around the front of his truck in hiking shoes, shorts, T-shirt, and a beat up red backpack. "Ready?"

I fixed my one and only baseball cap—the one I'd bought a lifetime ago when I'd first arrived at Notre Dame—on my head and tightened my ponytail. "Not at all."

He nodded toward the entrance, and I followed him up the path. A park map outlined all the different paths, but he didn't stop at the podium to study it like I did.

I hurried to catch up. "You know this park well?"

"Yep."

I sighed at his one word answers. "Is this how it's going to be?"

He kept his focus forward. "I come out here if I need to clear my head."

"Uh huh." I kept quick pace with him. "Mountain air, clear head, good idea. I personally do my best thinking in the shower."

He paused briefly, his gaze dropping below my neck. "Come on. This way," he said after a moment, directing me off the beaten path. "Watch your step."

We climbed quietly together through the wooded area, him easily pushing small branches out of the way, me avoiding big logs. The air in my lungs thickened as we ascended a steeper incline, and I swiped at sweat beading under my nose. "You actually enjoy doing this?"

He glanced over his shoulder at me. "What? You're not having fun?"

"No wonder why Sarah broke up with you, if you think sweating in the middle of the woods while mosquitoes feast is fun."

He stopped so I could catch up to him. "Sarah loves to hike."

I grimaced as I waved off another bug by my head. "Let me guess, she loves to drink beer and eat wings while watching football too. The perfect girl, huh?"

"Nah." He wiped his forehead with his forearm. "She'd never drink beer or eat wings."

"Right. Of course not," I muttered, ducking under a low-hanging branch. Sarah and her petite little fingers always picked at food. Once, after I slurped back my third free champagne while getting a pedicure during Ellen's bachelorette party at the spa, she had leaned over to tell me she never wasted her calories on alcohol. I, on the other hand, ate everything on my plate *and* drank free champagne whenever it was offered.

"What is it you like about her?" My tone must have given me away because he raised one bushy red-tinted eyebrow. "I'm sure she's a lovely person," I said, and he sniffed.

"Sounds like you're jealous."

"Yes, I'm jealous. She's marrying Tyler. I mean... She won't be marrying Tyler, but she's somehow got him wrapped around her posy pink-tipped finger." The path steepened again, and my breath momentarily left me as I tried to keep up with Zack.

"Are you sure this isn't about her?"

I hunched over. Cardio wasn't my favorite thing. "This is about Tyler..." I said between pants. "And not rushing into marriage with someone he barely knows."

"All right then, you tell me what you like about Tyler."

"He's brilliant and funny, dorky and sweet. And he's got great hair." When Zack let out a derisive sort of snort, I pointed at him. "Now *you're* jealous."

He shook his head and gestured up ahead.

When I finally traipsed through the trees to a clearing, I planted my hands on my hips. "You self-conscious of your ginger twigs?"

"Do I look like I'm self-conscious?" He gave me a haughty smirk—I doubted there was a self-conscious bone in his body—and found a spot of grass to lounge on.

I followed his lead. "Well, Tyler really does have gorgeous hair."

"You love the guy because of his hair?" He took out an aluminum water bottle from his backpack.

"I love him because...because I always have. He's my best friend," I said as he gulped from the bottle then offered it to me. Seeing as how I came unprepared, I took it gratefully. "What about you? Why Sarah?"

Without hesitation he said, "She's got a great ass."

I coughed on my swig of water when I laughed. "Oh, come on."

"You said Tyler's hair. I can't say Sarah's got a tight ass?"

I knocked him in the arm with the side of my fist, and both of our gazes dropped to his bicep, where my hand rested.

I hurried to cover it by passing him the water bottle back. He let it dangle from his fingertips as he stared out ahead of us at the horizon, which I only now noticed was pretty spectacular with the bright green below and clear blue above.

"She's really nice," he said after a while.

Nice. That word. I hated it. Women always had to be nice, but what if we didn't want to be? *I* certainly didn't want to be nice. I wanted to be strong and smart and bold. Nice was for the weather and comfy sweaters, not descriptions of women.

Instead of getting on my soap box, I rolled my eyes. "Nice? Really?"

He shrugged. "Yeah. She's always helping. Simple stuff like offering people rides and grocery shopping for her grandparents. She even adopted this diabetic cat, and he's blind in one eye. She's got to give him shots and all kinds of meds, and she has so much patience but..." He shook his head. "She was always upset I never wanted to go to her place because I didn't like the cat, but I'm allergic." He held his hands out as if the cat was in front of him. "I'm allergic to cats. Not that I don't like *this* cat."

"I don't like cats," I said.

He turned my way with that small tick of his mouth before it was gone, and he was regarding the horizon again. The sun began to set, the sky barely tinted orange at the edges. "I think she believed she could rehab me or something, make me better." He scratched at his beard. "I wanted to be better for her."

"Better?" When he didn't elaborate, I let it go but couldn't take my eyes off the side of his face, the few freckles on his nose, the one on his earlobe. "Did you put on sunscreen?"

He dug through his backpack and produced two protein bars of some kind, tossing one to me. "I did not."

I ripped open the wrapper to the vanilla almond bar. "You know the percentage of redheads who get skin cancer?"

His jaw worked on a big bite. "No, do you?"

"No, but it's probably, like, really high. Aren't you worried?"

His gaze settled on my bare arms, pale as the moon. "What about you?"

"I don't stand near a window without the highest SPF. You're lucky you even got me and my sensitive skin outside." When his eyes caught somewhere around my throat, I looked away. "It's nice out here though."

He agreed with a satisfied grunt, and we sat in amicable silence, sharing his water, eating the cardboard bars.

"So," I said eventually, "tell me something about yourself."

"Tell you something about myself?" He lifted the bottom of his T-shirt up to wipe at his mouth, and I couldn't help but notice the thick slab of muscle under the sweaty rag he wore. Tyler, all 6'4" of him, was basically Slender Man and had come about his lean physique from years of eating junk food while having the metabolism of a professional basketball player. Zack, on the other hand, was built like an ox, solid and thick. He could probably plow a field with his bare hands.

"I need to get to know you so I can help you get Sarah back." Half-lie, half-truth. I might have been more than a little curious about him. "How tall are you?"

"'Round five eleven."

I pursed my lips. Too bad.

"Why? Is it of interest to you?"

"What?" I wrenched my head back. "No. Not to me. No."

He eyed me in the same suspicious way he had done when he was in my apartment. "Notre Dame, huh?"

I reflexively tugged on the bill of my hat. "Yep."

"Did you go there?"

"Yeah." Technically, it was the truth. I'd attended Notre Dame University. I just didn't graduate.

His eyes never left me. It was unnerving. "What does a big Notre Dame brain have to do with a wedding dress shop?"

"Nothing." I curled my legs up and wrapped my arms around them. "I double majored in history and Irish language."

"I didn't know studying Irish language was a thing."

"Anything can be a *thing*," I said, flicking my finger in the air. "People go to school for a degree in ice cream making. They don't go to Notre Dame for that but, you know...anything."

"And your thing is Irish language?" he asked in a low voice like he was struggling to figure me out.

I wished him all the best of luck. Since I was still struggling to figure me out too.

"Hey." I pressed my fingers to my collarbone. "I'm supposed to be learning about you. How did this get turned around on me?"

His eyes made a circuit of my face. "We're a team, right? I've got to trust you."

The way he said the word *trust* stuck with me. Like it was the most important thing to him. And, weirdly enough, I wanted him to trust me.

"You tell me something about you, and I'll tell you something about me," he said, leaning back onto his elbows and stretching his legs out in front of him.

"My great grandparents came from County Cork in Ireland, and I was really close to Nellie, my great-grandmother, or as close as a little kid could be to a ninety-year-old. Her dad was a storyteller back home, and Nellie used to tell me those same stories about the Tuatha Dé Danann, Tir na nÓg, and Brian Boru. It fascinated me that their history—Ireland's history—was never written down, and only passed on generation to generation because of storytellers like Nellie's father. I wanted to learn it too, pass it on."

He raised his brows, allowing me to see how the flecks of brown and blue in his eyes truly did create an ocean of color in his gaze.

"Your turn."

He ran his hand over his hair then beard. "There isn't really anything interesting about me."

"Did you always want to be in heating and plumbing?" I asked, grasping at straws.

"It's a family business."

"But your sister told me your dad...?" My question trailed off when his eyes met mine, dark and irritated.

He sat up, shoulders rigid. "What did Chloe say about my dad?"

I shifted back at his sudden change in temperament. Until now, he'd been so introverted he almost verged on indifference, but I guessed still waters ran deep. This guy had layers, and I wanted to dig them all up, examine each one. Discover exactly who he was beyond Sarah's ex-boyfriend.

"Back when she was picking out her gown, she told me you were walking her down the aisle because you two were really close and your dad wasn't really around," I explained.

He squinted at me as if deciding whether or not to trust me. Shadows crossed over us. The temperature dropped and rose again. Seasons changed and birds migrated South before he finally spoke. "Her dad wasn't really around. He's been in and out of jail. I've never met my dad."

I winced. "Sorry, I didn't mean to bring that up."

He scrubbed his hand over his beard. "My mom had me when she was seventeen, my dad was older, in his twenties and as messed up as she was. He's not even listed on my birth certificate. The only things I know of him are memories of what my grandmother yelled about him when she and my mom used to fight."

"I'm sorry," I said again, but he waved me off.

"It's my uncle who owns the business, my mom's brother."

When I thought he'd continue, he didn't, and I left it there, surprised he told me that much. Zack's life was complicated, and even though I was interested in learning more about him as a person, I didn't want to dredge up any emotional trauma. All I needed from him was his help in putting a stop to a wedding.

"Okay." I clapped my hands to clear the air with a fresh start. "How can I help you get Sarah back?"

He chewed on the question for a moment. "She was always saying she wished I did more stuff for her."

"More stuff? As in buy her gifts?"

"No, as in spontaneous and romantic stuff, which...okay," he said with a comically baffled shrug. "I'd volunteer to do her dishes or buy her flowers sometimes, but I guess that's not what she meant." He shook his head. "We were on different wavelengths. I offered to take her on my bike sometimes, but she always turned me down."

"Your bike? Are we talking a ten-speed here?"

"My Harley."

"You have a motorcycle?" When he nodded, I drew an imaginary shape in the air, connecting the dots of their relationship. "And you thought it would be romantic to take Sarah out for a ride, and she turned you down?"

He nodded again, and I made a slash through my geometry. I guess if I *had* to defend her on this point, I could because sometimes you wanted to know the other person was thinking of you. But she told him to be more romantic, spur-of-the-moment, and he offered her motorcycle rides. It sounded spontaneous and sort of death-defyingly romantic to me.

Merely thinking of it had my heart beating faster.

"I guess she wanted weekend getaways," he mused quietly. "But I can't swing that."

"All right. We'll work on your romance and spontaneity. What else?"

"She always wanted me to shave."

"Really? I think the beard works for you." I circled my hand to encompass his body. "The whole thing works. The muscle, the hair, the tattoo."

He grinned then. An honest to god, panty-melting grin. "Yeah?"

I hoped I didn't blush and tried to correct him. "Not that it works for me. You're too short."

He jerked his head back. "'Scuse me?"

"Listen, when you're Amazon height, you need a guy who doesn't make you feel like a walking tree. It's, like, minimum six three for me."

He looked me up and down, evidently unconvinced.

"Well, I'm all scrunched up now," I said, defensively.

He stood and threw his backpack over his shoulder. "Come on, lemme see this Amazon at full height. We should get going anyway, while there's still light."

I got up, and he pressed his shoulder against mine, our eyes briefly meeting on the same plane. "Six three." He huffed. "You ever hear it's not the size that counts?"

We were basically the same height. "I've never found that to be the case."

He stepped away from me, making his way to the edge of the clearing. "Sounds like you never found someone who knows how to use it."

"Are we still talking about height here?" I followed him until I tripped on uneven ground, and he steadied me with a hand around my elbow. "Because we've drifted into innuendos, and to be honest, I'm a little confused."

He let out an amused sound, his eyes softening as if I was slowly endearing myself to him. I didn't need him to like me, but the fleeting thought hiccupped the tiniest blip in my belly.

"Let's go," he said. "But could you move over a little to block the sun? I could use your shade."

I pushed his shoulder on my way down the mountain. "I'm sure it was your incredible sense of humor that first attracted Sarah to you."

He smirked in my direction. "No. It was the size of my dick."

And I sputtered out a laugh.

Six

A house this size shouldn't have shocked me since Sarah had told me her dad was an executive in a pharmaceutical company, but this one was easily over seven figures.

"How many acres do they own?" I asked Tyler when I finally skirted the engagement party crowd to find him by the pool.

He slung an arm around my shoulders. "Hello to you too."

"There's a four-car garage and is that an actual pond with ducks in it?"

"Pretty cool, right?" He spread his hand out to the landscape. "I thought you'd love it. The original house was built in seventeen forty-something and was only two bedrooms. Every owner kept building and updating it. Sarah lives in the cottage back there."

I nodded at the fenced-in vegetable garden. "And what? She farms too."

"Yeah. She likes the whole organic, farm-to-table thing," he reminded me.

I forced a smile up at him. "Right. Of course."

"Come on. Mom was just saying how much she misses you." He took my hand, and guided me back toward the house, past the outdoor grilling area and makeshift bar, where staff handed out special cocktails including *Summer of Love* Sangria and *Marry Me* Mojito. I snatched a *Honey I Do* from the edge of the table, not knowing what was in it besides whiskey.

Inside, the blaringly bright white kitchen gleamed with marble countertops and huge windows. Another hired server was stationed behind the spread of canapes, offering shrimp skewers, beet and goat cheese bites, smoked salmon pâté, and miniature mushroom wellingtons.

"Tilly, baby!" Mrs. Rodriguez crowed, reaching for me, her tropical print caftan like a neon blinking sign in the stark kitchen.

"Hey, mama llama." I stooped down to encircle her shoulders while she reached around my waist. How Mrs. R. could have birthed three gargantuan children out of her tiny little body was beyond me. "How are you?"

She stretched up and forced my head down, smooshing my cheeks with her hands, kissing me between my eyebrows. "I'm fine, but I've missed your face. I haven't seen you in so long."

"I've been busy, and Tyler hasn't been home. I don't want to drop in without an invitation."

She laced her fingers with mine and yanked on my hand. "Come on now! Yeah, you can!"

I grinned at her, loving and missing her slight Bronx accent. Sylvia and Juan Rodriguez settled in Doylestown by way of New York City. Tyler worked and lived in Philly now, but he had always come back here once a week for family dinners. Although ever since Sarah entered into the picture, he'd been staying with her. I didn't realize it was in her parents' palatial backyard.

"Come tomorrow. We're having monfongo."

I glanced at Tyler, and he shrugged. "Sarah's never had it."

"I've got a lot of work to do for the shop," I lied, not being able to bear a Rodriguez family dinner with Sarah there, even with the temptation of delicious food. "Maybe next time."

Mrs. R. nodded. For a while after Mom's accident, Dad and I had survived on her cooking, and she'd even helped in the boutique a few days a week, keeping us afloat. "How's my Chelle-Chelle and Johnny?"

Right when I started to answer, Sarah popped up next to Tyler. "There you are, babe. I couldn't find you," Sarah said before quickly hugging me. "And here you are! I'm so glad you could come today." She snaked her arm around Tyler's, and I noticed their matching white outfits.

I could never wear all white—I'd look ridiculous—but Sarah's sun-kissed skin shone under the eyelet lace sundress. Next to Tyler in his striped white and gray T-shirt and white linen shorts, they could have walked out of a magazine.

Sarah poked her index finger into my wrist. "I have so many people to introduce you to, but first I need to steal him for a minute. Then we'll go meet my girls and my parents, kay?"

"Yeah, sure."

After the staring-into-the-sun-blissful couple strolled toward a few gray-haired people, Mrs. R gently tugged on my arm. "They look happy, huh?"

I didn't answer.

"I always thought we'd be having this party for you and Tyler," she said with a faraway smile. "The way you two were always together."

I swallowed the lump of regret and jealousy in my throat. He chose Sarah to become part of his family when I had been there the whole time. Throwing back my *Honey I Do* drink, I coughed and set the glass down on the counter. "Do you like her?"

Mrs. R. tilted her head side to side. "She's very sweet. Too skinny though." She glanced up at me and patted my hand. "Come on, mami, let's eat."

My eyes stung at the term of endearment. Sylvia and Juan had always treated me as one of their own. Now she'd be calling someone else mami. Someone with no hips who didn't shove two tiny mushroom wellingtons into her mouth at one time.

Mr. R. moseyed in as I swallowed down the salmon pâté, verifying I indeed hated pâté. He wrapped me up in a bear hug, and I grinned into his shoulder. Juan Rodriguez ran a residential construction company, and he had the roughened hands of someone who worked hard with the belly of someone who ate well. "I miss you, Tilly girl."

"Miss you too," I said, as he let go of me with a ruffle to my hair.

"I'm glad you'll be with Tyler every step of the way. That boy needs someone with a brain."

Mrs. R. playfully backhanded her husband. I laughed too. Tyler was brilliant, but being the baby of the family, he had a sometimes unwarranted reputation for being a dope. He was lovingly spoiled and mercilessly teased.

"I'll take care of him," I said, and Mr. R. winked.

"You always do."

Honey I Do threatened to come back up.

"Hey, Till," Tyler called from the sliding door, and I left his parents with a wave to trail him and Sarah around as they introduced me to friends and family. There were her parents, Charles and Beverly, her younger sister, Mandy, who was still in college and would be the Maid of Honor. My cousin Ellen was there with Austin. She was going to be a bridesmaid.

There were also aunts and uncles, co-workers, and Tyler's family, many of whom I already knew. Sarah sang my praises to all of them. She couldn't stop gushing over how sweet I was for helping her, and how she hoped we could become best friends like Tyler and I were. She didn't want to be a third wheel, she joked.

Little did she know, she'd be tossed right out of the vehicle soon.

A familiar tattooed arm slipped around my waist when I stopped at the bar again. "Hey, gorgeous."

"Hi, Ricky."

Tyler's cousin gave me that big grin of his. "You're looking beautiful as always."

"Thank you. You look...bright."

His eyebrows lifted above his Ray-bans. "You like it, huh?" He stepped away from me, striking a pose he'd most definitely practiced with one hand in the pocket of his cheetah print shorts and the other on the collar of his highlighter yellow short-sleeve button-down, which was left mostly unbuttoned. Ricky was hot, and he knew it. He was one of the few people who could pull off the *Fresh Prince of Bel-Air* style. "How 'bout taking a dip in the pool with me?"

"Nope."

He leaned in close, his breath minty fresh. "No?"

"Didn't bring a suit."

He lowered his sunglasses enough so I could see his playful brown eyes. He thought he was slick, assessing me in a way I'm sure most girls found flattering, but I'd known him for almost as long as I'd known Tyler. I wasn't impressed.

"One of these days..."

I shook my head. Whatever the end of that sentence was, it absolutely would not come true.

"So, what are we going to do for the bachelor party?" He

straightened to his full height, not much taller than me. "I can call my boys."

"No."

Ricky had boys all over the Tristate area. He'd grown up in New York City, and when we were kids he was often at Tyler's house on the weekends. Sometimes in the summer, I'd ride along in the Rodriguez family van up to the Bronx for the day to Ricky's mom's place. Ricky had always been the life of the party, flitting here and there and everywhere. I still didn't have a full grasp of what he did for a living...something about club and bar promotions.

"It's going to be low-key," I told him. "What Tyler wants."

"Right. Well." He looped his arm around my waist. "Long as you're there, it don't matter."

I pressed my lips together in a tight smile and slid out of his hold, right into Sarah. "Hey, doll," she said, pulling me by the wrist. "My dad wants to make a toast. Can you say a little something?"

"I...uh..."

She shoved me right next to Tyler, who grinned down at me. Charles clinked his glass, calling everyone's attention, and dozens of pairs of eyes focused on us. As Charles began to speak in a cheerful rumbling tone, welcoming his friends and family to celebrate his daughter's pending nuptials, the midday heat assaulted me.

I threw my hair up into a hasty ponytail in an attempt to offer my damp neck some air while Charles went on about the first time Sarah had brought Tyler home to meet them. How nervous he had been, stumbling over himself. I gazed up at Tyler, who laughed congenially, his arm draped around Sarah like a shower curtain. Jesus, she was so small.

We could not have been more opposite. She was bright and fresh, a dainty little daisy, while I was an overgrown and sweaty tomato in my red maxi dress. I pressed my shoulder blades together and stood taller. Might as well aim for the prize-winning-vegetable-at-the-fair size. I had a speech to give, after all. When Charles finally ended his toast and introduced me as Tyler's best lady friend, I stepped forward.

"Hi, my name is Tilly, and I've known Tyler almost my whole life. We've been best friends since first grade, when his family moved in next door. As soon as we met, we became an instant package deal: Tilly and Tyler. There is not one moment, good or bad, in my life which he has not been present for."

I glanced back over my shoulder, catching sight of Sarah leaning her head against Tyler's side. I plastered a smile on my face and faced the crowd once again. "Tyler was my first kiss." A few people laughed, and I nodded, dabbing my index finger on the tiny scar, barely visible, on my upper lip. "We were on the swings in his backyard, and he dared me to jump off. Told me I couldn't fly as high as he could." More laughs. "I took the dare because, first of all, I never say no to a dare, and, second, because whatever we did, good and bad, we did it together. If he was jumping, so was I."

"Aw, babe," Sarah cooed behind me.

I raised my voice. "Tyler jumped first and landed on both feet, no problem. Then it was my turn. Suffice to say, I did not land on both feet. He ran right over, and after I finally stopped crying, he wiped the blood away with the bottom of his T-shirt and kissed me."

I pressed three fingers to my mouth, and if I tried hard enough, I could still smell the crisp leaves on the ground and feel the early autumn breeze. I could remember how he had held my hand and smiled after kissing me, saying, "All better?"

"Tyler looks out for people," I said, continuing with my impromptu speech. "He's honest and kind, and always knows exactly what to say. He's the best friend anybody could have, and I am profoundly lucky to be able to call him mine. I love you, Ty."

I spun around to him as everyone in the crowd oohed and awed, and he wrapped his arms around me, lifting me up off the ground an inch, his mouth next to my ear. "I love you, Till."

I'd like to say there was no wobble of my chin, no blinking away of tears, but that would be a lie. By the time he set me back down on the ground with his hands on my shoulders, smiling so brightly it was hard to hold his gaze, I had my features set in place. "I mean it," I said. "I love you."

He nodded, not understanding. "I know. I'd do anything for you because I know you'd do anything for me."

I endeavored to keep my face composed, even as I sensed he was about to say something I wouldn't like.

"I'm really happy, beyond happy," he went on, as he held my hand, "but I was a little nervous about you and Sarah getting along, 'cause you know..." He shrugged with a laugh. "You tend not to like the girls I bring home."

His smile told me he was kidding, but the underlying message still irked me. "Because you don't bring them home. You bring them to your bed and then bye-bye."

He squeezed my fingers, checking over his shoulder that no one heard me. "I know, but that's all in the past. Sarah is it for me."

Sarah.

Is.

It.

For.

Me.

Each word was an arrow to my heart.

"Can we get together when I get home?" he asked. "The company's got me traveling this week, but I wanted to make sure we have some time together."

"Yeah, sure," I said, my words totally unaffected by the fact that we would be alone for the first time in months.

"And—"

"Hey, babe," Sarah called from a few feet away with a little wave. "Sorry to interrupt you two."

Tyler dropped his hand from me and turned to Sarah, who held up an empty glass, a sad lemon slice hanging off.

"Get me another?"

"Yeah, babe. Right there." Tyler kissed my cheek before scampering away to get Sarah another lemon water, and I hollowed my cheeks, pinching my lips together. They needed a break from maintaining the ridiculous smile.

It was like an alien had come down and played body-snatcher with Tyler. Sarah snapped her fingers and he ran? What was it she had over him? Whiskey flavored nipples? A gold vagina?

I sulked away, through the crowd, around the pool, down the hill toward the pond, and past the vegetable garden to Sarah's "cottage." With stone walls, a chimney, and paned glass, it looked like something out of another century. I tried the doorknob and found it unlocked. With a glance behind me to make sure no one spied me, I stepped into the Pottery Barn catalog.

The beams on the ceiling and wood floor was dark but everything else in between was open and light, pale pinks and muted grays, decorative throw rugs and tall vases of fresh flowers. I spun in a circle, mouth open. Not everyone was lucky to have money like this, and I didn't begrudge anyone, but if the Kellys weren't one percenters, they were definitely top fivers. Meanwhile, my parents' whole house was probably about the same size as this cottage, and I was still paying off college loans for a university I never graduated from.

It was hard for me not to resent Sarah and her family a little bit.

I explored the place, poking my head into the bathroom with the claw-foot tub, outside to the stone patio, and finally into her bedroom, with its pastel purple and French inspired décor. Her bed was huge, a California King. Tyler would have more than enough room to stretch out on it. He couldn't ever sleep in my bed. If, on the rare occasion, he passed out at my apartment, it was usually on my couch. On the other hand, his condo in Rittenhouse Square was even smaller than my apartment, but his bed could comfortably fit both me and him after a night at our favorite dive bar.

No wonder he spent so much time here in the lap of luxury. Who wouldn't? I wondered what their plan was after they got marr—

No. They would not be getting married. I didn't have to know what their plan was for living quarters.

Turning to leave, I ran into Sarah's cat. Or rather, it silently crept up to me, curling around my legs. This was the one Zack had told me about. The long-haired, gray cat was the only witness to my crime, and while it rubbed against my shin, I noticed the closet door was open. I couldn't help but snoop, searching for anything of interest.

And I found it.

A small box, covered in pretty pink and purple Parisian motifs. Inside were mementos, including birthday cards and photos, and right on top, a couple strips from a photo booth. I studied each little picture of Sarah and Zack. They appeared to be at some sort of carnival. She held a stuffed penguin under one arm, and a bloom of cotton candy in the other hand. In most of the photos, they'd put on silly faces, tongues out sort of thing, and maybe even more surprising than Sarah eating sugar was how happy Zack appeared with his eyes crossed as he held bunny ears behind Sarah's head.

I tossed the photos into the box and placed it back on the shelf before grabbing my phone to text Zack.

At Sarah's quaint little cottage home, found some pics of you and her in a memory box. Good sign I think.

According to those fair photos, Zack had been happy with Sarah at some point, and from the little I knew about him, he deserved to be happy. I wanted that for him. If it meant breaking up Sarah and Tyler, so be it. Everyone would be better off.

Seven

I loved growing up in a small town that was still so close to Philadelphia or New York City. A few miles in either direction, you could hit farms—actual farms with cows and barns —while our "downtown" had a walkable Hallmark movie setting with boutique stores and local shops, where the owners and customers knew each other by name. That's where Michelle's Belles was located, on the corner, across from a dance studio and catty corner to the bookstore. I parked in my usual spot, outside of the bank lot, and waved to Davey through the chalk-painted window of the coffee shop.

There could be worse places for me to live besides this picturesque town, but I wasn't given much of a choice.

Not that I regretted it.

While my mother recuperated, she needed someone to keep the shop running for income. My dad's high school teaching salary wasn't going to cover the bills, and with all of the rehab and necessary adaptations to their house, paying for my school was out of the question, let alone finishing it.

Second semester of my junior year was supposed to be a study-abroad in Ireland, but only a week in, I'd gotten the call.

A deer had jumped out on the road as my mother had driven home from a wedding expo, and she'd swerved right into black ice. Her car had flipped twice.

No way was I going to stay in a different country while my mother relearned basic tasks like feeding herself and brushing her teeth. I wouldn't let her dream of Michelle's Belles die.

There had been no other option besides coming back home to help.

And I would do it all over again if I had to.

Except everyone else had moved on while I was still stuck here, preparing to help my best friend's fiancée pick out her wedding gown.

If I had a choice between accepting this fate or doing something about it, I was going to do something about it.

Opening the door to the shop, the bell above the door jingled, and Jenny, one of our sales staff, waved to me from her place on the podium as a bride walked out of a dressing room in an off-the-shoulder Maggie Sottero with a beaded lace bodice and full tulle ball gown skirt. A princess gown, if I ever saw one. The two women with the bride leaped up to fawn over her while the bride herself had yet to face the mirror. I stuffed my purse under the wrap-up counter and made my way over to the group.

"Hi, I'm Tilly," I said, introducing myself to the trio of women.

"My manager," Jenny clarified, and then gestured to her bride. "This is Sydney, and her friends, Nikki and Vanessa."

"I'm so nervous," Sydney whispered, and I quirked an eyebrow at Jenny who smiled kindly at the bride.

"There is no reason to be nervous here," she said softly, patting Sydney's shoulder.

Nikki folded her hands under her chin. "Jay will love you no matter what you wear. He'd marry you in a paper bag, I think."

"You look beautiful," I said. Behind me, Nikki and Vanessa agreed, and I smiled at Sydney, whose fingers visibly trembled. "May I?"

When the bride-to-be nodded, I stepped onto the platform and fixed the straps a little lower on her arms and then fluffed the skirts to create more of an hourglass figure. "How about a veil?"

Sydney glanced at her friends before answering. "I don't think I want to wear a veil."

Normally, I'd talk a bride into buying one, but I refrained this time, not wanting to put any more pressure on a palpably insecure bride. "When is the wedding?"

"Next spring," Sydney said, caressing the soft tulle of the dress.

"Lovely. What's the date?"

"We actually haven't decided yet."

Vanessa spoke up then. "We thought if we picked the dress out, it would help her decide what else she wanted."

"Besides Jay, I have no idea what I want." Sydney shrugged, and I laughed but quickly lost my smile when Sydney began to cry.

"I never thought I'd see this day."

Her friends immediately moved to hug her. Nikki wrapped her arm around Sydney's middle while Vanessa pressed her head against the bride's temple.

"I'd dreamed of this day for so long," she said with a sniff, and I handed her a tissue. "I'm trans and growing up I never thought this day would have been possible." She glanced down at her gown, tears tracking down her cheeks. "Today is, quite literally, a dream come true."

I'd met Bridezillas on a daily basis and had become jaded by the wedding industry, but even my cold heart melted, and I pivoted away, clearing my throat of the emotion threatening to spill out as Jenny dabbed at her eyes. If Sydney dreamed of this day, I was going to make it perfect for her. We kept bottles of champagne for VIP appointments in the refrigerator in the break room, and I grabbed one along with some plastic flutes before returning to them. "I think this calls for a toast."

Vanessa clapped, her long curls bouncing. "Yes, yes, yes."

Once the champagne was distributed, Nikki held her glass aloft. "To dreams come true!"

I downed the champagne to dislodge the lump in my throat and went to work. Sydney was in flats, and I offered to find her a pair of heels to help her see the whole picture. Even though she wasn't sure she wanted a veil, I tied a Swarovski crystal and pearl headband around her hair, going so far as to loosely braid back the coffee brown locks. When I finished, Nikki, Vanessa, and even Jenny were awestruck.

"Okay," I started, "envision your wedding day with Jay at the other end of the aisle. This is what he'll see."

Gently, I nudged Sydney to turn around, finally seeing her dream come true, and her face lit up.

"Oh my god!"

"You're like a fairy princess."

"Everything is perfect, absolutely perfect."

"I love this skirt. It's so soft."

"And your boobs look great."

"Can you dance in it?"

Sydney bent over, shimmying here and there, and the other two girls joined in, so I stepped away. Jenny followed. "You're magnificent at this."

I checked my mascara, sidestepping her praise. "Make sure you tell her if she plans on wearing a necklace, it should be a thin, subtle chain, nothing ornate, and to wear it high, like, right at her collarbone. Long earrings, though, if she wants."

"Thanks!"

In the backroom, I found my mother at the computer. "What're you doing here?"

"Ordering more inventory."

Even though she didn't do any sales floor work anymore, she was still the big boss who signed all the checks and had final say on inventory, staff hiring, and general guidelines. She popped in a few times a week to check up on everything, square our numbers, and give me instruction. I didn't need it, but I knew it made her feel better to have her hands in the business as much as she could.

"I see Sarah has her appointment today."

I hooked my elbow around the steamer. "Yep."

"Maybe I'll stick around so I can meet her."

"Didn't you meet her at Ellen's wedding?"

She tilted her head, smiling. "Yeah, but that was before she was engaged to Tyler. He was practically another child to your father and me. I want to get to know her."

"Right." I leaned my head down on my bicep, remembering with a cringe how Tyler had texted me this morning, telling me to find Sarah a dress that showed off her ass. Ugh.

"Are you excited?"

I lifted my head and tacked on my saleswoman grin. "Sure. They should be here soon. Jenny's finishing up with her client now."

Mom stopped scrolling on the computer and regarded me over the top of her glasses. "Yeah? How'd she do?"

"Should be a good commission for her."

Jenny had a problem closing sales, and I'd been working on it with her, so I wasn't about to let my mother in on how she'd seemed to be struggling when I arrived.

"I'm glad, but we're behind on the target."

"I know, Mom, but it's the summer. Besides fittings and last-minute accessories, it's our down time. What do you expect?"

She rolled her chair backward. "Maybe we should run a sale on—"

"I'm already on it. I'm going to sort out jewelry and shoes from last year, and run some social media posts this week. I'll have Jenny change the window display to feature some of the bigger statement necklaces and maybe a pair or two of the Vera Wang shoes."

My mom reached for my hand and smiled up at me. "Of course you have it covered. You do a fantastic job."

I nodded and turned away. I was good at this. I just didn't know if I *wanted* to be good at this. Michelle's Belles was my mother's ambition, not mine.

After Jenny finished up with Sydney and her friends, I offered to clean up the dressing room if she took the flower girl fittings. We were a small boutique and couldn't carry every size of every gown, but we had a good amount, and I liked to personally inspect the racks to make sure every dress was categorized correctly. It calmed me to organize, and I needed all the Zen vibes I could get because when Sarah Kelly showed up for her appointment, she arrived with an army.

They came with magazines, sparkling cider, chocolate covered strawberries, and small chalkboards. Like the Grinch, I wanted to cancel the whole thing. I'd prefer to roll up all the gowns like a Christmas tree and stuff them up a chimney.

"Hey...everyone." I performed a swift head count then signaled Jenny over to find some folding chairs in the back. "It's...nice...to have you all here," I finally got out after each woman gave me a hug like we knew each other. There was Sarah, her mother, two aunts, godmother, sister, grandmother, and Cooper, her completely disinterested cousin. When Sarah explained to me that she needed his input, Cooper had deliberately plopped down onto a chair before proceeding to play on his phone.

This was shaping up to be a real rom-com fashion montage.

I couldn't have hated it more.

My mother rolled out onto the floor, maneuvering her chair with some difficulty around all of the crap they'd brought along.

"I'd like to introduce you to my mom, Michelle. She's the owner of this fine establishment."

"Oh my god!" Sarah lunged at my mother, hugging her around the neck. "It's so nice to see you again! I love it here. So cute. I love everything. The décor—Mom, did you see those little decorative bird cages in the corner and the window display with all those origami birds?" Sarah beamed back at me and my mom. "So adorable."

"Well, it's all Tilly," Mom said. "She manages all the day-to-day operations of the store."

Sarah and her mom both frowned and touched their hands to their hearts, probably making a connection between my mother's wheelchair and my name tag with the title of Manager on it.

"I opened the store about ten years ago now, but I had an unfortunate car accident so Tilly volunteered to step in where I couldn't."

"Aw, so sweet," Mrs. Kelly cooed with a pat to my arm.

"And so brave," Sarah added with a wave to my mom's chair. "To not give up."

I didn't even allow my mother to respond before I did. "It's not brave."

Sarah and her mother both shot me matching doe eyes. "What?"

I knew my mom didn't appreciate the condescension, but while she stayed silent, I refused to. "There's nothing brave about continuing to live her life, like you and I are doing. She owns a bridal salon. She's not getting on a rocket ship to explore the unknown."

My mom tapped my hand, wordlessly telling me to stop.

"Saying she's brave implies there is some innate weakness

or something wrong about how she's living her life when, in reality, there is nothing wrong or weird or weak. It's different, but she's still living like any other person."

"I'm so sorry," Sarah said. "I didn't mean to imply anything negative."

"Tilly," Mom said, barely concealing the admonishment in her voice. I'm sure I'd get a lecture later about good customer service. "Why don't you go to the back to help Jenny get more chairs?"

I did as she told me to but not before I heard the rest of the conversation.

"I'm sorry, Mrs. Mahoney," Sarah said.

"It's all right. No offense taken. I think Tilly is a little stressed out."

A little stressed out, to say the least.

I was stressed about a lot of things. About this ridiculous charade of a wedding and this whole outrageous appointment. Because who brings chocolate covered strawberries to a bridal boutique filled with white gowns?

People with either a lot of audacity or no common sense, that's who.

And, yeah, I know Sarah didn't mean it, but after the years of physical therapy and hard work to adjust to a new "normal" life, my mom didn't need anyone pointing out how she didn't fit in with some peoples' idea of normal. She was simply trying to make a living.

I was simply trying to make a living.

I inhaled a few deep breaths and followed Jenny out of the backroom with two folding chairs to earn my paycheck. Once the entire Kelly clan settled, and my mother gently requested they save the chocolate covered strawberries for later, I took Sarah aside to explore the racks of gowns.

"Tilly, I really am sorry. I didn't mean to upset you earlier. It's just wonderful to see someone go through what your mom did and be strong and prevail," Sarah said with shimmering eyes that had guilt bubbling up in my chest.

Sarah didn't strike me as a bad person. Not even a careless person who spoke without thinking. Though she did seem like a girl trying a bit too hard to please everyone around her.

"I know." I moved out of her grasp to sort through some gowns. "Like my mom said, I'm stressed."

Sarah shook her hands out before pressing them to her cheeks, screaming silently. "I know! Me too. If you're stressed, my god, how do you think I'm feeling?" She laughed as if she couldn't believe she'd admitted that out loud then looped her arm around my waist, squeezing me tightly. "I'm so happy to be here and doing this with you. I'm so grateful for your help."

I wiggled away from her and plastered on a smile. "Do you have any idea of what kind of gown you want?"

A funeral shroud, perhaps?

"Not really. Something sexy, for sure. My parents said I could get whatever I wanted, so we're not even going to consider price tags. It's whatever I love."

"Well, then..." I marched down the aisle to the Marchesas with the highest price tag. "Let's start here. If you see anything you like, let me know."

Anything she liked? She liked everything. I put her in over a dozen gowns. While my mother pointed out the details of each dress and her family scored them with their chalkboards, Sarah hemmed and hawed. The latest was by Hailey Paige with an off-the shoulder illusion neckline and open back with lace appliques on the long sleeves. I cinched it in at the waist and very carefully by her shoulders. She was so tiny.

Truthfully, Sarah was stunning in the gown. She looked stunning in every gown, but this one, in particular.

Standing next to her, I couldn't help but compare our bodies in the mirror. Her, in the ivory lace sheath, with a flat stomach and the defined muscles of her arms and back on display. And me, in my black knee-length, cap-sleeved dress, with the genetically-coded hips and boobs required to breed multiple children to farm the potato fields. If this was 1845 Ireland, I'd definitely survive the famine. Her? Definitely not.

Sarah twisted back and forth in front of the mirror. She pivoted to me, holding my hand. "What do you think?"

"This is your wedding gown. It doesn't matter what I think."

Sarah gave me an *Oh, you* wave of her hand. "But you know Tyler, what do you think he'll like?"

I'd rather take a dagger to the heart than answer what my best friend might think about his fiancée's possible wedding dress, and I stepped away from her, dropping our hands. "I honestly don't think he'll care what you wear."

She smoothed her hands over her hips. "Of course he will. He always comments on my clothes."

I jerked my head back. "He does?"

She nodded, speaking in a faraway voice as she became engrossed with the decorative buttons at the wrist of her sleeves. "I'm always in workout stuff for work, it's basically my whole wardrobe, and I don't really like wearing anything else, you know? Why wear real pants when I don't have to? We actually got into an argument about it. He can be kind of high-handed sometimes. Can we take these buttons off?"

It took me a moment to recover from her sudden change in topic. "We can remove the buttons if you want to."

"Since they're not functional, what's the point, right?"

Once I caught Sarah's reflection in the mirror again, I frowned. "Tyler's high-handed?"

She lifted her shoulder with an eye roll. "Yeah, you know him."

I quirked my brow. Maybe I didn't know him.

While I spiraled through a friendship identity crisis, she

went on. "He thinks I'll go along with whatever he says, but I'm training him, don't you worry," she said with a sassy smile. "He's so used to being a bachelor and the baby of the family, he thinks he can get whatever he wants, but he's got another think coming with me, huh?" She twisted side to side in the mirror. "It's hard that we're so different on some things. He likes one thing, and I like the opposite. But—" she winked at me "—I like this one."

I blinked off the conversation whiplash. "The gown?"

She spun to her family. "This is the one!"

She bounced gleefully as they all surrounded her while I leaned against the mirror, thinking back over my relationship with Tyler, examining it from a different angle to see if he'd ever been high-handed with me. He did have a tendency to always get his way, mostly because he'd charm people into whatever he wanted. Sometimes he may have been a little spoiled or a tad inconsiderate, and he was definitely slow on the follow through, but I easily ignored all that. He'd always been that way, and after a lifetime together, I wasn't sure if it really mattered.

I knew all of his bad habits and personality traits. Like he knew mine. But that's what good relationships were based on, loving a person in spite of their faults.

I tucked Sarah's small admission away to use at a later date and tried my best to celebrate this moment with her. Or at least pretend to celebrate.

Once Sarah finished her mini photo shoot in the dress, I helped her off the small platform and back into the dressing room. After closing the curtain behind us, I carefully took off the clips and unfastened the top button at the nape of her neck.

"I can't believe we only have ten more weeks until the wedding," she mused. "There's still so much to do."

Once I unzipped the gown, she slid her arms free of the

sleeves and held it up at her bust before spinning to face me. "I'm so behind on making a registry. It should've been done, like, yesterday."

"Well, that's not hard."

"It is when Tyler's so picky, but he's not around to help."

As I stepped away so she could dress, she stopped me with her hand against the door, caging me in.

"If I go tomorrow, will you come with me? I already talked to him about it. You could be his stand-in for helping me narrow things down."

I pointed at myself. "You want me to help you pick out what you and Tyler will use in your house?"

She nodded eagerly. She was always so excited.

I skirted my gaze around the small space, suddenly a little claustrophobic. "It's only towels and stuff. You really need me for that?"

"Towels and dishes and flatware and stemware and—"

"Okay." I stopped her from ticking off more items on her fingers. "All right." Even though this was yet another errand I dreaded, I figured it might be a good time to start dropping some doubts about this wedding at Sarah's feet. "Do you want to meet up somewhere? I'll bring my laptop."

She wrinkled her nose at me. "I'm not registering online. I'm going in person, which is why I need you, you goose." She poked my arm. "It's better for business to shop at brick and mortar stores. I like to shop local."

I couldn't disagree, especially since Michelle's Belles was indeed a small business. Tyler and I had always patronized our local shops. "Great. Where do you want to go?"

"I was thinking Macy's."

I snorted a laugh. "That's a national chain."

She blinked at me. So... She was serious.

"It's not shopping local."

"It's local to here," she said with a shrug and proceeded to shimmy out of the dress, her back to me. I slipped out of the dressing room and headed straight for the cash wrap, where I'd stashed my purse earlier and texted Zack. **I have an idea. Meet me here later?**

He responded immediately. **Where is here?**

Michelle's Belles, we close at 8.

Before I could wait for Zack's answer, Sarah's crew all attacked different sections of the store. Grandma went for a matronly blue number, Mrs. Kelly nabbed a tiara, while her sister and aunt pored over the bridesmaid dresses. Cooper lazily draped himself on the counter, near me, his phone still in his hand.

"What did you think of everything?" I asked him.

He propped his chin in his hand, heaving out a sigh. "Everything's over the top with my family."

"Yeah, I caught on."

He leveled me with a conspiratorial gaze. "And why wouldn't I want to be dragged along? I love fashion, right? Every gay guy does."

I didn't know what else to say besides, "Sorry, that sucks."

"I'm used to it." He reached for one of the pens in the holder, clicking it a few times. "Especially with her." He glanced over his shoulder in Sarah's direction. "Maybe she'll actually go through with it this time."

I barely held back from hurdling over the counter to get to Cooper's side. "What?"

"Don't you know?"

I shook my head.

"She's a serial breaker of engagements."

"I had no idea," I whispered, eyeing Sarah and her family, making sure they couldn't hear us.

"She was engaged twice before. The first time, right out of high school. That girl falls in and out of love faster than it takes us to remember their names."

This revelation had me sewing my lips shut so I didn't make any comment that would give me away.

"If you ask me," he went on, "I think she likes the attention, but when it comes right down to it, she's not in it for better or for worse. It's probably a good thing she has yet to make it down the aisle."

"Cooper!" We both jumped slightly at Sarah's voice. She held up a sequined white dress. "For the rehearsal dinner. Too much?"

He slanted his gaze to me with a secretive smirk then walked over to his cousin. "It's your wedding. There's no such thing as too much."

I tilted my head back and forth. There was such a thing as too much, but I didn't think Sarah *or* Cooper would care.

Eight

Another 45 excruciating minutes ticked by before I had Sarah's proper dress size ordered and the whole gang out of the store, a wreckage of tulle and pearls in their wake. After Mom left, I had Jenny help me with the new window display then told her she could leave early. We didn't have any more appointments scheduled, and I liked having the place to myself so I could sing off-key to The Cranberries in solitude. After dinner, I sold an off-the-rack dress to a mother of a bride and scheduled the first of our Summer Sale social media posts before straightening up the racks and vacuuming.

I didn't hear the door open so I startled when someone tapped me on the shoulder. With a hand to my heart, I whirled around, relaxing when I found Zack. "You're early," I said, and he shrugged, his motorcycle helmet in one hand. "You scared me."

He mumbled an apology, surveying the shop. "This is your store?"

"My mom's."

"You always listen to Van Morrison on full blast?"

I unplugged the cord and wound it around the vacuum. "'Tupelo Honey' is my favorite."

"I could tell you were having fun with your date." He motioned to the vacuum as I carted it to the closet. "Saw you two dancing together through the window."

"Creep."

The corner of his mouth twitched, and I ignored how that tiny reaction made me feel the lightest I had all day. After hanging the closed sign and locking the door, I nodded for him to follow me behind the cash wrap, where we settled on the two rolling chairs. I left my flats on the floor and extended my feet up on one of the open cubicles beneath the counter.

"How was your day?" I asked because it seemed like good manners to do so before we planned how to break up a wedding.

"Uneventful."

"I had quite an afternoon with Sarah," I told him, and one bronze eyebrow raised my way. "She's...a lot."

He stared at me. His unreadable eyes might have made him seem unapproachable for people who didn't know him, but it only made me more interested in learning what was inside his head. Right when I thought he wouldn't respond, his mouth curved up in a smile I almost missed before he wiped it away with his palm. "That's for sure." Then he nodded at me more seriously. "What's your big idea that brought me to a wedding dress shop?"

I set my feet on the floor and crossed my legs. His attention dropped to my toes, and I was suddenly self-conscious of the bright blue paint that was half chipped off. "She wants me to help her with her registry tomorrow, and I thought it would be a good time for you to run into her."

The journey his gaze took up my leg had me fidgeting with the hem of my dress at my thigh. When he finally met my eyes, he arched one eyebrow. "Run into her?"

"Yeah, you know, oops-didn't-see-you-there-so-sorry-to-bump-into-you-love-of-my-life-please-take-me-back."

He let out a cross between a laugh and a snort as he dragged a hand through his hair. The clothes he wore weren't much different than his work uniform, but his jeans were fitted and clean, his T-shirt wonderfully worn. He had showered, the tips of his auburn strands still wet, and whatever soap he used had me involuntarily leaning closer to him.

"That's how you see it going?" he asked.

I shrugged. "Why not? The oops-didn't-see-you-there usually works for me."

His stare was not a gentle caress. It was a heavy, tangible thing, and my skin prickled under the weight of it as if his fingers were dragging over my body from head to toes and back up.

I tugged on my necklace, uncrossing my legs, only to recross them again. Still, he didn't look away. He merely tipped his head thoughtfully. "I can't imagine how anyone wouldn't see you coming."

My skin heated, and I covered my throat with my hand, hoping it wasn't as red as it felt. "Is that supposed to be an insult?"

He gave a barely perceptible shake of his head then spun away from me, toggling his chair back and forth. I was tempted to put my hand on his shoulder to stop him. To ask him what it meant that anyone wouldn't see me. Did he mean that literally or metaphorically? And, more importantly, did he include himself as anyone?

But I honestly wasn't sure if I wanted to know the truth.

After all, there was no reason to read into it. He was getting back with Sarah, and I'd finally have Tyler all to myself. That was the plan.

"Do you enjoy doing all..." Zack waved his around to encompass the boutique. "This?"

I began to put my hair up but quit halfway through. "Sometimes."

He stopped swerving the chair, his big boots and knees facing me, his arms folded over his chest. "Sometimes?"

I focused on the small tear-away calendar next to the computer, ordering my thoughts. "I don't hate it, and sometimes it's really nice. Like today, I had this transgender bride come in who was really emotional and grateful. She was beautiful in a gown she never thought she'd get to wear. Moments like that are really great, but mostly it's nervous or pushy brides with families who aren't always nice." I forced my eyes up to his and told him the truth. "It's not the worst thing in the world. It's just not what I thought I'd be doing."

His index finger tapped his elbow a few times as if he was really thinking about my answer. Then he finally asked, "What did you think you'd be doing?"

I shrugged. "Living an academic life. Masters, doctorate, maybe write a book or two, teach somewhere."

Under the whiskers of his beard, his bottom lip disappeared behind his teeth for a moment while he assessed me. I didn't like how it felt like he could always see what I was thinking. Or, at least, like he was trying to. Especially when I couldn't see inside him. "But now you're living the *Say Yes to the Dress* life?"

"You know that show?"

He went back to swiveling the chair back and forth. "Chloe's been addicted since she was a kid."

I aimed my thumb over my shoulder. "Does that mean you're not afraid of all *this*, as you say?"

"Nope." He studied a poster stand-up of a bride and groom near the center of the room, next to a small settee and side table, where we placed bridal magazine and coffee table books from designers.

"Do you want to get married?" I asked because why not?

We were partners in crime now. I should know his most basic life ambitions.

He licked his bottom lip then scraped his top teeth over it as his eyes sort of glazed over for a few moments. Then he shook his head as if stirring from a sleep and briefly met my gaze before it skittered away again. "I don't know if I'll ever get married. I never saw that for myself since I didn't see it around me. I didn't know what a functioning relationship looked like."

"Oh." I raised my hand to stop him. He didn't need to explain his family situation again, but since he was mostly turned away from me, he didn't see my gesture and continued.

"When I met Sarah. She—" He cut himself off and swiveled his chair in my direction, clearing his throat. "I'd read a few self-help books before I met her, so it's not like she saved me or anything," he said like I needed to know he didn't need saving. I'm sure he didn't.

He nodded to himself. Or, possibly to me and my thoughts that I swore he could read. "But she convinced me to go to therapy to work through some family stuff, and I started to think..." He lifted a thick shoulder. "Maybe I do want to get married. Maybe I do want something for myself that was different than what I thought I could have."

"You go to therapy?" I asked, both surprised and proud. "Good for you."

His mouth tipped up playfully. "You never thought of going?"

I tossed him a look. "I'm planning on breaking up my best friend and his fiancée like a totally normal person."

He nodded sarcastically. "Right."

We exchanged a grin that knocked me on my ass, and he scooted his chair closer to me. "How 'bout you? Do you want to get married?"

"Yeah. For sure," I answered confidently.

"To Tyler?"

I huffed. "Why else would I be doing this?"

He licked his lips again, and it was becoming a real problem for me. Perhaps they were a problem for him too. Dry lips, that was the issue.

I dug through the drawer in front of me for lip balm, and when I found the small round tub, I applied it with my pinkie. He watched me without blinking as he repeated my question. "Why else would you be doing this? Hm." He made a big performance out of it, puffing his cheeks and stretching his back as if he *really* had to think about it. "I don't know, but off the top of my head? It could possibly be some misguided notion you have about love, friendship, and control?"

I chucked the lip balm at him, which he caught handily with a laugh like he knew he was right. Then he uncapped the pink container and brought to his nose for a sniff, humming in appreciation before screwing the lid back on with another goddamn lick of his lips.

"You could use it," I told him, and he merely stared at me, his attention dipping to my mouth for a moment.

"When you marry Tyler are you going to have a big wedding?"

I shouldn't have been surprised by the question since we'd been talking about weddings, but his sincere voice settling over me set off a flurry of goosebumps along my arms. I rubbed at them as I answered. "No. I think they're a waste."

As if to remind me what I did for a living, he plucked a discarded veil from the counter and held it out to me. "A waste, huh?"

I took it from him. "A wedding is for other people. It's not for the bride and groom. I know for a fact most couples don't really get to enjoy their weddings." I mindlessly fiddled with the veil, which had a rip in it, the reason it'd been tossed aside. "I want a marriage. I want love and adventure and fun. I don't need a big wedding with one or two hundred people eating bland chicken and asparagus while they stare at me cutting a cake."

I raised my gaze to the ceiling, picturing the day I'd imagined since I was a kid. "I only need my husband to look into my eyes and promise to love me forever. I'll wear a long, empire-waist chiffon dress. He'll wear plain black pants and a white shirt open at the collar. The wind will ruffle our hair, and he'll reach out to tuck loose strands behind my ear, and we'll laugh because my hair never does what it's supposed to."

I smiled dreamily and rested my head on the back of my chair, closing my eyes. "Then we'll kiss the most perfect kiss. It won't be any different than the millions of kisses we've shared before, but it'll be perfect *because* it's not any different. Because when we kiss each other, it's the most natural thing in the world, like breathing. Our bodies already know what our words have promised, that we belong to each other. And that kiss will be the first kiss of the rest of our lives, the first of millions of the same kisses."

Funny, I'd visualized my wedding day in detail so many times before, but suddenly the groom's face was blank. He was shaded as if I didn't know who it would be anymore.

Zack let out a rough sound, yanking me back into the present, and I sat up, blinking over to him. With his elbows resting on his thighs, his hands were folded as if in prayer, and he lifted his head from where he had it lowered. I raised an embarrassed shoulder and finished my thought with a shy smile. "Only him and me and maybe the sea or a river behind us. That's all I want."

His ocean eyes almost carried me away when he nodded, his voice like an incoming storm. "Me too."

Nine

"Don't let her get any dishes with animals on them," Tyler told me.

I stared ahead at the Macy's, holding my cell phone. "First of all, 'let her?' Since when did you get so bossy?"

His ratty laugh sniffled in my ear. "It's not being bossy. It's not wanting birds or some other animal staring up at me while I eat."

"Fine, no bird plates." He started to say something about coffee mugs, but I spotted Sarah getting out of her car.

"She's here, I gotta go."

"She's there? You see her? What's she wearing?"

I sighed and looked up to the heavens. "Oh dear, sweet Jesus."

"Are you praying a Novena over there?"

"I offer it up to you, Lord."

"Come on," he whined. "I haven't seen her in days, and FaceTime isn't doing it for me anymore."

"Tyler Emmanuel Rodriguez, I am not playing some weird go between for whatever phone sex thing you have going on."

"I don't want you to narrate phone sex," he said with a

chuckle, "although that might be kinda hot. I only want to know what she's wearing. Those tight dark jeans?"

I groaned and watched Sarah traipse toward the store, a big bag over her shoulder. "She's got on tie-dye pink joggers and a white shirt with a cut-out in the back."

"I hate those pants. They're so ugly. I don't know why she wears them."

"I think they're cute. I mean... She's a personal trainer, Tyler. She's not going to wear pencil skirts to work, no matter what your fantasies are." I couldn't believe words in defense of my mortal enemy were coming out of my mouth, but tearing down the patriarchy called for an armistice sometimes. "She wears what she likes, like you do, and not everyone has a personal shopper at their beck and call. I don't know why you care so much. You've never commented on anything I wear."

"I don't comment on what you wear because I don't care," he said, and *ouch*. "But..." He paused as if searching for words. "You like the person you're with to wear certain things, right? I can't imagine you'd ever be with someone who wore polka dots and stripes together."

"Yeah, but you can *like* when someone wears a certain something or make suggestions, but you shouldn't be forcing her to wear something."

"I'm not forcing her," he said like I'd wounded him.

"She told me you guys got into an argument about it."

"Oh, so now you two are talking about me?"

"I was helping her find a wedding gown. It's an intimate thing, and I can't help if she shares your business with me." When he didn't say anything, I filled in the blank for him. "Don't be a dick about what she wears. I get you want her to wear tight jeans, or a French maid costume, or whatever-the-hell, but you know she won't be hot all the time, right? I know you don't often interact with girls outside of your bed, but we don't all wake up with our hair and make-up done and our sexiest clothes on. Sarah isn't some fantasy, she's real, and if you're going to marry her, you better get used to her in sweats with zits and bags under eyes."

Although, in actuality, she probably never got zits or bags.

Tyler gave in with a mumbled apology. "You're right. You're right. Of course. Sarah is beautiful inside and out, and I promise to tell her so as often as possible. And, whatever, if she wants bird plates, get the bird plates."

"Right-o. Birds of the jungle plates, got it."

He laughed. "Have fun. Love you!"

I tossed my phone in my purse to meet Sarah inside. We had an hour before Zack was supposed to bump into us, so when she hugged me by the entrance, I ushered her to the kitchen section. The girl truly couldn't make up her mind about anything. No wonder she needed Tyler—or me as the stand-in—to help her make decisions. If I didn't narrow down the choices for her, this registry would've taken days.

Between the size of coffee mugs, colors of KitchenAid mixers, and patterns of linen napkins, I had completely forgotten about Zack and literally bumped into him. "Oh, hey," I said, moving away from the solid form of his chest. I placed a waffle iron back on the shelf before tipping my chin to where Sarah had gotten lost among the glassware at the other end of the section. "You ready?"

Instead of answering, he held up striped navy bed sheets. "What do you think of these?"

"They're fine." After a glance over my shoulder to make sure Sarah was still occupied, I lowered my voice, all clandestine like. "But you know you really don't have to buy anything while you're here, right? It's all for show."

"I could use new ones, so I thou—"

"Zack?"

We both whirled around to Sarah, who held checkered dish towels to her chest, eyes wide in disbelief.

"Hey, Sar," he said with an easy smile, as if we hadn't planned this exact thing. Even if he'd failed on the *oops* part, bumping into me instead of her.

"What are you doing here?" she asked with a hesitant step forward.

"You always said it's better to shop at stores than online." And he was good. Sarah softened before my very eyes, taking two more steps closer.

I played dumb. "You two know each other?"

She toyed with her gold hoop earring. "Yeah. We... We used to date."

"Really?" I waved a spatula between the two of them. "This is the famous boyfriend you told us all about at Ellen's bachelorette, huh?"

"You talked about me?" Zack cocked his head flirtatiously in Sarah's direction, and a weird tension settled between my shoulder blades. I didn't know head tilts could be flirtatious, and I didn't know why it felt like I slept wrong all of the sudden.

"Not much," Sarah said, fluttering her fingers.

I rubbed at my neck with one hand while pointing the spatula up in the air with the other. "If I remember correctly, she talked about how you were overworked but always found time to fit her in." When Sarah's shoulders sagged in relief, I amended my statement. "Or you fit *in* her, I meant. Right, *Sar*? He was *so* good in bed, that's what you said."

Zack stood taller in the satisfied way men do with his feet apart, arms crossed over the packaged sheets in his arms while Sarah stumbled over her words. "Well... I-I don't know." She turned to me with a nervous giggle. "Did I?"

I nodded. "You'd had half a glass of wine. Kind of a light-weight, aren't you?"

Her cheeks pinked as she plastered on one of the fakest smiles I'd ever seen. Which was saying a lot since I'd been donning them often as of late. "I don't like to drink my calories."

"So you've said. Many times." I could tell she wanted to bolt, so I gripped her arm before she could. Then I tapped Zack's shoulder with the spatula, knighting him. "Well done, sir." He narrowed his brows at me in silent reprimand. Maybe I was putting it on a bit thick, but I needed to get these two lovebirds back together and fast. I had no time to fuck around with niceties. "Listen, I'm going to check out the dinner plates. Tyler said something about birds, so I'll give you two a moment alone."

There were, in fact, no birds of the jungle plates, though I did find an excellent set with wolves. Since I had the scanner, I zapped those suckers while Sarah and Zack stayed in my peripheral vision. It didn't escape my notice that they finished up their short conversation with a hug. He shuffled backward, away from her and right by me as if we were strangers, but for some unknown reason I was desperate for him to acknowledge me. He didn't. He played his part. "See you later, Sar."

Once he was out of sight, I made my way back to her. "Well, that was unexpected."

She nodded a bit unsteadily, her gaze on the dish towels twisted up in her hands.

"Was it awkward?" I asked, and the question seemed to snap her into focus.

"Only the part where you brought up sex with him." She laughed good-naturedly and smacked my arm with the towels. I had to hand it to her; I didn't think she'd be one to roll with the punches, but so far, she had. She didn't mind my sarcasm or my attempts at embarrassing her. I was both exceedingly disappointed and a bit...relieved. At least Tyler hadn't fallen for someone who was all bad. Proof he wasn't completely off the deep end.

"Sorry," I said, not at all sorry as I stared in the direction Zack had gone. "He's cute though. Good for you."

Sarah snorted adorably next to me. "Not for me. For some other girl."

I shot my gaze down to her, disappointed and relieved once again. Although, it wasn't at all good.

I ignored how the knot at the top of my spine eased from her lack of apparent lingering feelings for him. I shouldn't have felt relief. Only one hundred and ten percent disappointment. Yet, the only disappointment I felt was on Zack's behalf. He wanted her back, and if she wasn't interested, I didn't want to hurt him any more than he already had been.

"Why not for you?" I asked with a scrunch of my nose.

"We just weren't right for each other," she answered with a shrug, which was a total cop-out. But before I could prod her for more information, she plowed right on. "We're going to need to register for a lot of towels. Tyler goes through so many in a week." She set the checkered kitchen towels down to lead me toward the bedroom area, where we discussed thread count and pillow shams for a while.

We eventually lounged on a mattress with a color blocked comforter, and Sarah skimmed her hand back and forth, her forehead wrinkling as she pursed her lips as if she was considering something.

"What's up?" I asked like we were buddies.

We weren't.

We couldn't be.

Yet she met my eyes with a weary frown. "Can I tell you something?"

"Yeah. Of course."

She leaned in closer to me, whispering, "Zack is really good at sex."

I started to grin, but her serious expression cut me off.

"*Really* good," she said, a little louder, and my heart rate sped up, cheeks ablaze. I fluffed the pillow next to me, so I didn't have to face her while trying to figure out why. I punched the decorative throw pillow twice then stuffed it behind my back, giving her my attention once again with a smile.

I wondered if it appeared as fake as hers did when Zack was standing in front of us.

"Sometimes I try to get Tyler to..." She circled her hands. "Vary it up a little. I know he's been with a lot of girls, but we aren't all the same, right?" She waited for my confirmation, and a reluctant laugh bubbled up at my best friend's sexual prowess.

"Yeah, right."

"It's like he read a how to step-by-step sex guide, perfected it, and now he can only do it that one way."

I wanted to defend Tyler, but I had—to my regret—no evidence to the contrary, so I seized the first thing I could think of. "He's real analytical, if you haven't figured that out yet."

She tapped one finger to her pouty lips. "I've been considering a boudoir photo shoot. Maybe it'll inspire him."

Maybe, but right this second, I was inspired to roll off the bed and walk away from her.

How many times had I thought about kissing Tyler? Really kissing him, not those friendly pecks on the cheek, or occasional sweet kisses to comfort me. I'd thought about having his hands on me. About me being able to explore that long, lean body of his. Sharing a bed, not only to hear him snore, but to spend hours naked and together.

And here she was *complaining* about having sex with him. I didn't know whether to be angry, jealous, mortified, or all three.

By the time she caught up to me in the bathroom section, I'd already added a shower curtain with a parrot pattern on it, and we continued filling in the rest of the registry. It took almost four hours, but we finished it, and I didn't feel a bit bad about sneaking in the back massager that looked like a giant dildo.

"I can't believe we ran into Zack today. He despises shopping and wears his clothes until there're holes in them," Sarah mused as we exited the store. "And even then, he orders everything online. Finds a shirt he likes and buys three of them."

"That's efficient. Good qualities in a guy, don't you think? Good at sex and not fussy," I said, hoping she caught the part I inferred, *unlike Tyler.*

"Meh."

Meh?

Good at sex and not fussy seemed like a pretty good combination to me, but all she had to say was "Meh." Between Tyler's need for inspiration and their supposed arguments over clothes, I don't know why she wasn't all over Zack.

If it was me, I would—

"Tilly!" Sarah yanked me back to the sidewalk as a car flew past us. "Hey!" Sarah shook her fist at the retreating vehicle. "Slow down! You're going to kill someone!"

I pressed my hand to my chest as I caught my breath. I hadn't been paying attention, my mind a million miles away.

"Are you all right?" she asked, holding my shoulders.

"I'm fine."

"Good." She offered me a sweet smile. "Have to be careful in parking lots. Some of these drivers don't watch where they're going." Then she searched her bright pink bag for a car fob, and the lights of a blue Tesla lit up when she unlocked it. I unlocked my old Chevy Cobalt, rusted by the tires.

"Thanks for coming with me today."

"No problem," I said, although I'd had to switch around the schedule at the boutique so I could scoot out early.

She hugged me tight, her head at my boobs. "Tyler's home

tomorrow, so we're going to get him fitted for his tux this weekend. Did you talk about it with him yet, do you want to wear one?"

"He said as long as I matched the color of his suit, he doesn't care."

"Okay, perfect, what do you want to wear then?"

"I'm going to get a jumpsuit."

"Yes! I love that for you." At some point during the day, I had gotten used to how touchy-feely she was and didn't even realize now how she held my hands between hers. I reminded myself that we weren't friends. Especially when she said, "And I so respect how you know exactly what you want and go after it."

She had no idea.

Ten

With Sundays being my one true day off—I didn't have to worry about running in to the shop to check something, or frantic phone calls from Jenny about how she'd ordered the wrong flower girl dress size, or buffering complaints from our grouchy tailor, Galina—I had planned to laze about, eat salt and vinegar chips, and rewatch *The Tudors* for the 1,375th time. But one call from my mom, and those plans were thrown right out of the window.

I arrived at my parents' to find soaked dish towels on the floor. Mom offered possible but probably not great solutions for what could be the cause of their leak while Dad fiddled with the pipes under the sink.

"What happened?" I collected the wet towels, tapping my dad's leg so he'd come up for air.

"We got home from church and there was water every-where," Mom supplied, exaggerating the damage. The water flowed from underneath the sink, slowly and consistently pooling on the tiled floor, but it wasn't *everywhere*.

"Did you turn the water off?" I asked.

"I...think?" Dad ran a wet hand over his face. He may have

been a gifted teacher and patient father, but he had no idea what to do when it came to household maintenance issues. So, I did the only thing I could think of. I called Zack.

I hadn't seen him for a few days, not since Macy's, and we'd exchanged exactly four text messages afterwards.

That worked out, I'd said.

Yep, he'd said.

Big plans coming up? I texted back.

Overtime, he replied.

It's why I startled when he picked up after the first ring and told me he'd be right over.

Fifteen minutes later, the doorbell rang, and I shouted for him to come in and enter the chaos. Dad had his shoes and socks off and his pants rolled up to his knees. I sat in front of a plethora of tools, not knowing what any of them did besides the hammer. Mom scrolled on the computer, randomly giving tips about water heaters and rusted pipes. Neither of which were the issue. Even I knew that.

Zack stood in the threshold of the kitchen, taking it all in.

"Hey." I swapped out another wet towel for a dry one. "Glad you could make it to the party. Mom, Dad, this is my friend, Zack. He's going to save us."

"I'll try," he said with a tip of his head. "What's going on?"

"We came home to water." Dad moved out of the way so Zack could lay down and stick his head under the sink.

"It's not the sink," he declared after a minute as he carefully avoided bumping his head on the cabinetry as he stood up from the floor, his shirt damp.

"The internet says it could be the drainage pipe," Mom said, wheeling to the kitchen table.

I plopped down next to her. "Well if it's on the internet…"

She knocked her fist against my arm with a cluck of her tongue while Zack wrenched the dishwasher out from under the counter like it was nothing. His face was completely placid as if moving a huge appliance was an everyday occurrence.

We watched him work, my parents out of curiosity, me for purely wanton reasons. The muscles on either side of his spine bunched and relaxed as he bent, and I was sure his arms were the envy of lumberjacks everywhere. When the bottom of his T-shirt rode up, displaying even more black ink tattooed into his skin, I tilted my head, trying to make it out, but that tease of skin disappeared again as he straightened.

He faced us with his hands on his trim hips. "It's not the drainage pipe. It's the supply hose."

Dad frowned. "Doesn't sound too good."

Zack wiped his hands off. "Did you use the dishwasher today?"

"We turned it on to run while we were at church," Mom said, and Zack nodded like that was the answer he was expecting.

"The reason you're having the constant water flow from under your sink is because it's delivering water to your dishwasher, so I'll need to replace it. Easy enough fix."

"Oh, thank god," Mom said.

"I don't have the right size hose in my truck, but I can grab one from the store and come back."

"It can be fixed today?" my dad asked.

"Yeah."

Dad smoothed a hand over his hair. "Well, in that case I'll let the professional handle it." He shook Zack's hand then pointed down the hall. "I'm going to change into dry clothes."

"Thank you very much, Zack," Mom said. "You really did save us." She followed behind Dad, with an exhausted yawn, "I've got to lay down."

I stood up and tossed all the wet towels to a heap in the corner. "It's been a hectic afternoon."

"Looks like it."

"Thanks for coming over so fast."

He scratched at his beard. "Yeah, sure. It's only my one day off this week."

"Sarcasm, duly noted." I stepped closer to him. "This was my day off too."

"Great. We get to spend it together, fixing a dishwasher."

"*We*? As in you and me?" I shook my head. "I don't know how to fix a dishwasher."

"Lucky for you, today is the day you're gonna learn." Then he curled his hand around my neck and flashes of a different kind of lesson ransacked my brain. "Come on," he said, escorting me out the front door, and I murmured an apology when I swayed into his side. But I couldn't help it. A gravitational pull had seized hold of me, closing the space between us.

His truck was parked in the driveway, and he gestured for me to get in.

"You want me to go with you?"

He nodded.

"I can't go out like this." I motioned down my body, and his gaze followed. I tried to pretend it didn't make me a tad self-conscious. I hadn't planned on leaving my apartment in my rattiest leggings and droopy tank-top, which revealed my orange sports bra. I wasn't exactly suitable for public display.

"Why not?"

To further my point, I stuck my pinkie finger in a hole at my thigh.

"We're going to Home Depot, not a fashion show," he said and got behind the wheel. "You're fine."

Once I was seated next to him, I hung my arm out of the open window in an attempt to dry off while convincing myself I was sweating because of the temperature and not because I was in the small cab of his truck while his mesh athletic shorts did nothing to hide his thick thighs or what was between them. I twisted my hair up into a loose bun, a few strands falling out of it. "We're going to have to work on your compliments if you want to get back in Sarah's good graces."

He glowered at me then reversed out of the driveway. "I know how to give a compliment."

Zack didn't really scream romance and poetry to me, and I angled my face to him in a challenge. "Yeah? Let me hear your best line."

"You hot?"

I sputtered a laugh. "You've got to be kidding. That's your best line?"

He shot me a bored expression. "I was asking if you're hot. Watch your arm." I removed my elbow from my window, and he rolled it up before cranking up the air conditioning, making sure the vents were pointed my way. "Better?"

When I didn't answer, he tucked a lock of hair behind my ear, the tip of his index finger barely tracing the lobe "You looked flushed."

Now that I was five degrees hotter, I plucked at my shirt. "Yeah. I'm good." My voice wavered only a little. "Thanks. Now, give me your lines."

He heaved a sigh like I exhausted him. "I don't have lines. It's not like I rehearse talking to a woman."

Tyler did. He had a few lines always at the ready, tested and perfected.

"If you're reciting lines like you're in a play, you don't really care about who you're talking to." He deliberately paused as if I should somehow connect his words to my own life, and I wondered if I accidentally spoke my thoughts about Tyler out loud. He swiveled his head left to right before he turned onto another street. "The worst type of guys play that game."

"And you're giving yourself some kind of back-handed compliment by saying you don't have to do that? What if someone isn't confident or afraid of talking to other people? I don't think there's anything wrong with practicing social skills. You—" I poked his arm "—don't come off as the most outgoing guy."

"First of all," he started, meeting my gaze at a stop light, "there's a difference between having low self-confidence and needing practice and being an arrogant dick who treats people as interchangeable objects."

Tyler had only begun practicing conversation starters because he was a tad awkward growing up. And I guess he kept it up because it worked for him—I mean, it obviously worked for him—but I didn't appreciate Zack's inferred insult about my best friend. "Is there a second?"

With his left hand on the steering wheel, he leaned his right elbow on the console between us, his shoulder and arm taking up so much room they brushed against mine. "Second, if I'm having a conversation with someone it's because I'm interested in learning about them, whether it's a woman or anyone else. I give a compliment when I mean it, not because it sounds like the right thing to say."

I couldn't argue with him, and we sat the rest of the drive in silence as I contemplated the hidden depth behind the beard and muscle.

"Was this really your only day off? I didn't realize you worked so many hours," I said after we hopped out of the truck in the parking lot.

He dropped his keys into his pocket. "Yeah. I've been doing a lot of overtime lately, and one of our guys is on vacation this week, so I got some more hours in. I could use the money."

"Well, I really appreciate you doing this. My parents and I are hopeless. You can expect a big tip." I permitted myself a pat on his back, where my fingertips lingered for barely a second. Two...three, tops.

He inclined his head toward mine, his shoulder dropping the tiniest bit as if wanting to keep my hand on him. "This one's on the house." Then he knocked the back of his hand against my hip as he steered me into the store. "But the next leak, I expect you to be able to fix."

"You can lead a horse to water..." I trailed off as we trekked into the wood and tool play land. It wasn't as bad as I thought it'd be, and I peppered him with questions about what different items were while pointing out others I liked. When we passed an especially cute art deco lamp, I stopped. "Ooh, I love that. It would look great in Michelle's."

He wielded the white plastic drain at me. "You haven't been paying attention to anything I've been explaining."

I took it from him. "This is a corrugated hose," I said, proudly recalling that one fact since I had to help him rummage for it, although I couldn't remember much of anything else. "And something about pressure heads and O-rings." I cupped my hand around my mouth, stage whispering, "I never would have guessed plumbing was so sexual."

His lips quirked, and he leaned close to me, placing his hand on my lower back to usher me away from the lamp section. "Honey, I didn't even get to the ball check valve yet."

What an astonishingly suggestive combination, his rough fingers under the hem of my shirt and weird plumbing terms. I barely held back a giggle, a little drunk on the stark smells of the store's wood and metal and the heat of his body radiating next to me.

"We've been here forever," he noted and pointed to the cash register. "Your parents are probably wondering where we are."

I stopped suddenly, the change in momentum crushing his chest to my back. "Oh no, wait. Can we get this?" I picked up the small succulent, potted in a ceramic baby deer, from the display at the end of the aisle. "It's on sale."

He grunted and rolled his eyes yet grabbed the deer from my hand, paying for it along with the hose. In the car, I felt comfortable enough—after our friendly outing—to ask him about our earlier conversation. "Before, when you said you could use the extra hours at work...?"

He glanced at me. "Yeah."

"What did you mean?"

He leaned his arm on the console again, the space between us barely there. I was burning up, even as the vents blew cool air at me. "I never went to college, and I don't have a mortgage, so I don't have a lot of debt to my name. I like to keep it that way."

"Smart."

As usual, his easy honesty felt anything but casual. "I'm saving for a down payment on a house, but I do have one credit card, and I used it to pay for my sister's wedding."

He had all my focus now. "You paid for Chloe's wedding?"

"Not all of it. Her in-laws take good care of her but—" he scratched at the center of his chest, wincing as if it hurt him to talk "—she's my baby sister, and I wanted to give her *her* day." He regarded me in a familiar way, like I understood. I did. Weddings were a big business.

"I wanted her to have the dress she loved, the flowers, the cake, the food. Hudson's parents paid for a lot, but I didn't want her to feel like..." He ran his hand over his beard a few times. "When we were growing up, we didn't have a lot. What little we had was because of our grandmother, and after she died, we were pretty much on our own. Our mother was careless about a lot of things, including when the food stamps ran out. Chloe was always so sweet and smart. Not like me." His laugh sounded more weary than angry. "I wanted her to know, for at least one day, she could have whatever she wanted, so I paid for what I could from my savings and put the rest on my credit card."

"That's incredible, Zack." When he tried to shrug it off, I shook my head. "No, really. I don't have a sibling, but if I did, I'd wish they were like you."

He cut his eyes to me then, unreadable, and the memory of his hand on my back seared into me suddenly. As if he'd branded me. I had heat in the form of five fingers on my skin, able to be evoked at any moment he wished.

Goddamn. I'd never think of Home Depot the same.

I stared at the side of his face for a moment, more than interested in the number of layers this onion contained. I wondered how many of them Sarah had uncovered before they broke up. She had to have known this about him, how he paid for his sister's wedding and worked a lot of overtime because of it, and I hated her for it. That she would ever tell this man he wasn't thoughtful enough or didn't do enough for her. What a selfish shrew.

"So, um, what did Sarah think of all that?"

He shifted in his seat. The mention of her name was a vacuum, sucking up all the oxygen between us. I was stupid for bringing her up.

But he answered anyway. "She didn't understand why I wanted to pay the credit card off as fast as possible, why I kept taking on overtime hours. She never had to worry about interest rates and savings accounts. To her, what was an extra fifty bucks here and there?"

"I totally get it. Tyler's always going out to eat, ordering anything and everything he wants, and it's not like he rubs it in my face, but when you're pinching pennies, going out to eat can be really expensive." I circled my hands as I explained, "I'd rather not pay for the charcuterie board when I could run to the grocery store for some salami and gouda, right?"

His mouth twisted into a half-smile. "Exactly."

After a few quiet moments he added, "Though, to be honest, I could've done more with her."

The abrupt change in demeanor confused me. "Sarah?"

"Yeah, I'm trying to save my money, but I should've taken her out to eat more or whatever. I could've been nicer," he said making quotation marks around the last word with his fingers. "I could've done it."

Maybe you didn't want to almost came tumbling out of my mouth, but I zipped my lips together, nibbling on the insides of them. I wasn't qualified to dissect their relationship, but it was obvious—in my highly unqualified opinion—that Sarah and Zack had different ideas about what it meant to be with each other. And maybe Zack didn't try as hard as he should have or could have because he didn't want to.

I lightly squeezed his bicep. "I think you're plenty nice."

He parked his truck back in my parents' driveway and sent me a very not nice leer. "If you say so."

Eleven

Inside, Zack operated on the plumbing with surgeon-like precision while I handed him tools. It took less than an hour, and when my dad tried to pay him, he resisted. "It was really no big deal. I'm happy to help."

"Stay for dinner then," Mom said. "It's the least we can do. We were going to order pizza."

Zack silently questioned me with a raised brow, so I sauntered over to the junk drawer, where all the menus were saved and held up my favorite. "Hope you like pineapple on pizza."

"Disgusting," he mumbled, hiding his grin behind his hand.

"I agree, Zack." Mom nodded. "I don't know who these two think they are putting fruit on pizza like it's some kind of dessert."

"It's a delicacy," Dad said.

"A delicacy?" Zack repeated incredulously as Mom shook her head.

"Yeah, right up there with frog legs."

"You two don't have our refined palettes. The sweetness of

97

the pineapple compliments the acidity of the tomato," I said in my best Food Channel voice.

"Exactly." Dad tapped in the phone number to order.

Mom angled her chair to Zack. "Do you like pepperoni?"

"Of course."

Mom gestured between me and Dad. "You two can eat your disgusting pizza. Me and Zack will share a pepperoni. And don't forget extra garlic knots." She nodded for Zack to settle in the living room. "Come on, make yourself at home."

He did, and over the next two hours Dad went on a tirade about how the History Channel barely played history shows any more, only antiquing and swamp people. Mom relayed a story about how she'd recently gotten her head bit off in her Hallmark movie Facebook group because she'd posted about how she wished the couples would kiss more. Some woman responded, "This isn't Skinemax."

Zack laughed so hard he choked on his piece of pizza, and I had to slap his back a few times. Then we all laughed more, and when I thought Zack would leave, my parents asked if he'd be interested in helping with their new puzzle, this one of Cinque Terra. The four of us sat at the kitchen table, forming the outline of the colorful houses on the Italian coastline.

Mom started her nightly routine at 8 p.m. sharp so she said goodnight with a kiss to my cheek and a pat to Zack's arm. Dad followed to help, inviting us to stay as long as we liked. Once they were out of sight, down the hall, I resumed my pursuit of the purple pieces. After a few wordless seconds, he did too.

"I like your parents," he said.

"Yeah. They're pretty okay."

When our knuckles collided over two pieces making up the roof of a house, his eyes met mine. He didn't pull his hand away. I didn't either.

"It still surprises me sometimes when I see families...being families. It's like finding Bigfoot," he said.

I assumed he wouldn't want pity for his family history—I didn't like being pitied for mine—so instead I futzed with the box. "Didn't do many puzzles growing up?"

He fit another piece in. "I didn't do much of anything besides fight."

"Really?" I rested my chin in my hand as he tossed a piece aside when it didn't match the house.

"I had anger issues." With a momentary pause to glance at me, he amended, "Still do," before going back to the puzzle. "I didn't know what to do with all of it back then. I ended up kicked out of high school and arrested for a couple of misdemeanors. After my grandma died, my uncle told me he would take me on as an apprentice if I got my G.E.D, and the only reason I agreed to do it was because of my sister. She couldn't rely on our mom, so I had to be the one she could rely on. Otherwise, I think I'd probably still be in a lot of fights."

With another layer peeled back, I could almost see inside him, to where he hid all his warmth and conviction. "I'd imagine punching someone might let out all the—" I flapped my hands by my chest, encompassing the anxiety "—angst. The one time I did throw a punch, the wall won."

His hands stilled, and he gazed evenly at me, waiting for me to continue.

"My mom was in a car accident and fractured her C6, C7 vertebrae," I said, mindlessly touching my own spinal cord. "After I saw her for the first time in the hospital, I came home and punched the wall." Guilt crept up, the way it usually did, stifling my thoughts and words from escaping, and I cleared my throat. "I knew everything had changed. We couldn't go back to the way it was. I couldn't go back to school and..." I closed my eyes, stiffly shaking my head.

Zack had been honest with me, and I wanted to be honest with him too.

"I was so mad," I told him. "Even though I had no right to be. I wasn't the one laying in the hospital bed. But, Jesus, I hated it. I hated that I had to leave school. I hated that I had to give up so much, too." Once it was out, I exhaled heavily, shifting my focus to the table. "I was angry—I'm still angry—because my mom was in incredible pain, but also because I was too. Everything I wanted, all my dreams, they were gone." I held up my fist, showing him the nearly invisible scars on my knuckles from where the wall won the fight.

He lightly rubbed his fingertip over them, such a small movement for such a big truth. When he dropped his hands and attention back to the puzzle, I blew out a breath and combed through the pieces too. After a minute, he gave me a blue bit for the section I worked on. "That's why you manage your mom's shop? Why you never got your Ph.D.?"

"I never even finished my bachelor's. I quit my junior year. I'd been studying abroad in Dublin." I tapped a piece of the puzzle on the table, nibbling on the inside of my cheek. "Do you think I'm a terrible person?"

"For being angry?" He huffed. "Of course not. You did what you had to for your family. It's okay to be angry about it."

"I know, but I'm not happy about it either."

He reached across the table to a piece he needed. "I get it. It's not like I wake up giddy to go install bathroom pipes. I got into it because I needed money, and it was an easy offer from my uncle. You're allowed to feel bad about losing something. I mean, you lost a lot of somethings, right?"

I squinted at him. "You're oddly wise about all this."

He stacked his arms on the table, ignoring the puzzle so I had the full weight of his gaze on me. "All the therapy."

I hummed knowingly, earning the smallest of smiles from him.

Under the table, his foot tapped mine. "I read this book about grief. The guy wrote it about the death of his daughter, but the idea of the book was more general." He paused to rub his bottom lip with his thumb twice before his tongue skated out to wet it, and I couldn't stop staring.

I had to stop staring.

I scratched at the hole in my leggings, forcing my eyes to my thigh.

"The author explained how lions hunt," he went on. "It's the female lions who do the actual hunting, but they basically set a trap with the male lion. He'll roar and scare the prey right into the line of waiting females, so the author said it would be better if the animal ran toward the male lion. They would have a chance to get away if they ran toward the roar, get it? We have to face our problems head on. We have to run toward the roar."

I nodded, though I still didn't want to face my problems, including but not limited to why my focus was back on his mouth.

"I don't think you're a terrible person for being angry about your mom's accident. I think you should acknowledge it and then try to move on from it."

"Easy for the guy who has a lion tattooed on him." I didn't mean to let that slip. It's not like I'd gotten much of a glimpse the day we went hiking. And I certainly didn't care about it... that much.

"I got it as a reminder." He tugged the collar of his T-shirt down.

This time I did stare. Blatantly. The black ink of the lion's mane covered most of his shoulder, with only the top of its face visible from under the weathered cotton.

"What about the one on your side?" I asked before I thought better of it.

He twisted on his chair so his right side faced me, and he lifted his shirt to reveal the Viking ship tattoo from the bottom of his ribcage to the top of his hip.

"Wow," I rasped, my mouth incredibly dry all of the sudden as I remembered at the last second to keep my hands to myself. I wiped my clammy palms down my pants. "Does this one have special meaning too?"

"Vikings are awesome," he said as if it were obvious. "What about yours?" He apparently didn't have the same hesitation about touching my skin as I did his. He drew a line down my left ribs, along my tattoo made visible because of the low cut on the sides of my tank top. "What is it?"

I sat taller, tingles from his feathery touch echoing in my belly and between my legs. "It's Ogham. Remember when I said I wanted to study Irish language?"

"I remember." He tilted his head, presumably to get a better view of the markings.

"It's the ancient Irish alphabet, read from top to bottom. They only used it for a few centuries before the Middle Ages." I raised my eyes to the ceiling in thought. "Not beyond the fall of the Roman Empire, if I remember right, because they started using Latin then. And there are only three hundred or so inscriptions left, I think, but academics have been able to translate them."

"What does it say?"

"Most of the inscriptions, including this one, are names of places or people." I blinked down to my tattoo, which probably looked like a bunch of hash marks on a vertical line to anyone who didn't know what it was, then back up to his murky green-blue-brown eyes.

"What does it say?" he asked again.

"Alive like fire." I pressed my hand to the markings that

had been carved into a stone centuries ago and now graced my side. "This was someone's name, and it meant alive like fire."

Sometime during my mini history lesson, he'd leaned into my space. With one hand on the table and the other on the edge of my chairback, his breath mingled with mine and my skin prickled with desire.

"It's really incredible," he said, his voice low and vibrating, sending mini tidal waves over me, and I shivered. He dragged a finger over my bare shoulder, setting off another tremor. "You're incredible."

His words sent my already galloping heart into overdrive, and I smiled, holding onto this connection like it was a lifeline. "You want to run toward the roar. I want to be alive like fire."

He smiled too, one that reached all the way up to his eyes so they crinkled at the corners. A stray curl of auburn hair fell onto his forehead, and I brushed it back. "Don't ever cut your hair shorter than this," I said, a vague memory wiggling loose in my brain about Sarah telling him to cut his hair. But honestly, I didn't say it because of Sarah.

I said it for me.

There wasn't one thing I'd change about Zack.

His eyes drifted back and forth between mine, his jaw moving as if he wanted to respond, but he didn't, and I was starting to get confused about what we were doing here. What I was doing here, with him. What my plans were.

I inched away from him to catch my breath and get back on track. I blinked a few times then moved back even further. He just took up so much room. Or, maybe, it was all in my head that his presence surrounded me.

"I guess, um, we should talk about our next steps, huh? I'm going to hang out with Tyler this weekend, and I'll start putting some bugs in his ear. Then maybe we can go shopping? Get you some new threads to impress your lady?"

He combed his hands through his hair a few times and

stood up, patting his pockets for his keys and cell phone. "Yeah, so... I guess I'll talk to you later." I followed him down the hall, and he stopped at the door. "Tell your parents thanks again."

"No, no. Thank you. I owe you one."

He waved me off and started to his car, but I stopped him.

"Wait. Don't forget Bambi." I ran back to the kitchen to grab the succulent from the counter.

He eyed the planter. "You're the one who wanted it."

"Yeah, but you've seen my place. I have enough plants." When he didn't move, I marched over to him and took his hand in mine, turning it up to place the deer on his palm. "It's a proven fact. Caring for plants improves a person's mood. I can't believe you didn't read that in one of your books."

He smothered the tilt of his lips with his other hand. I hated he always did that. He had a great smile, and I tugged his hand away from his beard.

"All right." He raised the fawn to me in a salute. "See you."

I made my way back to the house and leaned against the doorjamb as he walked to his truck, the summer sun almost faded into night. With his door open and one foot inside, he tipped his head to me. "Hey."

"Yeah?"

"I had fun today."

"Me too."

"And you're not nearly as tall as you think you are."

I smiled. "Is that a compliment or an insult?"

He offered me half a grin then settled into his truck.

"I'm going to take it as a compliment," I called out, and I swear I could hear him laughing even as he drove away.

Twelve

"You're a sight for sore eyes." Tyler hauled me to him with one arm, and I tucked my face against his shoulder.

"Missed you too."

Once he let go of me, he closed his apartment door. "I feel like it's been ages since I've seen you."

"Because it has." I tossed my purse by the door to his bedroom after we released our hug, and I trailed him to the living room, where I made myself at home on the end of his beige couch. He laid down at the other end, his bare feet in my lap. "How was your trip? Where'd you go?"

"Oklahoma." He flipped through channels on the television. "It was all right. I'm not sure how much more traveling I want to do."

"Yeah?"

He'd been going on so many trips because he'd been aiming for a promotion from project manager to systems engineering manager. Although I still wasn't sure what either of those roles did, he'd said he required the experience to move up the corporate ladder.

He settled on the Phillies pre-game and met my eyes. He

hadn't shaved in a few days, his sharp jaw softened with the beginnings of a dark beard. "I don't want to be away from Sarah so much."

"What about the promotion?"

He took his glasses off and removed something from one of the lenses before cleaning them with the bottom of his shirt. He placed them back on with a blink. "I talked to Davis about it, and he said Tom is retiring next year so it's not like I *need* to keep the schedule I have now. They know I'm a team player. I don't necessarily have the years of experience they'd like, but I've put in more than enough miles. At least, in his opinion."

"And Davis is your boss, right?"

He nodded through a yawn. "Sorry," he said, yet his grin didn't appear repentant. "Sarah picked me up from the airport and she stayed over last night. I only slept for a few hours."

I examined his apartment more closely, finding proof of her everywhere. A pair of women's sneakers by the front door. A wedding magazine underneath two empty cups on the coffee table. A pink frame with a close-up photo of the two of them. Oversized sunglasses. A fancy artisanal candle Tyler would never ever buy on his own.

"She was here? Is she still here? Does she know I'm here?"

"Calm down." He held his hand out as if I was a wild horse. "She had clients this morning, so she left a while ago. And, yeah, she knew you were coming over. Jesus," he sniffle-laughed, "you're acting like you're the other woman."

"I kind of am."

He sat up, putting his feet on the floor and his arm around me. "You are not. Sarah knows we've been friends forever. She doesn't have a jealous bone in her body."

I tugged at the ends of my hair, my stomach flipping into knots, feeling insecure in my grand plan. Not for the first time. "Maybe she should."

He lightly knocked his head against mine then got up to head to the bathroom. He didn't bother closing the door. "She says you've been great." His voice was loud enough that I could hear him over the sounds of him peeing. "She refuses to tell me anything about her dress but said she tried them on for, like, two hours."

"Yeah." I laid my head back on the cushion, closing my eyes. Sarah seemed like the type of woman who would be mortified to let her boyfriend know she had any bodily functions, and here was Tyler, having a conversation with me while he was in the bathroom. I wondered if she ever had Tyler buy her tampons. He'd run into the grocery store for me a time or two to grab a box of the jumbos. Didn't even freak out the one time in high school when I'd gotten my period unexpectedly, and the back of my plaid skirt had a huge blood stain on it. He'd skipped class to drive me home, and got a week's worth of detention for it.

"She can't make a decision to save her life," I said, remembering my conversation with Sarah's cousin, Cooper.

When Tyler finished in the bathroom, he crossed the apartment to the kitchen. "What do you want to drink? I still have that bottle of wine you opened forever ago, but it's probably not any good anymore, huh?"

"The last time I was here was in February." I huffed a laugh. "No, it's not good."

He tugged the cork from the bottle and let the liquid spill out into the drain. "I don't know anything about wine. That's why you should drink whiskey. It gets better with age."

I helped myself to inspect his fridge. There again was more evidence of how Sarah's life had integrated with Tyler's from the Icelandic yogurt to the snack sized servings of hummus. I grabbed a beer and sat at the eat-in counter.

After putting a few dishes in the dishwasher, he opened his

own beer and leaned against the oven, facing me. "How's everything going with you?"

"The same as it always is," I said, which was the truth. My life was always the same. For seven years, it'd been like walking in circles, forever moving but going nowhere. Every day, I got up, worked a job which was more obligation than passion, paid bills that were never ending, and hung my hat on a hope that someday this man would finally see me as something more than a friend.

"I was able to refinance my student loans though so..." I added some jazz hands for effect. "And I had this bride yesterday who got into a nasty fight with her maid of honor about the guest list." I ducked my head down, my voice an octave lower. "Apparently, the maid of honor has been sleeping with the bride's brother's ex-wife, and she—the maid of honor—wants to bring her—the ex-wife—to the wedding."

Tyler stilled with the beer halfway to his mouth. "I never realized how insanely dramatic the wedding gown business was."

I tipped my bottle to him in agreement.

"And I can't believe you still work there."

A little offended he would speak my internal conflict out loud, I scowled at him. "Why?"

"Because..." He lifted his hand as if to encapsulate the world then let it thump down on the counter. "You could be doing so many other things."

The tips of my ears went hot. "What's that tone for?"

"I don't have a tone."

"Yes, you do. You have your condescending Tyler tone."

His eyebrows raised toward his hairline. "I do not have a condescending Tyler tone."

"You get it sometimes because now that you're in a higher tax bracket, you think you know something."

"Whoa." He jerked his head back.

"Sorry," I mumbled, and he gripped my arms to untangle them from how I'd crossed them then held onto my hands.

"Why are you getting all worked up?"

"I'm not, but you know why I'm still at Michelle's." I specifically used the name of the store to remind him my mother was the reason I worked there.

"You could go back to school," he said as if I didn't know it. As if we hadn't already had this conversation a thousand times before.

I slipped my hands out of his grasp and folded them together. "You know how many more years I have before I pay off my student loans?"

He shook his head. Between scholarships, grants, and his high-paying job now, student loan interest wasn't in his vocabulary.

"Five more years," I told him. "Five more years until I can pay off my incomplete education. I don't necessarily want to add on another decade or two of payments. Plus, it's not so easy to go backward. It's not so easy to return to an academic life. What do you expect me to do? Go knock on Notre Dame's door and pick up where I left off?"

"It's not impossible."

"But it's not realistic either," I snapped, turning away from him.

"I don't want you to waste your life, that's all."

Heat flashed over my skin, anger momentarily blinding me, and I pressed my hands into my eye sockets until I could rein in my bitterness. I didn't want to have to defend my own shame—my innermost thoughts that I was indeed wasting my life—so I didn't.

I pivoted instead and picked at his scabs in retaliation. "You know Sarah was engaged before?"

Tyler was unbothered, long used to my distractions. "I know."

"Two times."

He straightened and took a sip of beer. "I know."

"And you don't care?"

"If she doesn't care about the girls I was with before her, I shouldn't care about the two guys she was engaged to," he said, swiping at the hair that helped him land all those girls.

"What about Zack?" I asked, hoping this wedge was big enough to cause a divide between them.

"What about him?"

"She was with him days before she met you."

Tyler placed his hands on the counter, unimpressed.

"Sarah and I ran into him while we were doing the registry."

His shoulders rose infinitesimally. Any other person wouldn't have noticed, but I did.

"She didn't tell me," he said.

I leaned back in my chair, mentally scrubbing my hands together like a cartoon villain. "She might not have a jealous bone in her body, but I know you do."

He snorted, aiming and missing for indifference. "I'm not jealous of him."

I eyed Tyler.

"I'm not," he repeated, louder. "He's a dick with anger issues. She told me he's in therapy."

"So?"

As if it should be apparent, he raised his hands. "He's trailer trash."

I had never wanted to hit my best friend, but there was a first time for everything. "Oh my god. That tone!"

"All right. Okay." He walked around the counter to sit next to me, his chest rising on a deep inhale before he met my eyes, repentant. "It doesn't matter where he lives, I don't care, but, yeah, I guess I am a little jealous. I think everyone kind of is when it comes to the person you love, right?" He played with the label on his beer bottle. "I'm not dumb enough to think Sarah's life started when she met me. Mine certainly didn't start when I met her, but I'm a little jealous of everyone she's been with before me. They got to have experiences with her and know her in different ways than I have. I love her so much; I want all of her for myself. I want every laugh and smile. I want every time she's cried to be with me so I can fix it. I want every birthday with her, and every Halloween to wear matching costumes. I want to bake no-sugar-added desserts and have so many Christmases with her that I end up learning she likes certain kinds of socks and buy them for her every year so it becomes our own inside joke."

His dark amber eyes met mine, and my own jealousy grew out of my chest to my limbs, incapacitating me from looking anywhere but right at him.

We had cried with each other.

We had worn matching Halloween costumes before, and even though I didn't bake, I could learn.

We had twenty years together.

"I don't care that she's been engaged before or had a lot of boyfriends, but I am jealous they've had any of her time because now that I've found her, I feel like I've missed so much. I don't want to waste another minute without her."

My eyes stung with tears, and I blinked them away before downing my beer.

Goddamn it.

I hated it. Hated the whole monologue and how it made such perfect sense. Hated how he'd suddenly transformed into a romantic, and that he was so infatuated with her, he couldn't see what was right in front of him.

Me.

I sniffed once. "Pretty crazy that after only a few weeks, you feel this way. Sounds like you have everything settled. Bank accounts, where you'll be living, and number of kids."

"Well..."

His hesitation hung like a bell on a rope between us, and I rang it. "What?"

"We haven't decided where we'll be living yet. She wants me to move into her place at her parents' house."

I played devil's advocate. "The cottage? It's cute."

"It's at her parents' house," he said a little too evenly.

"No mortgage though," I added.

"Yeah, and she doesn't care about being under her father's thumb, but I'm not okay with that."

I offered him an award-winning face filled with sincere curiosity and worry. I really should've gone into theater.

"She doesn't have any of her own credit cards. Her dad still pays for everything for her." He splayed his hands flat on the counter, apologetic. "I know you think I'm a dick for judging Zack about living in a trailer—not that I give a shit about him —but I do feel bad, Till, if I've ever said anything to make you feel like I look down on you for not graduating college. You know my parents never went to school. I don't care about any of that. But her dad is such an asshole. He's a nice guy in that multi-millionaire way, I guess."

"Can multi-millionaires be nice?" I asked, this time honestly curious.

"In the isn't-it-so-nice-my-daughter-is-marrying-someone-who-isn't-white-so-I-can-show-him-off-to-my-Republican-friends kind of way."

"Oh." I cringed. "No, you can't live there."

"No. Absolutely not."

"What does Sarah say about it?"

His answering sigh was resigned. "She doesn't see it like I do. She says it can be a honeymoon period, where we figure out where we want to go, but I know where I want to go. Here." He tapped his index fingers on the counter. "I know the apartment is small, and I offered to sell this place so we would find something together, but I want to stay in the city. I told her she should start trying to get clients here, maybe work out of a gym, but so far she's refused." He gave me his puppy dog eyes. "I was thinking...maybe if you talk to her—"

"You want *me* to talk to her?" I choked on my sip of beer.

"She trusts you," he said, and I slapped at my chest, still coughing.

They were supposed to be getting married in a matter of weeks. If they weren't able to solve basic issues, they had to realize rushing was a bad idea. "Fine." I cleared my throat. "I'll talk to her."

"Thanks," he said, squeezing my knee. "You're the best. Really. You hold me together."

Exactly, I didn't say. *It's why you should be with me.*

Tyler, for all his rational logic, had a tendency to think everyone would see the world the way he did. He believed what he wanted was best, which in this case about the living situation, I couldn't disagree, but at some point he had to come to terms with not being able to convince everyone else into getting his way. Especially when he wasn't good at confrontation. He was paradoxical in that he never wanted to hurt anyone's feelings but sometimes spoke without thinking about how his words might come across. Hence, why he had no problem shooting straight at me and then immediately apologizing when he knew it hurt me. I was positive that when it came to Sarah, he was walking on eggshells, knowing what he might say could hurt her, so he was avoiding it at all costs.

Sweet but misguided.

I tapped the neck of my beer bottle against his. "You want another?"

He checked his phone, tapping out a text message with his thumbs. "Actually, I told Logan we'd meet him for drinks. Ricky's in town too."

I only realized I'd been pouting when he got up from his chair. "What's the face for?"

"I thought it was going to be you and me today."

He plucked my nose before heading to his bedroom. "It'll be a pre-bachelor party party. Let me change quick and then we'll go."

With a dejected sigh, I got up for my purse. Tyler's bare back was to me as he snagged a shirt off one of the hangers in his closet, and the little mole below his left shoulder blade sent a pang of longing through me.

I wanted to wrap my arms around him and press my cheek against his back. I wanted to be the one he spent his birthdays and Christmases with. Hell, we already had inside jokes, so it wouldn't even be a big transition. Our histories were already intertwined. Like ivy, sometimes it was difficult to know where I ended and he began. He knew my mind as well as his own.

It's why, when he spun back around to me with a navy polo shirt on, his lips sloped down in a playful frown. "Hey. Please, don't be mad at me." He threw his arm around me, and like always, my head found his shoulder. "I'm sorry for what I said about you wasting your life. I didn't mean it."

"I know."

"You're so talented and beyond brilliant, I want you to be able to do whatever you want, and I know that's not working at Michelle's."

I stayed silent, chin dipped down so he didn't see my eyes water.

"I think we should put a pin in the conversation about student loans until tomorrow. How about I run some numbers for you? See if we can't do something about your loans. If you want to go back to school, I want to make that happen for you."

I nodded and rubbed at my burning nose before tipping my chin up to smile at my best friend. "Thanks, Ty."

He kissed my forehead. "Of course. So, tonight we'll go out for a couple hours and then it's only me and you as soon as we get home. Movie marathon. I'll even let you pick."

"Good, because I wasn't planning on getting drunk, and that's the only way I can get through Guillermo del Toro movies."

Tyler gasped. "He's one of the greatest filmmakers of all time."

"If you like beastiality and monsters with eyes on their palms who eat children."

"It's allegory!" He laughed, tugging me out of his apartment.

I wished the rest of the evening went as Tyler said it would, but once we got to the bar, two drinks became three, and Ricky had called more friends, and suddenly I was in the middle of a drunk bro-fest. To top it all off, I was starving.

I tugged on Tyler's sleeve. "Let's go get pizza."

He bent his knees, lowering his ear to me. "What?"

"I'm hungry. Let's go home."

"Yeah, okay. After this inning," he said, pointing to the television above the bar. The Phillies were in extra innings, not that I cared. I'd passed hangry half an hour ago, and lost my patience around the time Ricky offered to take me home. His cousin had been willing to leave a bar to take me home, but my best friend wasn't.

"We've been here for hours."

"You could order food here." He slid the bar menu to me with the few measly food offerings before going back to conversation with one of the other dudes.

Annoyed, I fisted my hand at my side, darting my focus around, asking myself if I had any more patience to scrape from the bottom of the barrel. And, no. No, I didn't.

I tugged on Tyler's wrist, gesturing toward the door. "I'm going to go home."

He finally pulled away from the group. "What?"

"I'm going to head home."

"All right," he gave in eventually. "Give me a few minutes to say goodbye to everybody."

"No. I mean I want to go home home."

He held onto my elbow, closing the space between us so we could hear each other better. "*Home* home?"

"Yes, my home," I said against his ear.

"Are you sure?"

I nodded. He obviously didn't want to leave the bar and his friends. "Yeah."

"All right. Text me when you get home, so I know you're safe."

I didn't expect him to beg me to stay, but I assumed he would put up a little more of a fight. I snorted a laugh in irritation. "Sure."

"Bye, Till," he called out to my back. I didn't turn around, only raised my hand on the way out of the door.

Thirteen

Sunday morning, I woke up in my own bed, hoping Tyler was miserable and hungover. I'd rearranged my work schedule so I could go down there yesterday with the plan to stay over and spend time with him, only for it to blow up in my face. I wasn't quite sure what I was more upset about, the way Tyler always pushed me aside or the fact that he had a wedding coming up. Either way, I was exhausted.

With less than two months to the Kelly-Rodriguez wedding, I'd made no headway in separating them. However, I was convinced I could use Tyler's jealousy to my advantage. Unplugging my phone from the charger, I ignored the drunk emojis he'd sent me last night after I'd messaged him that I got home safe, and pulled up Zack's number. He answered after a few rings.

"It's a little early for plumbing emergencies."

I smiled up at the ceiling. "I called to check on Bambi. Are you taking care of her?"

"How do you know it's a her?"

"She's got those pointy leaves," I explained, picturing him holding the succulent outside of my parents' house, "with that

117

pretty purple-ish center. Hard on the outside, sweet on the inside, it's definitely a girl."

His thoughtful hum sounded in my ear. "Are you describing the plant or you?"

"It's also a little early for introspective conversations." When he didn't laugh or make any other equally charmed noise, disappointment unexpectedly flooded my veins. I wanted him to find me witty or, at the very least, mildly entertaining. We were friends, comrades in arms, teammates.

I wanted him to like me. A little bit.

"What are you doing today?" I asked, yawning.

"I went for a hike this morning."

"But it's—" I checked the time "—not even ten o'clock."

"Yeah, I wanted to enjoy the trail before it got crowded."

I sat up, contemplating an existence where someone would purposely wake up on their day off to go outside.

In the middle of summer.

To climb a mountain.

"Why?" I asked.

"I told you it helps to clear my head."

"Got a lot on your mind, do you?"

He stayed silent for a moment, and we were back to square one. All of those hours when we'd talked and confessed and teased, it was like they'd never happened.

"I can hear you brooding," I said after a while.

"I'm not brooding. I'm hungry."

I slipped out of bed and shuffled to the kitchen, tugging the refrigerator door open. "Well, *that* I understand."

"You eat breakfast yet?"

"I just woke up," I said, purposely avoiding what it meant that I called him first thing. "Of course I didn't eat yet."

"Do you like waffles? They're from a box mix."

I let the fridge door close and raised my hand in question

as if he was right in front of me. "Did you... Are you offering to make me waffles?"

"I'm making them for myself, and yeah, I'm asking if you want to come over for some."

I spun in a tight circle, taking account of myself in my pajamas with bedhead. He couldn't see me, though my body reacted like he could, my skin hot, my heart rate spiking.

But I played it cool. "Yeah, sure. I'll come over for waffles. I can take a peek in your closet to see what we need to turn you into Sarah's perfect man."

He ignored the suggestion and hung up with a curt, "I'll text you my address."

I showered and changed, not even bothering to do my hair, instead wrapping it up in a bun on the top of my head. My biological response to any temperature above eighty degrees was immediate sweating, and in the few minutes it took my car to cool down, a pool had gathered between my boobs. Unlike my slimmer sisters, I could never go without a bra, and I already regretted my decision to wear a romper. The material of my bra soaked up my sweat, while the cotton of the one-piece trapped it all inside. I was a walking ShamWow.

And I was about to go see a man who ignited my internal temperature with one arch of his eyebrow.

Might as well wring me out.

Zack lived in a trailer park, and some of the homes were worse for wear, but Zack's had wooden steps leading up to the front door that appeared to be new. Although, the screen door barely clung to its hinges.

I poked my head in the open door. "Hello?"

"Hey," he said from the right of me. "Come in."

I stepped inside and the screen door slammed behind me. "Sorry."

He waved his fork in the door's direction. "I haven't got around to fixing it yet."

I walked into the small kitchen area, where a well-worn wood table was set with two plates, napkins, and glasses of orange juice. "Smells great."

"Have a seat," he said, and I did, taking in his home.

"It's bigger than it looks from the outside." The carpets needed to be cleaned, and the wallpaper had to be from decades ago, but it was in good shape for the most part. Bambi resided by the window, soaking in the sun from under what probably used to be white lace curtains. In the living room area, a framed photo of Chloe in her wedding dress and Zack in a dark suit sat on a scratched up end table.

"It was my Grandma's. My mom was sometimes gone for weeks so me and Chloe lived here with her," he explained and opened the waffle maker to remove four square waffles, adding them to an already towering plate next to him.

"How was that?"

"Cramped." He set the plate down in the middle of the table, next to the syrup. "There're two bedrooms, and I slept on the couch." His eyes flickered in the direction of a small burgundy couch. "There used to be this old sofa there, covered in blue flowers. Scratchy as hell."

He wrinkled his nose, and I relaxed with a smile. He nudged the waffles toward me to help myself.

"What was your grandma like?" I asked, taking two.

He shot me an unimpressed look and added another to my plate then put four waffles on his own and slathered them in syrup. "Too sweet-natured. My grandpa died of a heart attack when I was real little, and she was on disability, so she didn't work. She took care of us as best she could, but Mom walked all over her."

I nodded, chewing on a bite of waffle. I was raised with two loving parents and the safety of a roof over my head and food on the table. We may have had our struggles, but I was lucky.

And an ingrate for ever being unappreciative.

"What about Chloe?"

Zack gulped down his orange juice, and then proceeded to absolutely gush over his sister. It was the only way to describe it. He went on and on, in between bites of food that seemed to only refuel him in order to spout more adoration.

They were six years apart, he said, and he had loved her since the moment he saw her all wrapped up in a soft pink blanket, like she was his baby doll to take care of. For a while, he had believed she was an actual baby doll until she didn't stop crying. Chloe's dad had a temper and would scream to "shut that kid up," and sometimes hit their mom, so Zack took it upon himself to keep her quiet by singing songs and holding her for hours. During one of Chloe's dad's stints in jail, when their mom had taken off, their grandmother brought them to live with her. Chloe was little, in first grade or so, but by then Zack was older, wiser to the ways of the world, and he'd begun to turn into the things he saw around him. But not Chloe, she had always been kind and saw the best in people.

He recalled, in detail, when she had lost her first tooth by biting into an apple, and how he'd stolen a candy bar from a convenience store to leave under her pillow. When she questioned him about it, he'd invented some story about how the Tooth Fairy gave out candy to make sure children's teeth rotted and fell out in order to get more. The story, which he made up to cover his theft, ended up scaring her. She'd been afraid of the tooth fairy for years after that, he said with a laugh.

He told me how she always made the honor roll and had wanted to be a nurse since she was a little kid. She currently worked in labor and delivery, and he was happy she'd met Hudson in high school because she'd been able to get out from under their mom's influence. He described how Hudson had been a bumbling mess, a kid—only twenty-one-years-old—asking if Zack would approve of him and Chloe getting married after they graduated.

Zack gestured around the trailer, holding memories of their childhood, probably some nightmares too. He said he was glad his sister married a straight-laced accountant who would give her more than she grew up with: a perfectly boring life with a house and a fenced-in yard, with a three-legged dog they'd adopted, where no one raised their voices, let alone their hand.

"Is that what you want? A boring life?" I asked.

He stood up, taking the dirty dishes with him. "Yeah, like what you told me the night in your shop about what you want for your wedding."

I gasped, playfully pressing my hand to my heart. "You think my wedding will be boring?"

With his attention on soaping up the dishes, he shook his head. "No. You said when you kiss your husband at your wedding it will be like all the other kisses you've had before, but that's why it's perfect."

I blinked.

And then blinked again.

My heart thudded in a funny way.

My romper was strangling me.

"I want boring." He rinsed off the dishes and lined them up on a drying rack. "I want stability." He turned to me with a dish towel in his hands. "I want to wake up to the same kiss every morning and go to bed with the same kiss every night and have every kiss in between, knowing the person I love most is safe and happy."

His gaze focused on me then, and I told myself to breathe.

I thought lungs were supposed to work involuntarily, but mine were having trouble. I tapped my breastbone to make sure they were doing what they were supposed to under there.

Somewhere, far, far away from the pull of Zack's stare, something buzzed. But I didn't move.

I didn't want to.

He inhaled deeply, his chest visibly rising and falling beneath his black T-shirt.

I inhaled too.

He blinked and shifted his focus toward my purse on the floor.

I blinked too.

"Is that your phone?"

"Oh." I moved for the first time in centuries. "Yeah." I tugged my bag on my lap and located my phone, almost groaning at the name on the screen. "It's Sarah."

And just like that, whatever spell he'd cast over me—or the one we'd put on each other, I don't know who bewitched whom—was broken.

I stepped outside. "Hey, Sarah."

"Thank god," she said. "I've been texting you all morning."

I took a quick peek at my phone, there were five messages from her. Between the waffles and the whole drowning in the ocean of Zack's eyes thing, I hadn't noticed.

"Settle something for me. I told you how I want to DIY the favors, right?" She went on without pause. "My sister and I are having an argument over what we should do. I think little pouches filled with wildflower seeds are cute, but she thinks people won't actually plant them."

"Well—"

"She thinks I should do a homemade honey or jam. That's a good idea, but I don't know who has an allergy or who hates berries. If I do the seeds, I'll just put them in envelopes, which is cheap and easy. But if I do the honey or jam, I'll have to buy mason jars, and I don't think people will actually keep them. Unless they like to bake or cook."

"I keep mason jars," I said.

"So you think I should do honey or jam?"

Strolling in a loop around the small driveway, I let my hand trail over the leather and chrome of Zack's motorcycle. "I don't really use honey."

"What about, like, a raspberry jam?"

"I like raspberry jam, but I don't know, Sarah. What does Tyler say?"

"He thinks we should buy the favors and be done with it. Give a candle or beer Koozie, but those are so impersonal."

Stopping in the middle of another circle, I spotted the little succulent in front of the window. "In my opinion, it's all kind of impersonal. No one actually cares about favors. Some people will use or drink or eat what you give them, and other people won't. If it were me, I'd use the money as a donation to a place that's important to you, like..." I took a stab at a charity she might take a shine to. "An animal shelter and make little placards for each person, or even put it on the back of their table number cards."

"Ooooh my god. Yes. I love that idea."

I tucked a stray, curling hair behind my ear, irrationally annoyed that she unknowingly interrupted my time with Zack to talk about wedding favors.

I wanted to yell at her that no one cared. *No one gives a shit, Sarah!*

Out of spite, I threw a dart, hoping it might land on the bullseye. "Listen, Tyler would kill me if he knew I was telling you this, but I don't think I should keep this to myself."

"What?" she asked, concerned.

"Tyler is really uncomfortable with the idea of living with your parents."

She huffed, a small aggrieved sound. "We wouldn't be living with my parents. My house is completely separate."

"Yeah." I stretched the word into three syllables. "But

don't you think it would be hard to figure out how to be married with your parents a few yards away?"

"No," she said quickly, "and I'm a little bothered he had this conversation with you."

I smiled at her terse voice. Honestly, this was too easy. "Well, I'm his best friend."

"And I'm the one he's marrying," she snapped. "Why would he talk to you about it instead of me?"

"I don't know." I rubbed my forehead, trying to ignore the guilt creeping up the back of my neck. As much as I didn't want to admit it, Sarah was a good person. And clearly too trusting. "Maybe it all comes down to what you're used to and what he's used to is different. He mentioned not really seeing eye to eye with your dad."

"My dad? What does he have to do with it?"

"Well, you're...kind of..." I paused, finding the right word. "Privileged."

"Okay?"

"So, put yourself in Tyler's shoes." I kicked at a loose pebble in the driveway. "He's really proud of where he came from and what he's earned for himself, and I think it might be difficult for him to think of himself as your partner when he's living next to your dad, who still pretty much provides for everything for you still, right?"

"Yeah, but—"

"Tyler wants to provide for you," I said because she evidently didn't get it. "He wants to take care of you."

"I want to take care of him, too." Her voice was quiet, chastened. "That's why I thought it would be good to live at home. We can save money and figure out where we want to go. I—"

"I totally get why you want to live at home. I really do, but you're getting married in seven weeks," I said, interrupting whatever her argument was going to be with a not-so-gentle prompt. "These are big decisions that will affect the rest of your lives. You guys have got to figure it out before then or you might as well call it off."

After seconds of silence, long enough for me to check I hadn't lost the connection or accidentally hung up, she finally said, "You're right." Then she added a lighter, "As usual."

"All right, well, I'll talk—"

"Hey, you want to go grab a coffee?" she asked, and I froze mid-stride to Zack's door.

"Huh?"

"You've been so helpful to me, and I need to repay you somehow."

I tilted my head back, squinting up at the bright sky. "No, that's all right."

"Oh, come on. Please. I want to get to know you better. Once Tyler and I are hitched, we'll basically be sisters."

I swallowed down the guilty lump in my throat.

"He loves you, and I love you," she said, and then I didn't feel too bad anymore. Someone as fickle as Sarah Kelly fell in and out of love easily, with everyone apparently. Even me.

Fourteen

Renewed in my solid belief that Tyler and Sarah were absolutely not right for each other, I marched back into Zack's trailer.

"What was that about?" he asked, from the chair in the living room.

"She is a fickle creature, isn't she?"

"Yeah. I guess."

"Well, let's get you ready for the ball, Cinderella." I tapped the back of his chair, but he only ticked up his eyebrow. "That way to your bedroom?" I motioned my head toward the back of the trailer.

When he didn't answer or budge, I grabbed hold of a thick forearm, attempting to yank him up. He merely tilted his head to the side, a shadow of a smile beneath his beard.

"What? Are you made of cement?"

"Mostly," he said, finally relenting. We ended up chest to chest, eye to eye, and I had trouble remembering why I had a height rule for the men I dated.

"You're going out," I told him.

His mouth was close to mine, and I could smell the sweet scent of maple syrup when he licked his lips. "Am I?"

"Sarah wants to buy me a coffee. You'll be there too."

His nostrils flared on a breath as if he didn't like that idea. "Another oops?"

"This time you have to bump into her. Not me."

He narrowed his gaze, and just when I thought he would speak, he didn't. He only pointed over my shoulder, silently directing me down the hall. I about faced, passing a bathroom, and the second bedroom, which was a mess of boxes, junk, and a bench with some weights. His bedroom, at the end of the hall, had one single window with crooked blinds and some clothes hanging out of a laundry basket.

"Got a whole mountain man thing going on," I said, picking up a red plaid button down from the basket, then spying two more almost exactly like it in light blue and navy hanging in his tiny closet. I flipped through more hangers. Denim, and plaid, one white dress shirt, and more plaid. "You certainly have *a* style. But do you have anything green? A dark hunter green would be good. I think it'd bring out your eyes and with the—"

When I circled around with a particularly ugly orange and gray flannel in hand, I bumped right into Zack.

"Oops, sorry," he said with a crooked smile, and I pressed the shirt into his chest, a little harder than necessary.

"If you really wanted to make *that* work, it's got to be more natural. But I thought you didn't play those games." I added quotation marks over the last three words.

"I don't." He backed away from me, sitting on the edge of his unmade bed with familiar striped sheets. "And I don't know why you're still going through with this whole thing."

"Because Sarah and Tyler don't belong together."

"How do you know?"

"Because they've only been together for a few months, and

I know Tyler. I know all of his quirks and how he thinks, and I know, right now, he's blinded by her shininess." I helped myself to his drawers in the small dresser under the window. "Sarah has a way of making everyone feel special." I closed his underwear and sock drawers, searching for his T-shirts. "The way she cozies up to you with her tiny little body and those big cow eyes, kind of makes you want to put her in your pocket and take her home, right? She's sweet and fun and made of pixie dust. She's basically Tinker Bell. She's—you dated her." I flapped my hands around my head, scoffing at myself. Even I was blindsided by the little sprite. It was easy to see how someone like Tyler, who fancied nice things, would fall hard and fast.

I shook a bunch of his T-shirts at Zack. "Do you own any that don't have your company logo on them?"

"I doubt it."

Him and his T-shirts didn't deserve my rancor, and I sunk down next to him on his entirely too mushy mattress. I worked to temper my tone. "Tyler thinks he caught her, that he could keep her, but I know she won't stay around. She didn't stay with you." Speaking those words out loud grated at me because why wouldn't she want to stay with him? He was handy, caring, and surprisingly funny. But he didn't appear as offended by his ex's terrible life choices as I was, and I threw my arm out. "She barely waited a few days before she moved on from you!"

"And yet you're scheming to get us back together."

I didn't want him to get back with her. She didn't deserve him. Zack should be with someone who appreciated him. Someone like...

I shook my head. "I want her to see what she's missing."

He regarded me with an indecipherable glower before rolling his shoulders back like he'd come to some sort of decision and slowly perused my body.

I took it as an invitation to openly stare back at him. Sarah was missing out on a lot.

A whole lot of a lot.

Arms built from hard work, with fingertips rough enough to feel when he undoubtedly squeezed *just* a bit too tight while he kissed with those goddamn lips that looked soft and almost too plump for a man. Lips like that were wasted on a guy. Unless, of course, he used them well. And I imagined how his beard might scratch on the most intimate parts of me, only to be soothed by his mouth.

Then there were those thighs, huge and hard, and sitting so close to him, I was tempted to rest my hands on top of them. His right leg pressed into my left, and I giggled as Sarah's whispered conversation about Zack being good in bed came back to me.

"What?"

I shook my head. "Nothing."

"You snorted."

"I did not."

"You did," he said, but the quirk to his mouth told me he didn't find it nearly as embarrassing as I did. "What's so funny?"

"I was thinking of what Sarah said about...you." I thought my dramatic pause would have filled in the blank but he inclined his head *and?*

I tried to think of something else: instruments of the Bronze Age, different types of root vegetables, how to recite the alphabet backwards. Anything other than the feel of his heavy gaze on me, of what it would feel like to have his heavy weight on me. How I *knew* it—he—would be good.

My blood thrummed, my skin flushed, my nipples pebbled. "And, um, how you're good in bed."

His focus dropped to my breasts, and I refused to move, crossing my arms over the evidence of what his attention did to me. His teeth scraped over his lip, and I pressed my thighs together, shaking my head to rid it of the image of his teeth on me.

"And that's funny to you?" he asked, meeting my eyes after an eternity.

I couldn't tell him the truth of how my imagination had run head first into a veritable sex dungeon, so I did what I did best. I lied. "I would've guessed you have sex like a Taylor Swift song."

"What's that mean?" He leaned back on his hands, shifting beyond my peripheral vision, forcing me to slant my body to the side so I could see him.

Waving my hands in front of my face, I painted an illusion. "All face-to-face longing and gauzy lighting."

He tilted his head to the side. "What's wrong with that?"

"Nothing."

His knee nudged mine. "Why did you laugh about it?"

"Because..."

"Because?"

"Because," I said all beleaguered like I didn't put myself in this exact position—discussing his talents in bed—by being unable to set my jealousy aside, "you're the one who said you wanted boring."

His voice dropped dangerously low when he said, "Not *everything* is boring."

Fuck. I hated Sarah. I hated Tyler. I hated everything about this. I wasn't supposed to be attracted to Zack, my best friend's fiancée's ex-boyfriend. My life was complicated enough without wanting to climb this ginger mountain man like a goddamn tree.

I should have said goodbye, should've shut this all down. Instead, I dove head first into my fantasy. "So, there's no gauzy lighting or face-to-face longing for you?"

He rolled his head up toward the ceiling, his chest rising

and falling with each deep breath, and I imagined resting my head there, right between his well-rounded pectoral muscles. "Gauzy lighting and face-to-face could be good sometimes," he said then didn't move for a long time, and right when I thought I'd made my way out of the lust-filled haze, he dragged me back in by sitting up and tracing the strap of my bra. "And sometimes it's even better to be a little rough."

He slid his hand over my shoulder and throat, his palm forming to the curve of my jaw. And I hated myself for being right. His fingertips were rough yet gentle, and I closed my eyes at the pressure spreading out from my core. At the need to have his fingers on me, dragging over me, pumping into me.

What he gave me was a rough tug on my elastic so my hair fell around my shoulders. His answering groan of appreciation was followed up by his hand fisting the mass of unruly strands, tugging my head back a bit. Then his mouth was at my ear, his beard scraping my cheek. "Like this."

I was delirious, practically panting, and I had trouble catching my breath. Panic started to well up inside me. I couldn't make heads or tails of this situation, of my feelings for Zack, and I needed out.

Maybe he heard my internal conflict, or maybe he felt me stiffen in his hold. Either way, he let go, and I jumped up from the bed.

I tied my hair back up and made an attempt—admittedly, not my best effort—to appear perfectly unaffected.

"Well then, I guess she was telling the truth. You do know what you're doing." This trailer was in desperate need of more air conditioners, and I dabbed at the sweat on my upper lip. "Good for you. Okay." I clapped my hands, signaling the end of this conversation and possibly my blood circulation. "Let's get to work. Where's your beard trimmer?"

"I'm not shaving."

"I don't want you to, but have you seen your cheekbones?" I pointed to his reflection in the mirror mounted on the wall. "They could cut glass. I bet there's a jaw under there, which also might be able to. You should bless the world with the shape of it, at the very least."

He tossed me a suspicious glare but directed me to the bathroom, where he dug out the trimmer from under the sink. He plugged it in and handed it to me. I happily obliged.

Inch by inch, I cut down his Viking beard and shaped it to his face, close enough to see and feel the angle of his chin and jaw when I combed my fingers through the short, coarse hair. "Surprise, surprise," I said, "you have lips."

He smirked. "You didn't know?"

I supposed I needed to cut my thumb off because it had grown a mind of its own and traced over the curve of that cocky smile.

And I found myself right back in that lusty haze. Because now I knew how soft his lips were, how his hot breath felt on my skin, and I wasn't sure I'd ever be able to find my way out again.

I didn't know if I even wanted to.

But I did know that learning the details of his face with my fingers, like some cheap knock-off Lionel Ritchie music video, was *not* the point of today.

I dropped my hand and yanked the plug from the outlet. "You've got two," I said, referencing his lips because I had exactly two brain cells left. "The regular number."

"That's good." He cleared his throat and skimmed his hands over his newly shorn beard and down his throat, studying himself in the mirror. "You did good."

Back in his room, I laid out a clean pair of jeans on his bed with a heather gray V-neck as I heard the distinct sound of the shower turning on down the hall. He was about to be naked, and I had to hightail it out of there before my brain lost the last two working cells it had to worship at the altar of Zackary Olsen's body.

I stopped at the bathroom door, my farewell halted on the tip of my tongue because Zack had his shirt off.

I lost my valiant fight to keep my gaze above his neck.

But only for a moment.

And just to study the lion more closely.

Barely one second to take in the ridges of his abdomen.

Less than that on the line of hair leading below his shorts.

"I'm heading out." I forced my attention on anywhere but him: the open shower curtain, the faucet taps, the water hitting the tiled floor. "You should add more green to your wardrobe," I told the towel hanging on the wall.

"I don't have a wardrobe," Zack said, and I unconsciously turned toward him. "I have work jeans and non-work jeans."

My traitorous eyes found their way back to his chest with a smattering of copper hair among a constellation of freckles. His skin was as fair as mine, except for wherever it had been tanned by the sun.

What was the line from the Bible? If your right eye offends thee, pluck it out? Guess both of mine had to go.

"Meet me at The Coffee Club in an hour," I said, not even waiting for him to agree before I flew out of there like my pants were on fire.

More accurately, like my underwear was drenched.

Fifteen

I could've gone home to change out of my sweat roll-up but instead drove right to the coffee shop. I didn't need caffeine to further crank up my nerves, yet I ordered a large iced latte anyway. It was something to keep me company while I contemplated how I got to this place where I directed and starred in my own screwed up version of *A Midsummer Night's Dream*, trying and failing to rearrange couples falling in love.

Sure... I guess I liked Sarah, but it didn't change the fact she would never work with Tyler in the long run. They were fundamentally different, in how they viewed the world, and what they wanted out of it.

And now that I knew Zack, I didn't want him to go back to her either. He'd evolved from a kid with anger issues to a generous and perfectly *boring* man. To give up so quickly after an argument, Sarah either didn't see what a good guy he was, or worse, she did and didn't care. Which was a goddamn shame.

Before I fell too far down the mental rabbit hole of figuring out exactly where that left me, the roar of a motorcycle grew closer, and I turned in my seat to spot Zack—which was weird, that I knew it was him even obscured by a leather jacket and helmet—riding into the parking lot.

About the same time as Sarah found a spot.

Right on cue.

Through the window, I watched Zack remove his helmet—shampoo commercial worthy with the way he tucked it under one arm and skimmed his hand through his hair with the other—and the subtle falter in Sarah's steps in reaction.

She lifted her hand to him, and after he closed the distance between them, they spoke for a minute or so then entered the coffee shop together. Next to each other, they looked good.

Ugh.

She smiled wide when she saw me. "You'll never believe who I ran into again!"

"What a coincidence," I deadpanned, and he slanted his head to the side, a wry smile gracing his lips.

"I know. Bizarre, right?" Sarah bobbed her head between the two of us as if waiting for confirmation on how it was indeed bizarre that Zack kept spontaneously running into us.

"Is it?" I asked, and her smile skewed into a pensive frown as she slowly shook her head.

"I wanted to pay for your coffee, but you already got some," she noted. "Can I get you something else? How about a muffin?"

"Sure. I'll take a muffin," I said, and she dropped her purse in the chair next to me, to take only her wallet up to the counter. Alone with Zack, I tipped my chin toward the window. "Now *that* move has to be practiced."

When his brow crimped in confusion, I mimed removing a helmet and brushing my hand over my luscious locks.

"I have no idea what you're talking about."

I rolled my eyes and shoved the straw of my drink in my

mouth, speaking around it. "You have seen yourself, right? You know you look good."

As if the guy needed any more confidence, he puffed his chest out and seemed to grow taller before my very eyes. Then he tapped the table twice next to my elbow and squinted in a half-wink before stepping in line behind Sarah.

They spoke to each other while waiting for their orders, and I was either terrible at reading lips or Sarah really did say, "You're letting your hair grow longer."

That was what she was focused on? I rolled my eyes.

They returned to the table a few minutes later with a hot tea in a white mug for her, and something in a to-go cup for him, and I gestured to the other open seat. "Do you want to sit with us?"

"No, thanks. I'm headed over there." He pointed to the men's clothing store across the street with his drink. "Someone gave me some advice to wear more green."

"Oh, yes," Sarah agreed, clutching his wrist, and all three of us looked to the point of contact between them. She released him with a nervous smile. "Sorry, but you should definitely wear more green. Remember the sweater I bought you for your birthday?"

He nodded.

"Do you still have it?"

The pregnant pause implied the answer.

"It's okay," she said with a wave. "I didn't expect—it's no big deal." Her cheeks brightened in a red hue I'd never seen out of her before. "Only cashmere."

He had the good graces to wince at her awkwardness. "If it makes you feel better, I gave it to the men's shelter."

A fleetingly pained smile disappeared, and she became mesmerized by her tea.

His gaze slanted to me, and I shrugged. He didn't strike

me as the type to wear cashmere, so it didn't surprise me that he gave it away. "Guess I'll get going."

I would've rather spent more time with him, but there was no easy way for me to get away. "Have fun," I said breezily then mouthed over Sarah's bent head, "Text me later."

With a nod, he was gone, and I held my chin in my hand. Sarah sat unusually silent.

"He looks good, huh?" I prodded. "Different without the big beard."

With her eyes cast down, she squeaked out a quiet, "Yeah."

"The universe works in funny ways."

At that, she raised her gaze to me, but I still couldn't decipher her mood.

I broke the blueberry muffin she bought me in half. "You break up with him and are getting married but suddenly he's everywhere. Looking like, you know..."

She shook her head. She didn't know.

I tossed a piece of muffin in my mouth. "A snack. A delightfully ginger-haired, probably able to build you a house with his bare hands, snack."

She stared out of the window for a while before saying, "Tyler and I talked for hours, and you were right, we needed to."

I leaned my forearms on the table. "Yeah? What about?"

"Living together." She settled back in her chair, facing me. "I'm going to move to Philadelphia with him. I'm nervous, but it'll be fine."

She didn't sound quite convinced it would be fine.

"Are you sure?"

"No, but I have to trust it'll be. I have faith."

I didn't think platitudes were a great basis for a marriage, but I nodded anyway. "Right. How about everything else for the wedding? Are you all set?"

"Oh! Let me show you." She whipped out her phone,

scrolling through pictures she had saved of centerpieces and flower arrangements. I was more invested in eating the muffin than her plan to pour sand into a jar at the ceremony.

"So, you're good for Thursday?" she asked after a while.

"Hm?"

"The cake tasting on Thursday? It's at four o'clock?"

I didn't know when exactly I'd agreed to that. Must have been the *Uh huh* or *Yep* I threw in while daydreaming.

Most definitely not about the sound of a motorcycle. Or riding one.

"It would be such a big help," she said, touching her flat stomach. "I need my dress to fit perfectly, so no cake for me."

"You're not going to try your own wedding cake? A few bites of cake aren't going to change any of your measurements," I told her, though vanity didn't follow logic.

"Tyler will be there, and you will too. I trust you guys."

If eating a dozen different cakes was a sacrifice I'd have to make, I guess I could do it. Offer it up to the Lord. "I'll be there."

"Thank you! You're the best." She reached across the table to hug me.

After we said goodbye, I went home to my apartment, searching for my high school yearbook. When I found it, I flipped to the the superlatives page, grinning at the decade old photos of Samantha Lazinski for best eyes and Bradley Salva, who was most likely to succeed. And there, in the middle, were Tyler and I, voted best couple.

It was a joke. Everyone knew we weren't together, except we were *always* together. So they'd all voted for us. I think more than a few of our friends were convinced we'd end up together. I did too.

Truly, the universe was funny like that.

With a tired sigh, I put the yearbook away and settled on the couch.

A few hours later, I received a text from Zack. It was a picture of him wearing a hunter green T-shirt in the reflection of his bathroom mirror at home. Smart-ass smile included.

I really didn't need any more fuel for my dreams, but there it was.

There *he* was.

I saved the photo and opened my nightstand drawer for my vibrator.

Job well done.

Sixteen

I thought I'd be having more of an enjoyable time while sitting in front of five pieces of cake. But with Tyler on one side of me dissecting the nuance of every flavor combination and Sarah on the other side asking for a play-by-play, I was ready to toss them all in the trash.

"Pick what you like best, not what you think other people will want." I licked the cream cheese icing off my plastic spork.

"You know chocolate is my favorite," he told me then gestured over to Sarah. "But the almond is delicious."

"Is it?" Sarah asked me for verification.

"They're all good. I'd eat any one of them."

She wrinkled her nose at me, unsatisfied. "But which one do you like best?"

"The carrot cake."

Tyler gagged on purpose. "It's dessert. It shouldn't have vegetables in it."

I propped my elbows on the table. "Okay, then go with your tired old chocolate on chocolate."

Sarah opened the photo album the owner of the bakery left with us for cake decoration inspiration. "But don't you think chocolate is kind of..." She circled her hand in the air. "Generic?" She pointed to a certain page in the album. "Look. Look how gorgeous this cake is. Then we'll cut into it, and it's brown?"

I speculated if the quicker death would be stabbing myself in the ear or eye with the spork. "All right, then go for a more sophisticated flavor like vanilla bean or almond with layers of fruit."

Tyler wielded his spork like a sword. "No lemon."

"Cake or filling?" Sarah asked, considering another page of the book. "And are we sure we want to go with the ribbon? I kind of like the deconstructed style of this one? And square? No one has a square cake, it's really different, right, Till?"

Instead of opening up the display case and tossing the first cake I could get my hands on at Sarah, I stood and laid down my spork, rather than lodging it in anyone's throat. "I'm going to go outside and give you two a few moments. If I were you, I'd get a four layered square cake—" I turned my attention to Sarah "—with the white icing and ribbon motif—" then raised my brows in Tyler's direction "—and alternate chocolate with chocolate ganache and almond cake with your preference of fruit layers."

With that, I found a seat on the bench outside of the bakery door. Behind me, through the window, I could see the two of them flipping back and forth through the book. Tyler had opinions. Sarah had none. He second-guessed his opinions because of her, and she was too afraid to make a decision on anything in case it was the wrong one.

They were hopeless.

When my phone buzzed with a text, I dug through my purse for it and found a message from Zack. **How about this?**

After he'd sent the selfie of him in his new green shirt the other day, our messages had devolved to pictures of random pieces of green clothing for him to purchase. From a lime green plaid suit on his suggestion to a polyester highlighter green shirt and tie from me, we'd kept each other up late, scouring the internet for more and more ridiculous suggestions. This time he sent me a Grinch costume.

I texted him back. **I hear the Grinch is a kink for a certain subset of people.**

I bit back a grin at his response. **By certain people you mean you?**

Maybe after a few drinks I could be convinced, I replied.

A minute later he sent me two screen shots, both of purchase pages. One for a case of wine and another for the Grinch costume.

I snorted. **Stop.**

He texted back, **What?**

You didn't, I said.

I did, he said.

Without thinking, I pressed the button to call him. "Zackary Olsen, tell me you didn't buy that."

"What if I did?"

"I'd say I think that subset of people with that particular kink is small, and it does not include me."

"You're a mean one, Mr. Grinch." He leaned into the rhythm of the song, and I melted a little bit.

"What are you doing right now?" I asked.

"Hanging out at my favorite place."

"You're hiking?"

"No. I'm at Home Depot."

"Without me?"

"Yeah, but it's not the same." He sighed, and I melted a little bit more. "No pain in the ass following me around."

"You miss me," I cooed.

"Not really."

My laugh was hastily cut off by his follow-up question.

"Want to hang out later?"

I turned and spied the owner of the bakery who was now sitting at the table with Sarah and Tyler.

"I can't," I said in a slight whine. "I'm with Tyler and Sarah at their cake tasting, and I'm not sure how long it's going to take." Silence filled the line, and I wanted to make an excuse or joke. Anything to make him feel like he wasn't a piece in a chess game I played. He was a real person. An important person. "Maybe another day?"

"Yeah, sure." The background noise on his end changed, as if he'd gone from somewhere quiet to a place filled with people. "I gotta go."

Before he could hang up, I stopped him. "I'm sorry."

"For what?"

"I'm not sure," I answered honestly.

He huffed.

"Everything," I said.

"Even world hunger?"

If his sarcasm was aimed for a guilt trip, he hit the bullseye. "No, but I am sorry I dragged you into this." When he didn't say anything, I went on. "I'm a terrible person, and now I'm taking you down with me."

"You're not a terrible person, and you didn't drag me. I volunteered." The way his words slowed sounded like he left something off at the end.

"Uh huh?"

"And I think you should give up," he said after a while. "It's not working."

I snuck another peek through the bakery window, and it looked like Tyler and Sarah were finally wrapping up. "You don't want Sarah back?"

"I thought I did, but I don't."

It would have been a lie to say I wasn't happy to hear it. "When did you figure it out?"

He let out a quiet grunt, and I visualized him carrying a stack of wood on his shoulder with one arm. "Somewhere between finding out she was marrying someone else and actually seeing her again."

I twisted a loose strand of hair around my finger, creating a timeline in my head. "So... Before the oops at Macy's?"

"Yeah."

The equation didn't make sense to me, but something that felt a lot like hope bloomed in my chest. "And you went anyway?"

"Yeah."

He didn't elaborate, and I filled in the blanks like a mad lib to build my own story. I assumed he teamed up with me on this outlandish plot to break up my best friend's wedding, not because he wanted to get back with Sarah, but because of *me*.

The idea filled me with absolute glee and also left me completely guilt-ridden.

I wanted to be the reason he kept up our charade, yet I felt like I was being disloyal to Tyler by expanding my horizons beyond him.

I shook the confusion from my head when a few beeps sounded on Zack's end and to someone else he said, "Thanks," then to me, "I needed new bed sheets."

So much for my theory of him going to Macy's because of me. My heart plummeted to my stomach.

"Tilly, I really do have to go right now. I have one last appointment for the day."

"Yeah." I breathed out a sigh. "Okay."

We hung up, and even though I required more time to solve the geometry problem of me and Zack *and* Tyler *and* Sarah, I didn't have it. Sarah flew out of the door, happy as a lark. "We did exactly as you said, but I added sugar flowers in pale pink. There's going to be so much gray and white everywhere, I thought it would be a nice touch."

"Sounds great," I said, and Tyler dropped down next to me on the bench.

"Let's go get something to eat."

Sarah checked the time on her leopard print smart watch. "Can't. I'm filling in for a fitness class at six, but you guys go and have fun." She laid a kiss on Tyler's lips then one on my cheek. "See you back at my place later, babe? We'll start packing my stuff."

She added a little butt wiggle, and Tyler clucked his tongue. "Sounds good."

As he watched her walk away, I watched him. The way his smile lingered, higher on his left side than right. The number of times he tapped his middle finger on the bench, four. The relaxed set of his shoulders underneath his robin's egg blue shirt, the one I'd bought him two years ago.

When she finally got in her car, he poked my knee. "So, dinner?"

After the cake appetizer, I was still hungry, and I nodded. "Rob's?"

"Read my mind," he said, taking my hand to stand up.

We drove separately and met back up at his brother's hipster burger joint. The steak fries were the stuff dreams were made of. After a hug to Rob, he seated us by the kitchen, and I ordered my usual falafel burger before Tyler and I fell into silence.

Conversation had never been difficult between us, but ever since Sarah had come into his life, we played a stilted game of catch up.

"I wanted to apologize for when you came down to Philly," he said, eyes on his hands as he fiddled with his napkin. "Everything's been moving so fast with the wedding, and we've barely gotten to spend any time alone." He adjusted his glasses and met my gaze. "I really did want to hang out with you, but I also hadn't seen Ricky and everybody else in a while and..." He shook his head, frowning. "I'm sorry."

I hated that I forgave him so easily, but I wasn't about to start holding his feet to the fire now. Not when he gave me those puppy dog eyes.

"But bro code. I get it."

His frown twitched north to a tremulous smile. "If I ever followed a bro code, you helped me write it."

"That's me. A bro," I said, sick and tired of being his bro, but obviously that was the only role Tyler ever saw me in. I had just been too stubborn to see it.

He must have caught my frustration because he flicked his straw at my hand. "You know what I mean. You're my best friend."

Best friend. In all of our twenty years, from when we were too small to ride roller coasters, through our awkward years with braces and acne, and especially during the dark time after my mom's accident, I never doubted what it meant. Until now.

Until our ivy vines began to diverge.

My life had changed so much in the last few years, I'd been desperate to hold onto the past. And maybe I'd held onto it a little too tight.

Tyler reached for my hand. "I love you, Tilly, but it's going to be different between us, and I guess there'll be a learning curve until we figure it out. I don't want to lose you."

We locked our pinkies. "I don't want to lose you either."

"Then we won't. You know the call."

Before I could stop him, he tucked his arms up at his chest and angled his head back, letting out a ridiculous howl. I laughed despite myself, and he did it again, his impression of a T-Rex. He used to do it down the halls in high school. Mrs. Woods gave him detention for it.

"Life finds a way," I said, quoting Jurassic Park, a movie we'd watched a million times over, and I was determined to find a way. "Can I tell you a secret?"

With his arms crossed on the table, he dropped his head down. "Of course."

"Sarah isn't filling in for a class tonight. She and her bridesmaids are learning a dance for the reception."

His eyebrows erased off his face.

"It's to some country song."

He pressed his hand against his mouth.

"She's planning on doing it before you take the garter off."

His cheeks puffed up.

"A lap dance will probably be involved."

He closed his eyes, his words muffled behind his palm, and I pulled on his wrist to lower it.

"What?" I asked.

"I don't think it's nice to speak ill of my own fiancée."

I didn't have that same reticence. "She's a terrible dancer."

"I know!" He cradled his head. "You have to talk her out of it."

"I've basically planned your whole wedding, played messenger between you two like we're in elementary school, and now you want me to convince her not to do the one thing she actually decided on her own?"

He took off his glasses and rubbed the heels of his hands into his eyes. "It's going to be terrible."

"Absolutely."

"She has no rhythm," he said.

"I know."

"She thinks she's really good though."

I nodded. "I guessed that."

"She's not."

"Well..." My brain took off, picturing Sarah gyrating on Tyler, her rump shaking off beat in front of four hundred of their closest friends and family, and I started giggling. I couldn't stop.

He laughed too.

"You guys are nothing alike," I said, still grinning.

"Yeah." He wiped away the last of his laugh with a knuckle at the corner of his mouth. "But I love her."

"I only pray your kids inherit your dance ability."

The waiter arrived with our food, and Tyler leaned back in his chair, giving him more room to set his plate down on the table. "We haven't quite settled the kids question. She's not sure if she wants any."

"Tyler."

He squinted at me. "Don't give me that face."

I thrusted a fry at him. "It's August twenty-first. You're getting married on September twenty-sixth."

"Thanks for the reminder."

"You realize there is a marriage after the wedding, right?"

He bit into his burger, refusing to answer, and I was no marriage counselor—I wasn't even in a relationship—but why these two yahoos couldn't grasp the basic concepts of building a relationship beyond "you're cute and smell good" didn't bode well. But what did I know?

I was the woman trying to break them up.

Right?

That's what I was supposed to be doing.

I'm not sure exactly when the idea of ruining my best friend's wedding started losing its luster, but I was positive it was around the time I took notice of Zack's shine.

"Do you expect me to talk to her about the kids you want to have too?" I huffed. "Should I pass her a note in fifth period?"

"You don't get it," he said, his mouth full. He swallowed and squirted ketchup on his plate. "You have to make a lot of compromises when you're with someone, and it's hard sometimes. You'll understand when you finally have a relationship."

I snatched the bottle out of his hand. "Don't patronize me. Being engaged has made you kind of an asshole."

"I'm not patronizing you." He swirled a fry in ketchup.

"I know what compromise is. I also know if you want to spend the rest of your life with someone, you should probably make sure your basic life goals and dreams are the same. Or at least, moving in the same direction."

"We can learn. We're going to grow together," he said, and I thumped my drink on the table after a sip.

Somewhere along the journey to Break-Upland, I had started trying to make Tyler and Sarah work. If only by accident, since they were determined to make it *not* work on their own. They were so desperately mismatched, each of them assumed it would all work out by sheer force of will without ever putting any energy into rolling the ball along.

It was like Tyler had never taken Mr. Murray's Economics class in high school, when he made us do the "family planning" unit. But I knew he did. We completed the project together. Both of us cutting coupons and planning for a family of four. Maybe that was why Tyler had shit for brains when it came to thinking he could convince Sarah to have kids. A Catholic school's idea of family planning was to make sure your van was big enough for all the kids you'd have without birth control.

"If she doesn't want kids, I'm pretty sure she's not going to agree to the three or four you've always wanted," I told him.

He shook his head, but there was no way around this. Tyler had always wanted to be a father. He was one of three boys and close to all of his extended family. He wanted a big family.

"You shouldn't have to compromise on that," I told him. "I don't think you can."

"I'm working on it. I'll wear her down eventually," he said and took another big bite of his burger.

I pressed my hand to my forehead. "She's not a pencil you can sharpen how you want. I highly doubt she'll suddenly change her mind about it. I have ovaries; I'm kind of an expert."

"You're not—" chomp "—an expert on—" chomp "—Sarah though."

"Jesus, Mary, and Joseph. Stop talking while you're eating."

Tyler closed his mouth, chewed, swallowed, and took a gulp of his iced tea. Then he grinned. "Nellie came through right then."

I played with her mother-of-pearl pendant at my collarbone, giving into a smile. "She'd say you're a feckin' eejit."

Seventeen

The following week, I closed the boutique late after cataloging inventory for next season. All the new gowns Mom had ordered arrived within three days of each other, and I unpacked, steamed, and hung over two dozen dresses, half of which were heavy, beaded, and multi-layered ball gowns. Apparently this winter, bridal fashion was going full on Belle from *Beauty and the Beast*.

I skipped taking a break for dinner, working straight through in order to finish up so Alice and Fatima didn't have to deal with any dresses laying around in the morning when they opened. My stomach rumbled as I trudged through my door, but there wasn't much in my fridge besides some wilted lettuce, water-logged watermelon, and a sad piece of leftover chicken. I pulled up the online menu for my favorite take-out place, Picasso's, with a picture of Hawaiian pizza in the corner of the page.

The last conversation Zack and I had left me discombobulated, and I needed to know what direction I should be pointing. Right now I felt like a kite, at the mercy of the wind, so I reached for an anchor. I texted him. **Did you eat yet?**

His message back was immediate. **Nope just got home.**

My thumbs flew over my keyboard as I walked into my bedroom. **Me too. I'm hungry. Want to come over for pizza?**

Depends.

On what? I asked.

Pineapple.

I took off my work clothes before replying. **Don't worry, I won't offend your sensitive taste buds.**

Be over in a bit.

I sunk to the bed, my eyes on my reflection in the antique floor length mirror I'd found at a yard sale. A crack in the glass bisected almost the whole thing, and the owners had sold it to me for a few bucks, deeming it unusable. Over time, beloved objects were bound to wear and tear, but it made them more interesting. More beautiful in the story they told. Not that I thought this mirror's fracture had an interesting story, it probably simply fell over one day and now it lived with me in my apartment of misfit furniture.

Much like me, a misfit. Not quite fitting in anywhere and a little bit broken. A little bit like Zack too.

I threw on shorts and a T-shirt, not bothering to redo my make-up. Zack had already seen me at my worst—inviting him to shred my best friend's relationship—so there was no point in trying to impress him now. Yet I still tucked a bit of my shirt into my waistband. Couldn't help it if I came across artfully undone with my hair down around my shoulders.

The pizza arrived the same time my phone rang with Tyler on the other end.

"Hey, what's up?" I popped a piece of pineapple in my mouth.

"You think Sarah would like a honeymoon in Costa Rica?"

"Um, I don't know. Why don't you ask her?"

"I think I heard your eyeroll," he said with a laugh.

"Good."

"She wants me to surprise her. Do you think she'd like Costa Rica?"

I wasn't an aficionado on the geography of Central America, but a beach was a beach was a beach as far as I was concerned. "Yeah, I guess."

"You paused," he said, and I could almost picture him pointing an accusing finger at me. "You did your Tilly pause. You're lying."

I sunk down onto the couch. "I'm sure it's beautiful, and you'll probably rent out a little bungalow on the water which costs more than a year's worth of rent, but you know me, I'm allergic to the sun."

"Yeah, remember when we road tripped down to Florida?"

I raised my arm, twisting it side to side as if the sun blisters were still there. "How could I forget?"

He laughed. "I thought you might never recover."

"I almost didn't. It hurt to wear clothes for weeks."

"I still have a picture of you, cherry red, sitting in the ice water bath."

I cringed, recalling the pain and embarrassment of that weekend on the beach. I had been 20 and invincible, thinking I could get by with the sweet-smelling Copper Tone SPF15. I had worn a tiny bikini and baked myself into a gigantic lobster the first day on the beach. Tyler had promised not to leave me alone, swearing that Spring Break wouldn't be fun without me. So we stayed in the hotel room for the rest of the trip, watching movies and getting drunk.

"I learned my less—"

I was cut off by the buzz at my door, and Tyler perked up on the other end of my phone. "Is that the doorbell I heard?"

"Yeah, I have to go."

"Tilly. It's a Friday night. Do you have a date?"

"No."

"Liar."

I hung up on his chuckle and tossed my phone on the couch before opening the door. Two months ago, Zack had arrived to "fix" my toilet in boots, jeans, and an Olsen company T-shirt. Tonight he wore boots, jeans, and a soft olive shirt that brought out the flecks of green in his eyes.

"Hi," he said, not hiding the fact that he surveyed me up and down.

"You're late."

He closed the door behind him and followed me to the kitchen. "I didn't know I was being timed."

I gestured to the pizza on the small bistro table and then to the television where the episode of *Barbarians* was already halfway through. His gaze coasted around the rest of my apartment like he did the day he first came over, but this time he carefully considered everything.

"You're a fire hazard," he said, referring to the lit candles on every available flat surface.

"Am not."

He bent to study the black and white photo of Nellie and Sean. After a moment, he straightened with it in his hand, "This is Nellie?"

I nodded.

"You look exactly like her."

I'd always thought she was rather beautiful in a wild, I'd-burn-your-house-down-if-you-crossed-me sort of way. "Thanks."

He set the photo back, among the nest of others like it, old pictures from Ireland and other family members. He met me in the kitchen, where I handed him a plate and told him to help himself. I snagged a piece of Hawaiian and sat on the couch, pressing play on the Netflix show while he searched through my cabinets until he found a mason jar. He cracked a few ice cubes into it and opened one of the three cans of soda I had in the back of the fridge.

"Had to get pineapple, didn't you?" He sat next to me with two pieces of pepperoni.

"I got half and half. I told you I wouldn't harm your taste buds."

He set his plate and soda on the coffee table before unlacing and removing his boots, and there was something so natural and sweet in the action, I couldn't help but smile. As he made himself comfortable next to me, he gave me another one of his suspicious expressions. I think they were my favorite, like I was some foreign creature here to amuse and confound him. I hoped that if he was curious enough to figure me out, he would keep coming back for more, but there was no way I could tell him that. Instead, I burrowed down into the cushions, biting into my pizza.

We watched three episodes of *Barbarians*, in relative quiet, only interspersed with comments on the bloody fights or what we thought of the actors until he asked me how long the Roman Empire lasted. And then, because I had too much of my father in me, I spouted off any and every tidbit of information I had stored in my brain about the Empire's fall and how, in my opinion, Ireland saved civilization in the Dark Ages after Rome was sacked and burned. I described the work of the monasteries and how they preserved philosophical works and literature which might not have survived otherwise.

Though, he didn't appear to mind my stream-of-consciousness diatribe. He didn't even try to stop me, or reach for the remote to continue watching the show when the prompt filled the screen.

"Fun fact," I started as Zack combed his hand through his auburn hair before settling his arm on the back of the couch, his fingers near my ear, "it's believed the original Celts had black hair and brown eyes. It was the Germanic tribes who brought over light eyes and hair. The Vikings gave Ireland red hair. It's one of the things people associate with Irish people, right? Having red hair and blue eyes. But it wasn't even ours to begin with."

He propped his knee on the couch, leaned in toward me, and lifted those fingers by my ear to graze my temple. "Your eyes are blue."

I instinctively drew closer to him, unable to stay away even if I wanted to. He was a carving in stone I needed to examine closer.

"So you have some Viking in you too," he said, and I swallowed thickly when his other hand landed on my knee. He didn't say anything else, only let the tension settle between us. For me, the girl who couldn't shut up when she was nervous, simply being in the moment was difficult. Sitting in silence, even harder. But he challenged me too.

Without filling space and time with my words, my senses went into overdrive. My eyes couldn't find enough to behold, between the shine of his wavy hair falling over his forehead and the freckles dotting his skin like faerie kisses. My ears attuned to his breathing, and my skin adjusted to the heat of his hands.

And I was starting to understand the magic that the ancient Irish believed in. The pull of the natural world, the connection of spirits, the light that dwelled in all of us, I felt it in this space where I was being reborn. Under Zack's gaze, I felt whole and new and *right*.

He pinched a lock of my hair between his thumb and forefinger. "Want to go for a ride?"

It was almost midnight. "Right now?"

He nodded once, and it could have been three in the morning, but with the way he stared at me I still would have said, "Yes."

"You have to change."

"I do?"

He dragged his hand down over my shin to my ankle, stopping at where my feet were buried under a pillow next to his thigh. "You've got to put on pants."

"Why?"

"Road rash."

I jerked away from him. "You think we're going to crash? Why would I want to go with you now?"

He smiled indulgently. "Just a precaution." He squeezed my ankle once. "I'll take care of you, don't worry."

Jesus, Mary, and Joseph, I was worried. Except not about crashing a motorcycle.

I'd fallen headlong into Zack's murky eyes, lost in their depth. I'd been more and more desperate to peel his layers back, but now I was far too deep. I couldn't find my way out.

I didn't think I wanted to.

"Come on." He pulled me up with him when he stood and wrapped his hand around my back. "I want to show you something."

My chest was pressed lightly against his, our hips level, and I feared if I touched him now, I wouldn't be able to stop. So with my hands at my sides, I nodded and turned away.

As I changed in my bedroom, I could hear him blowing out the candles one by one around the apartment, dousing us in darkness, until there were only two left by the front door. I tugged on a zip-up over my T-shirt, and with jeans and sneakers on, I held out my arms for inspection. "Good?"

"Perfect."

I blew out the remaining candles when he opened the front door, and I didn't hesitate to take his hand when he offered it.

He led me out to his bike, where he opened a compartment in the back for a spare helmet and fit it to my head. One single street lamp above us illuminated his face, but underneath his brows that were bent in concentration, his eyes were dark pools. "There are footrests behind mine. You should put your feet on them and hold on to my waist," he instructed. "I won't be able to hear you, so if you want me to stop or slow down, tap my shoulder, okay?"

My voice was sandpaper. "Yeah. Okay."

"You scared?" he asked, finishing up with my helmet.

"No."

His mouth kicked up. "Liar."

"A little," I admitted, and he gripped both of my shoulders in his strong hands.

"I'll take care of you. Do you trust me to do that?"

"Yes."

He slid the little visor down over my eyes. "That's my girl."

Eighteen

Zack helped me on the bike before he settled in front of me, and as directed, I placed my feet on the pegs and held onto him. He revved the engine, and my blood thrummed in my veins as the motorcycle came to life underneath me. I was plastered to his body, my chest against his back, my hands clinging to his hard torso, and the heady combination of energy, fear, and lust swirled in my belly until I was practically trembling.

It was only after he patted my hands that I noticed I'd twisted his shirt into the balls of my fists. He twisted his head to me, as much as he could with his helmet, a move which I assumed was to make sure I was all right.

I most certainly was not all right, but there was no way I was getting off this motorcycle either. With my thighs bracketing his and my arms around his middle, it didn't feel so scary, especially when he squeezed the side of my thigh. A reminder that he would take care of me.

He eased out onto the street, and after one more pat to my leg, he sped off.

The wind whipped against me, and I tucked my head into Zack's back, every inch of my body coiled in tension. But nestled against his shoulder, I relaxed with every exhale before I could finally lift my head. I blinked my eyes open and sat up, a little bit more comfortable in my hold, even when we leaned left or right, weaving through the town with the stars as our guide.

We rode past cornfields and a horse stable, over a few hills, and around a lot of bends. Beneath my fingers, Zack was steady and strong, and I shifted closer in an attempt to burrow into him. Maybe it was the fact that we were one wrong move from death or maybe it was the fresh, cool air releasing the jumbled thoughts inside my brain. Whatever it was, I didn't want to let him go. Even after he slowed and turned off the main road onto a dirt path to park by a wooded area.

He removed his helmet and stepped off the bike before helping me, and I was glad for it, a little unsteady, even with both feet on the ground again. He took off my helmet and smoothed my messy hair back away from my face, his fingers lingering on my shoulder.

"How do you feel?"

I breathed deep and long, yielding to the glow that seemed to emanate from some ancient place inside me. "Alive like fire."

His hand cupped my neck, and I knew he could feel my thrashing pulse. I felt it. Everywhere. My chest, my fingertips, my core.

A reminder of *life*.

I had been still for so long, and now I was hurtling forward, headed directly for change. It wouldn't be easy, and it would most likely hurt, but I couldn't stop.

I didn't want to stop.

I held my arms out wide and tipped my head back, accepting all that had happened and giving in to what would come. The full moon above was the only source of light, and I soaked it in before righting myself. I found Zack's eyes, even in the dark, and anchored my hands to his side. Then I kissed him.

I not only felt alive like fire.

I *was* fire.

Heat spread from my center, licked up my spine and raced down the backs of my legs. My skin burned under his fingertips at my cheek and lower back. Those soft, plump lips of his chased mine, urging my mouth open, and when our tongues met, I sighed in relief. He tasted faintly of soda, and I drank him in, sipping until I was full and out of breath.

His teeth scraped my jaw, his beard scratched my neck, and I tunneled my fingers into his hair, holding him to me as he blazed a path to my throat, nipping and sucking a line of possession. My knees were weak, and he tightened one arm around me, the other roaming the dips and curves of my side. I was a panting, gasping mess as his fingers spanned my ribcage, his thumb teasing the swell of my breast, and I needed more. I needed to be closer. Dig down deep inside to discover if he glowed too.

I clung to the soft material of his T-shirt, but before I could lift it up and over his head, he stopped me with a rough grunt. He rested his forehead against mine, breathing hard and harsh against my lips. "I didn't take you out here for this."

"No?" I laughed, punch drunk. "This wasn't all part of a grand plot?"

He growled his answer into my mouth, scoring my lower lip with his teeth. "No." He left me wanting and leaning into him, dizzy with desire, as he took my hand. "I told you, I wanted to show you something."

With our fingers linked together, he guided me farther into the trees, but it cleared after a few yards, leading out to a lake. The moonlight reflected off the water so pretty it could have been a painting.

"This is gorgeous," I said, and he nodded. We sat down on

the tall grass, our only company a distant owl and a few fire-flies staying up late.

I removed my sweatshirt and crossed my legs, soaking it all in. "How did you find this place?"

"On a drive a few months ago. It was winter and the lake had frozen over."

I thought I'd spotted a For Sale sign among the weeds, but it was impossible to be sure in the darkness. Though it didn't look like much now, I could imagine this stony ground might be the beginning of something wonderful.

"Why'd you want to bring me here?" I turned to Zack to find him staring at me as if he could see me perfectly clear even through the blanket of navy surrounding us. He was reclined back with one hand behind him, the other rubbing his beard, still cut close to his jaw. I liked that he'd taken my advice. Not that he had to. He was handsome before. Still was now.

"I'm going to build a house here," he said quietly, although with only the two of us here, it might as well have been surround sound. "It's my long-term plan."

"Are you going to build it yourself?" I asked for no particular reason other than fodder for my imagination. Him shirt-less, cutting logs and hammering things.

"I'm not that skilled."

"No?" I pouted. "Too bad."

He shifted to lay on his side, cradling his head in his hand. "I'd love to know what goes on in your mind."

"No, you wouldn't."

"Yes, I would." He wrapped his left hand around my leg, urging me to lie down next to him.

I stretched out, fitting into the space next to him like the ground had been carved for us. "I was thinking about how you'd look really good building your own house, all sweaty and buff. Chopping down trees, carrying them on your back."

"I like how strong you think I am."

"Shh." I pressed two fingers to his lips. "Don't ruin the fantasy."

When he nipped at them, I jerked away, but he pulled me back, so I flipped on my side too. His warm hand glided under my shirt. "What else is going on in that head of yours?"

We'd been together for more than a few hours tonight, and the names of Sarah and Tyler hadn't come up at all, so I hesitated to tell him. But he curled his finger around one of my belt loops and tugged, goading me.

"I was thinking about the day we went for a hike, and you said you wanted to be better for Sarah."

He waited for me to go on. This man, he was so patient. Almost too patient for me and the mess going on in my mind.

"What did you think you needed to be better at?" I finally asked. "You're pretty okay to me."

"Okay?" His voice was laced with amusement.

"More than okay," I corrected. *Perfect*, I didn't say.

"Okay," he repeated with a squeeze of my hip. My eyesight had adjusted to the darkness, but I still could only see the outline of his features and had to rely on his voice to understand him. Listen for his rumbling laugh or pregnant pauses. "We met at this fitness fundraiser thing, where she was doing a demo class," he started after one of those such pauses. "I'm not big on group workouts, but my friend's wife was working at one of the booths, and Sarah was introducing herself to everyone, inviting them to come take her class."

I regretted asking him and hated how fond he sounded for her. Especially when my tangled thoughts reminded me that Sarah kissed him, touched him, *had* him.

I loathed her. "I'm sure she was sunshine in a bottle, and it was insta-love."

"Not quite." His hand moved up my side possessively, and I loathed her a little less. "I took her class, and she was so peppy, I didn't like it at all. But once she decides she wants you, she's like a koala. She doesn't let go."

There was no better description for her. I was in her clutches now, too.

The geometry of this situation was already awkward, I didn't want to imagine them in the relationship, let alone intimate. And now I had to figure out how to retract Sarah's koala claws when I'd been previously trying to sink them in further.

It wasn't easy being a puppet master.

"We were good for a while," Zack continued. "Except at some point, it felt less like she was in it for us and more like I was a lost cat she'd rescued. She wanted to fix me. After we broke up, I thought if I worked on myself more, she'd want me back."

I groaned, and his hand drifted up my ribcage as if to tell me I didn't need to be jealous. He was tracing each of *my* ribs. I was the one he wanted now. Or, at least, that's what I hoped it meant.

"I think she liked the idea of me being a reformed bad boy or something, but when she realized my life wasn't all that exciting, she lost interest. I realized it wasn't about what *I* was or wasn't doing. It was about what *she* wanted."

"She doesn't even know what she wants," I said, and he agreed with light pressure to my spine, urging my hips forward to meet his, and then our thighs were touching. I could feel his firm muscles through our denim, and I bent my leg, resting it on top of his. He grated out a soft but proprietorial hum and curled his hand around my ass.

"What do you want?" he asked, his voice giving nothing away.

"I want to hate Sarah."

He let out one single chuckle, almost like he didn't mean to. "Why?"

"She knew you." I let my hand drift across his chest. "*Knows* you."

"Not anymore." He closed the last bit of distance between us, so every inch of me pressed against every inch of him. With his hand gripping my thigh, he repositioned my knee higher on his hip, allowing him to slot between my legs. He ground the growing bulge of him against me, a crude partner to the chaste kisses he left along my jaw. It was a chaotic contradiction, sort of how I felt most days.

And I never wanted it to stop.

"I mean, what do you want for yourself?" he asked, pushing me back against the ground, deliberately rolling his hips into mine, pulling a gasp from me.

"What do I want?" Well, it was difficult to concentrate when his big hand worked under my shirt to my breast. He plumped me over my bra, swiped his thumb over my nipple, and still he stared down at me like he was waiting for an answer.

There were a great many things I wanted, so he needed to narrow it down. "In life? For the long-term?"

He lowered his mouth to my throat, laving the dip of my collarbone with his tongue, sucking on the soft skin under my jaw. "Let's start with Tyler?" he rasped against the shell of my ear. "What do you want with him?"

Then he levered up over me, his hands caging me in on either side, silently demanding more room as his knees spread my legs wider.

I knew he was waiting for my answer. Waiting to give me what I wanted.

The problem was I didn't know exactly what I wanted or needed from Tyler anymore, but I did know whatever it was, it wasn't anywhere close to what I wanted and needed from Zack. I'd been fooling myself in believing it was ever the same.

Tyler was familiar to me. He was my comfort blanket in

my time of need, and I'd been clinging tight to him because I didn't know how to handle so much change. I had wanted just *one thing* in my life to go according to plan since nothing else had. But now I knew I couldn't plan this.

I couldn't avoid change. I could merely run toward the roar.

Echoing Zack's words from the other day, I told him, "Somewhere between meeting you and kissing you, I realized he isn't what I want anymore. I love him, we'll always be friends, but I don't want him like I want you."

His answering groan spurred on my clawing desperate need for him, and I bowed into him when he lowered his weight back on top of me, his fingers gliding back and forth across the waistband of my jeans.

"Please, Zack," I murmured, and he obliged, unfastening the button, skating the zipper down, sinking his hand below my underwear. He teased at my opening, spreading me wide, his thumb skating over my clit.

His breath hitched. "You're so hot here."

"I'm burning up," I told him, scraping my nails along his scalp and the nape of his neck.

"I'll take care of you," he said and pushed two fingers inside me as he pressed his thick length into my hip. He kissed his way down to my chest, wrestling with the collar of my top until he could finally lick over the swell of my breast, mumbling words about how soft I was.

I reached for his jeans, but with him refusing to budge, I had a hard time undoing the button. He didn't seem to care. He was relentless in his pursuit of my pleasure, his mouth searching and sucking, his fingers circling and petting until I was squirming underneath him.

"I'm...I'm..." I didn't know what I was. My mind was gone, empty of everything except for Zack and the flashes of light when he twisted his hand, finding the spot deep inside me that set off sparks behind my eyelids.

"Let me take care of you," he crooned, and my body automatically responded, my muscles releasing their spiraled tension, my thighs widening, and he smiled into a kiss against my mouth. "That's my girl."

Now that I'd relinquished control to him, he shifted over, allowing me to palm the outline of him through his pants. Between his kisses and his fingers, I was an uncoordinated disaster, but he didn't care, groaning his satisfaction when I finally wrapped my fingers around his cock.

I stroked him up and down in time to our mingled inhales and exhales, both of us lost to each other's touch. We kissed, but it was sloppy, our lips frantic, our tongues useless for anything save for murmured words of *yes* and *like that* and *oh god*.

I was so swollen and wet that when he worked my clit, I cried out, my hips reflexively arching up, my insides raging to reach the peak. He ducked his head, his ragged breaths in my ear as I swept my thumb over the bead of moisture on his tip then curled my fingers tighter around his cock. I sank my teeth into the damp skin of his neck, the taste of salt and earth on my tongue.

"Tilly, come for me," he demanded on a moan. "I need you to come for me."

He flicked his fingers, turning me into some wanton creature, writhing and moaning as I stared up at the starry sky, rocking into his hand, giving into the most natural thing of this world. I soared higher and higher, through puffy clouds and whipping winds, finding heaven even as my back never left the ground.

"That's it, that's it, that's it," he chanted, the muscles of his neck corded below my fingers, and he wrenched out of my hold, his hand forcing mine away to wrap around himself, aiming his release onto the ground as he sighed, his eyes closed tight.

I licked my dry lips, rested my palm over my racing heart, but I couldn't be bothered with righting my clothes or hair.

Once I'd found my breath again, I gently held onto Zack's forearm. He peered over his shoulder, a smile tugging at the corner of his mouth. "You okay?"

"Yeah." My voice cracked, and I cleared my throat. "I'm okay."

But I was more than okay. I was exultant. On a different plane. In another universe.

He sank down next to me. "I really did want to talk," he said, and I heard the smile in his voice as I nestled into his side, laying my head on his shoulder. "I brought you here so you could see what I want. So you'd know what my long-term plan is because I want to know yours too."

I didn't answer, and he twirled a lock of hair around his finger, ever patient.

"I... I don't know what my-long term plan is," I said honestly—maybe a little too honest because of what we'd done moments ago—but I couldn't stop it now. He hadn't buttoned his fly, and I scratched my fingertip along the waist-band of his underwear, more truth pouring out of me. "I got lost, and I haven't been able to find my way back. Sometimes when I think about it, I get overwhelmed and just... I give up."

He turned on his side, cradling me in his arms, and I tipped my chin up to meet his gaze. It was easy to find his eyes in the dark now, like we'd shined a light on each other. He caressed my lower lip and chin with his fingertip, and being here with him made it easy to confess a secret. "I'm afraid of the future. Of the unknown."

I hadn't ever told anyone else about that fear. Not even Tyler.

But Zack merely nodded, holding my face tenderly in his hands like he was holding my secret.

"What about right now?" he asked, his thumb skimming my cheekbone. "If it scares you to think too far into the future, what do you want right now? If you could do anything, what would it be?"

I turned my head toward the lake and focused on a land far away from here. "I'd go to Ireland. Run through green fields. Get drunk in a pub and dance to a reel the locals play in the corner. Find the village my great-grandparents were from. Explore ruins, maybe even find this stone," I said, rubbing my tattoo before nudging him away so I could sit up.

My nose burned, and I wasn't usually so emotional, but I was laid bare here with him. I'd wanted to peel his layers back and ended up shedding mine instead. I wrapped my arms around my bent knees and made sure my voice was dry before I spoke. "I was supposed to spend the whole semester there. I got one week, so if I could do anything right now it would be to go back there and experience everything I never got to."

He sat up, quiet for a long time before expelling a low breath. "Wow." Then he dipped his chin toward his chest, huffing a laugh. "I was going to say I'd go swimming in the lake. Yours is much more poetic."

I gave into a smile. "I don't know about that."

When I stood, he shifted to look up at me, and before I could think better of it, I shimmied out of my clothes, having been half way there anyway. "I'm sure there've been poems written about swimming under the moonlight."

I stripped off my top and lobbed it at his face then took off running into the water in only my underwear and bra. The lake was lukewarm, but I'd scarcely gotten that far in before Zack splashed behind me.

"There better not be any fish or creepy crawlers in here," I said as his hands found my hips below the water.

"No, there's nothing in here," he assured me, tugging my back to his bare chest. He molded himself to me and fisted my hair, pressing kisses into my shoulder. "Your skin looks perfect under the moonlight."

I tilted my head to the side, giving him better access to my neck and melted against him. The simmering coals in my belly ignited, and fire consumed me again. I wound my arms behind his head and dug my fingers into his hair, holding him to me. Trying to remain in this place of freedom for as long as possible.

"I've thought about you nonstop," he said against my ear, sending shivers down my spine. "Ever since the first day in your apartment. I thought you were crazy." He slid his hands across my stomach and up to my breasts, and I laughed into a kiss, maybe a little too maniacally, because he lifted his head away from me.

I spun to face him, locking my arms around his neck, and sucked his bottom lip between mine, biting it hard enough that he hissed. With a soft grunt, he lifted me up off the ground, holding one arm under my butt, the other around my waist, and I didn't hesitate to wrap my legs around him.

"You don't come from Irish freedom fighters and a great-grandmother who drank whiskey with lunch every day and not end up a little crazy," I said and kissed him.

"A little wild," he amended into my lips.

I'd been such a fool to ever write-off this man because of my height. My own insecurities might have prevented me from kissing or touching him, and what a loss that would have been.

He kissed with his whole body, with his arms wound around me and murmured words against my neck and ear. He consumed me, and I never wanted it to stop. I'd offer myself up on a platter, if he asked.

"What the fuck!" He tore his mouth away from mine and

scrambled back with me still in his arms. I shrieked as we both fell down, submerged completely.

When I found my footing, I popped back up, gasping. "What?" I wiped my face. "What happened?"

He slipped twice, arms flailing, before he stood upright, his eyes searching the water. "Something touched the back of my leg. Something slimy."

I hid my laugh behind my hand. "I thought there was nothing in here."

"Lesson learned," he muttered with a grimace. "Come on." He grabbed my hand to haul me out of the lake behind him. Once we reached dry land, I realized we didn't have any towels. I hadn't fully thought through our tryst in the water.

Zack shook off like a dog and skimmed his hands down his torso, sluicing droplets off him. It was too dark to see the detail of his tattoos, but I tried my damnedest anyway before letting my gaze drop to his wet boxer briefs which were practically a second skin.

"Are you sure you don't know how to build a house?"

He froze in the middle of scrubbing his hands through his hair and eyed me. I couldn't tell where his focus had landed, but my body went on high alert anyway, my skin puckering, nipples tightening.

"Maybe I could learn for you." He had his arms around me in two strides, bending to kiss me. Yet before his lips met mine, he stopped suddenly. "You're cold." He rubbed his hands up and down my arms. "Let's get dressed and get you home."

"You going to tuck me in?" I teased, and he palmed my ass, nipping at the corner of my mouth.

"If you're a good girl."

I was, in fact, not a good girl, unable to keep my hands off of him as he drove us back to my apartment. It was like they had a mind of their own, wandering the plane of his stomach, along his thighs and in between them. When he'd parked and stepped off the bike, he shook his head in dismay, though he couldn't keep the amused tremble from his lips.

"I promised I'd take care of you. Kinda hard to do that when you're distracting me from the road."

I shrugged. "Sorry."

"No, you're not."

"No, I'm not," I confirmed, and he clucked his tongue. "Brat."

So, much to *my* dismay, he did not tuck me in, but he did walk me to my door and dropped a sweet good-night kiss on my forehead.

And later, when I laid my head on my pillow, I didn't think about Tyler or Sarah, or wedding gowns and cake. Tonight, I thought of romantic rides on a motorcycle, spontaneous night swims in a lake, and a ginger-haired mountain man building me a log cabin.

Nineteen

With three weeks until the wedding, Sarah's dress had been delivered, and this time she came alone to try it on. Thank god.

As always, she greeted me with a hug, but her concentration was lodged on the gown. I'd hung it up in a dressing room, and she stood a few feet from it, hands at her mouth.

"That's..." Her shoulders rose and fell on a breath. "That's my dress." She crept forward and touched the sleeve reverently. "That's the dress I'm getting married in." She turned to me, her eyes wet. "I'm getting married."

"You are."

Her smile tipped down a bit, bordering on a frown. "I'm getting married," she said again, a little less enthusiastic. "In twenty days."

"Yeah, are you okay?"

She shook out her arms and legs like a runner setting up at the blocks. "Yes, it's, you know...really overwhelming. I'm finally getting married."

"Are you sure? Because it sounded like a question." I

repeated her sentence, raising my voice at the end. "I'm finally getting *married?*"

She waved me off with a very un-Sarah-like giggle, low and a little manic. "No, no, I'm getting married." She set her shoulders and faced her dress. "I will be Mrs. Rodriguez. I love Tyler. I love him."

I nodded because only people who were very absolutely sure of what they were doing needed to talk themselves into it. Seemed like my plan was finally starting to take hold.

And I didn't feel good about it.

"Do you want some water?" I asked since I had nothing else to offer. I didn't know how to rewind what I'd put in motion.

Her shoulders slumped. "Water would be perfect, actually. Thanks."

Leaving Sarah with her dress, I snatched a bottle from the break room before hurrying to the backroom, afraid to leave her too long. I tapped on the doorframe, stealing Mom's attention from her discussion with Galina. "Sorry to interrupt, but Sarah's here. Do you want to come out?"

My mother nodded, and I was grateful. I felt a little dizzy like I'd spun around too fast. Which I guess I had. The pivot was disorienting.

After Sarah greeted my mom with a hug, I handed her the water and sat her on a chair. Her hand trembled slightly. I only detected it when she struggled to unscrew the cap from the bottle.

"How are you today?" Mom asked, motioning to her gown. "It's always an exciting day to put on your dress for the first time. When you try them on, they aren't yours, but I've always loved when our brides come in for *their* dress. It's a special moment to be a part of. Don't you think so, Tilly?"

I leaned more towards disillusion than enchantment when it came to wedding gowns and this business—this huge money-making business—but I agreed anyway, hoping to ease Sarah's obvious nerves.

"I think I'm a little stunned," she said, tugging on the diamond stud in her earlobe. "It hit me all at once, you know? It's happening. It's really happening."

"But..." I paused, attempting to be delicate. "Weren't you engaged before?"

She tossed me a sheepish glance. "Yeah, but I've never gotten this close to the altar."

"It's okay to be nervous. It's scary," Mom said, rolling closer to hold Sarah's hand. "You're about to change your life, and that is really scary, but you're also not doing it alone. That's what getting married is about, joining together so you don't have to be alone when you're scared or nervous. You have Tyler now." She nodded to me. "And you have us now too. We're here for you, however we can help."

Sarah slanted her eyes up to me, appearing to need more reassurance. I wasn't the person she should be talking to since I'd been trying to break them apart, but I gave it my best shot. "I'm not married. I have no advice. But I know Tyler loves you. He wants to make it work." I stared down at my feet, guilt washing over me for what I had tried to do. I supposed the best thing I could do now was be honest. I lifted my gaze to hers. "I don't believe in soul mates. I don't believe there is one person floating around out there for each of us. But I do believe you choose people to love, and if they love you back, you try your best every day to do the best for each other."

I smiled to myself, the scent of waffles and maple syrup filling my memory. "I don't think love is about weddings and parties and exciting things like first kisses and butterflies. I think it's all the boring stuff in between, when you wake up every morning and go to bed every night with the same person. It's doing your taxes together and grocery shopping and deciding if you're going to save your points for gas or a turkey." I wrapped my hand around the back of my mom's chair. "I don't have good advice, but I've never seen two people who have made a marriage work more than my parents, and I hope one day I'll have what they have, which is an everyday kind of love filled with tuna sandwiches and puzzles. I hope you and Tyler have that too."

Mom pursed her lips, blinking rapidly. "That was beautiful, Tilly."

Sarah agreed, her chin quivering. "Is that your Best Man speech? It should be." She jumped up and hugged me, whispering, "Thank you. Thank you."

I returned her squeeze and moved her to the platform. "Now, you ready to try on your dress?"

She clapped and nodded enthusiastically, yet as I ushered her forward, the bell over the door rang, and Tyler called out across the store, "There're my girls!"

Sarah squealed and flung herself in the dressing room. Tyler strode closer, grinning. "What are you hiding for?"

"I'm trying on my wedding dress," Sarah called from behind the door. "It's bad luck to see me."

"You don't have it on yet," I pointed out with a glare at Tyler mouthing, *You know she's a nut, right?*

He shrugged good-naturedly. *Yep.* "I brought you flowers."

Sarah popped her head out, spied the bouquet, and carefully closed the door behind her before throwing herself at Tyler. Literally. He caught her, and like some romantic comedy, they kissed and laughed together, spinning in a circle.

If marriages were measured on enthusiasm alone, they'd be fine, but I had a feeling Sarah's mini breakdown a few minutes ago wasn't the first or last.

Tyler set Sarah on her feet and handed her the huge bouquet. He leaned down so she could kiss his cheek, and he snagged two flowers. "Michelle," he cooed, sinking down to hug and kiss my mom. He'd been my one and only friend ever permitted to call my mom by her first name. "For you," he said, handing her an orange daisy. "I would bottle up the sunshine for you, if I could."

She laughed, sounding decades younger. "You're too charming for your own good."

He grinned at her, knowing exactly what he was doing. Then he straightened and offered me the second flower. "And a white rose for my white rose."

My mother was absolutely right. Too charming.

I knocked his shoulder. "Roses are my least favorite flower."

"But perfect for you." He slung his arm around my shoulders, singing, "Every rose has its thorn."

"Rude." I elbowed him in the gut, and he pretended to keel over.

"Come on, hon," my mom said to him. "You can check out the computer for me while the girls do their thing." She led him to the back. "It's been acting weird since it updated."

Once they were out of sight, Sarah and I got back to work, with no more signs of anxiety. As I buttoned her up, she prattled on about her sister's new boyfriend coming to the wedding and her bachelorette party this weekend, which she invited me to, but I declined, using the excuse of work. In reality, I didn't think I'd make it through a weekend getaway to Atlantic City with Sunshine Sarah and her merry band of bridesmaids. Besides, I'd rather spend time with a certain someone.

The dress fit her almost perfectly. It only required a hem at the bottom, and I called Galina over to pin it. When all was said and done, with the simple raw edge veil and hair comb, she looked beautifully vintage and simplistically chic.

"You're gorgeous," I said truthfully.

Sarah pressed her hand to her stomach, slowly breathing in her nose and out her mouth. "Everything will be fine."

Clearly, the self-assurance was not about the dress. The dress was more than fine. I'd make sure of it. Everything else? That had me worried.

"Could you give me a moment?" Sarah asked, and I left her alone, unsettled in my own thoughts.

Like the koala she was, she'd grown used to her. I wanted to hate her, but I couldn't. I possibly even liked her.

A little bit.

I still thought she and Tyler were absolutely wrong for rushing into marriage though.

"Hey." Tyler met me in the front by Sarah's dressing room. "How's she looking?"

"Perfect."

"Yeah?" A goofy expression crossed his face and remorse pushed me to tell him the truth.

I knitted my fingers together behind my back as I searched for the words to explain how I'd tried to derail his wedding out of my own selfishness. I regretted it.

Now that I'd gotten my own taste of what it felt like to be alive, I understood how wrong I was for wanting to take that away from my best friend.

"Tyler, I—"

"Tilly, can you come help me, please?" Sarah interrupted my confession, and I held my finger up to Tyler before heading to the dressing room, where I assisted her out of the gown. I pivoted away to hang the dress up in the garment bag from her while she dressed.

"Let's all go out to eat since Tyler's here," she suggested. "It'll be so nice for the three of us to be together."

"No, it's all right. I don't want to be a third wheel."

"You're not a third wheel!" She playfully smacked my arm, and I swung back around to her. With her usual smile in place, she held onto my arm. "Tyler loves you so I love you, and we're taking you out to eat. Do you like sushi?" She slipped out of the door before I could answer. "Babe, I told Tilly we would treat her to dinner, but she doesn't want to come."

Outside of the dressing room, I found Tyler, Sarah, and my mom all staring at me like I'd insulted them.

"Come on, Till," Tyler said.

I held up the garment bag. "I'm working."

"I'll stay and close up with Alice," my mom said, tilting her head toward Alice, who was behind the cash wrap. "You go ahead. You always close up, leave it to someone else for once."

"Yeah," Sarah agreed, as if she knew my work schedule. "Good managers have to be able to delegate."

"Delegate." Tyler snickered. "She'd have to stop micromanaging to do that."

I sneered at him as I marched to the back to hang up Sarah's dress with Galina and returned with my purse. Holding Tyler's gaze, I shouted to Alice. "Can you be sure you clean the windows tonight?"

"You got it," she said brightly, and I waved goodbye to my mom before striding out of the store.

See? I could delegate.

Twenty

The stark 80s décor of the White Lily endeared me to the place. There was something about those glass blocks I loved. Not to mention the neon blue and green flower behind the bar.

After we ordered edamame and some rolls, Sarah tapped her chopsticks on my water glass. "You know, I've been in your store twice, we've hung out a few times, but we've never talked about Michelle's Belles." She smiled so earnestly, I couldn't help but smile back. Until she said, "You really are so good at your job."

I shifted my gaze to Tyler, and he winced apologetically.

"Do you plan on taking over from your mom?" she asked.

"I don't think so."

"Aw. Why not?"

I glanced at Tyler again, and he smiled encouragingly. Though we never got a chance to finish our conversation in person, he had emailed me articles to read about going back to school as an adult and sent me an excel sheet with columns of numbers I had trouble deciphering. He'd texted me a long message about how he had always been proud of me and would always be but reiterated that he knew I wasn't happy.

In return, I'd sent him the thumbs up emoji like the mature and level-headed adult I was.

Now, I told Sarah, "I do like working there, but probably only because of some fashion gene my mother passed down to me. I don't love it."

She set her chin in her hands, apparently very invested in my career. "If you don't love it, why are you still there?"

"The million-dollar question." Tyler raised his hand to Sarah as if she proved the point he brought up all the time—that I should not be working there.

I fiddled with my paper napkin, tearing it up into tiny strips and rolling them into balls. "I'm there because it's easy, and my mom needs my help, so I do it for her."

"I think you're scared to leave," Tyler said.

The waitress arrived with our edamame, and I aimed a pod at him. "At least buy me dessert before you start analyzing me."

"I didn't know there was an etiquette to it."

I chucked the empty pod at him. "You never took the class."

"Okay, let's talk about something else," Sarah suggested, like a mother duck directing her chicks. "Why aren't you bringing a date to the wedding?"

"Oh." I purposefully stuck another pod in my mouth, finagled the beans out with my teeth, and chewed slowly. I very well couldn't tell them about—

"Zack?" Sarah gaped over my shoulder.

I whipped my head around, and there he was, in all his Viking glory. "Hi."

The corner of his mouth tilted up, but before he could say anything to me, Sarah spoke. "That's three times we've run into each other now."

Tyler shifted in his seat, making his presence known, and the two men exchanged not-so-friendly glances.

"What are you doing here?" Sarah asked. "You hate sushi."

"Yeah." Zack shrugged. "But Chloe loves it. I usually order tempura." Then he turned his gaze on me. "Hey, Tilly."

Tyler gestured between the two of us. "You know each other?"

I ground my teeth, completely torn about what to say or do. I was in over my head in this love square. "Yeah, Zack helped me with a few plumbing emergencies."

"Convenient." Tyler pushed his glasses up his nose and extended his arms out, one across the table toward Sarah and the other over the back of my chair. Zack's attention settled to the left of me, where Tyler's fingers rested next to my shoulder. He might as well have pissed a circle around Sarah and me.

After a moment, Zack arched a brow up at me. We'd only known each other for a few weeks, but already I could read each change in his features. His eyes blazed with blatant possession, setting my skin on fire.

"We've never had the pleasure of meeting," Tyler said, condescension dripping from every syllable, and I rolled my eyes as he extended his hand over me to Zack. "I'm Tyler, Sarah's fiancé."

"Zack." His biceps bunched when they shook hands, and I caught Sarah's eye over their arms. With a pinched face, her eyes ping-ponged back and forth between them.

"The ex-boyfriend," Tyler added.

"If it makes you feel better."

The tips of my ears burned. And not in the good way. Zack had said he didn't want to get back with Sarah, so why did *If it makes you feel better* sound so combative? Like the two of them were about to challenge each other in a duel for Sarah's hand.

"It does, actually," Tyler said, and Zack's eyes skirted off to the side, bored.

"Whatever, dude." He crossed his arms then brought his gaze back to the table. First to me then to Sarah and Tyler. "I'm here to have dinner with my sister. Sorry, if it intimidates you."

"Me?" Tyler bristled. "I'm not intimidated."

Zack nodded slowly, visibly uncomfortable. "Okay." He directed his gaze at me one last time, his eyes so dark I couldn't read them. "Enjoy the rest of your night."

Then he strode to the back of the restaurant, where he met a familiar dark-haired girl. He hugged his sister and sat at the table, his head turning back in our direction. Although I couldn't tell if he was staring at me, Sarah, or Tyler.

I slugged down some water, hoping to dislodge the lumps which had found a home in my throat and chest.

"What the fuck is that guy's problem?" Tyler spat, flinging a piece of edamame down.

Sarah shushed him. "Not so loud. There are kids at the next table."

"You were the one who started it with the caveman stuff," I said.

"Caveman stuff? What did *I* do?"

"Oh, come on." I twisted away from him in my seat. "You were so patronizing and, like..." I trailed off, waiting for Sarah to jump in, but she was in a different world, her eyes glazed over. I scowled at Tyler. "Don't deny you were trying to start something with him."

The waitress appeared at our table with a big plate of rolls and sashimi, and Tyler fluttered his chopsticks at me. "He didn't need to squeeze my hand that hard when we shook."

I feigned outrage. "How very ungentlemanly."

"You're supposed to be on my side."

I stuffed a spicy salmon roll in my mouth, avoiding any

more of this conversation. I had no idea whose side I was on anymore.

"Babe," Tyler said, finally yanking Sarah from her trance, "can you pass the soy sauce?"

I continued to stuff my face, pretending I didn't know why Sarah looked like she was about to cry while Tyler told a story about his elder brother, Eddie, and their robovac eating and proceeding to make a mess with their baby's dirty diaper.

"Monica was so pissed," he said, chuckling, "she won't let him change a diaper now for fear of him forgetting about it and leaving it on the floor." He paused, considering his words. "Maybe he did it on purpose to get out of diaper duty."

"Yeah, but there was baby shit all over their floor," I pointed out.

His laugh sputtered into a cough around the piece of California roll in his mouth. "Gross, Till, I'm eating."

"You're the one who told the story to begin with."

When Sarah didn't acknowledge the diaper debacle, he affectionately caught her chin between his thumb and index finger. "You okay?"

She sniffed and wiped her napkin over her mouth. "Yeah. Got a big bite of wasabi. I'm going to go to the bathroom."

From where we sat, Tyler and I could both watch her walk to the bathrooms at the back of the restaurant and stop at Zack's table. She leaned down to hug Chloe, and then put her hand on Zack's shoulder. He nodded at whatever she said, and then she bent to hug him too.

Tyler's eyebrows raised to cartoon proportions. "What's that about?"

I answered honestly. "I have no idea."

Whatever it was had the sushi threatening to come back up. I didn't have any entitlement to Zack. We'd made no declarations or had any conversations about us, but I was as

SOPHIE ANDREWS

concerned as Tyler to find out what she'd said to him. And especially about their overly familiar hug.

When Sarah finally made her way back to the table, after using the restroom, she appeared to be back to rights. Tyler paid the bill, and I offered a quick good-bye, already anticipating the argument between the two of them.

At home, I changed into comfy clothes, watered my plants, then lit some candles and tried to relax, but all I could think of was dinner. Awkward from beginning to end.

I couldn't be sure of the cause of Sarah's anxiety and hesitation about the wedding, yet I had a feeling it was my fault. I lamented that I may have put doubts into her mind and that my terrible, horrible, no good, very bad plan might have actually succeeded. It was wrong of me to think I could or should try to control Tyler's life. He'd made his choice, and no matter if I agreed with it or not, I loved him, so I should have supported him. Like a best friend would do.

Even more, I was frustrated with myself that I'd dangled Zack in front of her like a piece of meat. Like a dog with a bone, I wanted him for myself. I wanted to bury him in my backyard so no one else could have him. The catch was I didn't know how he felt. We'd spent those hours together, talking and laughing, and making each other glow, but I had no idea what he felt for me.

My first instinct was to call him and ask what Sarah had said, but that was a very girlfriend-y thing to do, and I had no rights to claim. Especially when I'd been using him for my own evil means.

I'd backed myself into a corner, painted myself as the villain, and I didn't know if it was possible to make up for what I did or didn't do to Sarah and Tyler, while also somehow finding a path forward with Zack.

After moping around for most of the night, I plucked up my courage and called him. I meant to have a real conversation, but when he picked up I lost my nerve and did the only logical thing.

I lied.

"I have a leak."

"It's almost ten o'clock," he said. "You have a leak. Right now?"

"Yep."

"Is it your toilet again?"

"How'd you know?"

Guess he didn't think my light-hearted pitch was cute because he responded with a curt, "What do you want, Tilly?"

"How's Chloe?"

"Good."

I wasn't afraid to poke the bear, but I did want some kind of assurance I didn't completely mess everything up. "Was tonight one of your twice a month dinners? Doesn't her husband usually tag along?"

"Tilly." His voice had a warning in it I'd never heard before. Commanding, with a hint of the anger I knew he still sometimes carried around with him.

"You sound mad."

On the other end, he grunted as if he laid down, and I imagined him on his ridiculously soft mattress which may as well have been a water bed.

"Are you mad?"

"No, I'm not mad. I..." He heaved a sigh. "I have a lot of stuff on my mind."

"Too late to go for a hike," I noted, stating the obvious. When he didn't laugh or make any other kind of amused sound, I tried again. "What's on your mind?"

"You called me. You first."

I sank to the floor, leaning against the couch and crossed my legs in front of me, playing with the tassels of the rug.

"You're a puzzle to me," he said when I didn't answer.

"Any stranger, I think, would describe you as confident. You fill up a room. With your wild hair and those stormy gray eyes, you're so beautiful, sometimes it's hard not to stare. And you're never at a loss for words. I love listening to you talk. No matter what it's about. I love hearing your voice."

I smiled to myself, lighting up from the inside out.

"Except now," he said, bringing me back down to earth, dimming my glow. "You're so bold about certain things, like going for a ride with me, letting me give you an orgasm in the middle of the woods. I mean—" he huffed "—you asked me to break-up a wedding with you, but then there are these times when you're so afraid to say what you actually want or mean, you'll lie instead."

I didn't know whether to be impressed or offended he had me pegged so easily.

I stayed silent and he practically growled his next words. "Just say it."

One second passed.

Two.

Three.

"Why did you call me, Tilly?"

I squeezed my eyes shut and hoped I didn't sound like a jealous girlfriend. "I want to know what Sarah said to you."

He didn't hesitate. "She told me I seemed happy."

My eyelids popped open. There had to be more. Not that I timed them, but she stood at their table for at least a minute. "And?"

"And she hoped to see me again."

"What's that supposed to mean?" I asked, unable to keep a shrill edge from my voice.

"I don't know. She said at this rate we would."

"At this rate we would..." I repeated, mentally examining the sentence for meaning. "She's obviously wishing for it." I sounded like a jealous girlfriend now.

"I highly doubt we will see each other again. Today was total coincidence and the other two times were *your* doing."

I palmed my face, internalizing my scream. "I know! Regular old Machiavelli here." He only grunted in response, so I turned the tables. "What's on your mind?"

"Not much different than what's on yours."

"Yeah?" I sat up a little taller. "You're filled with self-inflicted mistrust and envy?"

"Tilly," he said slowly as if I didn't get it. "You were having dinner with Tyler and Sarah, the couple you're supposedly trying to break up because you're in love with him."

"I'm not trying to break them up anymore. They're doing a fine job of it themselves," I said, skipping over the love part because I couldn't truthfully say I wasn't in love with Tyler. I'd loved him my whole life, it's not like I could set those feelings aside. I think a tiny part of me would always be *in* love with him.

"It was weird to see you three at a table together with a whole complicated history between all of us. I dated Sarah, and you..." He stopped, refusing to go on.

"I what?"

"You looked really pretty. I wanted to tell you, but Tyler was there acting like a dick. Like you were both in his harem or something."

I nibbled on a hangnail. "He doesn't think of me like that."

"You sure?" His voice was low and menacing. "I use to get in fights with guys like Tyler. Those preppy asshole types, who thought I was below them. I could—" He stopped himself and when he came back over the line, his voice was more reserved. "You guys have been friends a long time. It's hard to believe he doesn't think of you that way."

I didn't know how else to explain it other than tell him about how Tyler hopped in and out of women's beds for the better part of the last decade, even if it was me he was leaving and coming back to. I hadn't exactly been a nun, but I never allowed myself to enter into anything serious, on the chance that Tyler would come back to me for good. We'd been physical and cuddly, but since he'd grown up in such a physically demonstrative family, it wasn't anything special. It didn't mean anything, even though it took me a while to understand.

"I hate to point out the obvious," Zack said, "but it seems like you've been much more loyal to him than he has been to you."

"What?" It wasn't obvious to me.

"He's been doing his thing all these years, coming and going with you as he sees fit, but you haven't been doing the same."

True.

"And he's a goddamn idiot if he's had you in his bed and left to go with another girl. Maybe I should've smacked him around like I wanted to at the restaurant."

"Stop. That's not nice," I said, although it was impossible to keep the smile out of the rebuke. "Then I would have had to fight to defend his honor. It would've been really unpleasant."

"Kill me with those Amazon skills?" He sounded intrigued.

"Mm-hmm."

We both went quiet, and I screwed my courage to the sticking place. "For the record, it's your bed I want into."

"Good," he said, his voice deliciously husky. "You want to go on a hike with me tomorrow? It's supposed to be really sunny, and I'll need the shade."

"Your sense of humor still needs some work, I see," I said and hung up on his low laughter.

Twenty-One

"How do I look?" Zack held his arms out with the borrowed, paint-stained apron tied around his neck.

"Adorable." I tapped the tip of his nose to make the point, and he caught my wrist, towing me closer to him. After some haggling on our hike yesterday, I got him to agree to attend Booze & Brush with me.

"You do this a lot? Take art classes?" With his mouth so close to mine, I could smell the mint he'd popped in his mouth after he'd snagged it from the bowl on the counter when we had entered. He snatched the ties of my apron from my fingers and looped the extra-long strings around my waist, knotting them in the front.

"I wouldn't really say I take art classes." I curled my fingers into the soft cotton of his shirt. "Some people like to hike. Others get drunk and paint."

He flattened his lips, suppressing a slow-growing grin, and I smiled brightly in return. Tension hummed between us. It'd been a few days since the sushi fiasco, and after only exchanging texts and phone calls, it felt right to be with him again. To be drenched in heat. Death by fire. As if he could feel my desperation, he skimmed the tip of his nose down the length of mine then pressed a kiss into my lips. Tame but oh so delicious.

A skinny woman with a dark pixie cut and denim smock waved from her position at the front of the room. "Hello and welcome! I'm Skye, and I'll be guiding you in your artistic journey to Margaritaville tonight."

Giggles erupted around us, coming from all sides. There were a couple of gray-haired women, a trio of barely legal girls, and a large birthday party behind us, tittering with excitement.

Zack inched his stool closer to mine. "I've never even had a margarita before."

"Really?" I whispered while Skye instructed everyone to have a seat and make sure our supplies were accounted for. "How's that possible?"

He shrugged, stretching his neck to peer over his easel toward Skye, who showed off the painting we were supposed to recreate tonight. A margarita with lime set at the beach, palm tree included.

I opened up the small bottle of wine I'd brought and poured some into a cup before holding it out to him, but he shook his head. "No, thanks."

"But that's the whole point, getting sloshed and painting crap."

"I'm not a big drinker, but I'll watch you get sloshed and paint crap." He followed along as Skye demonstrated how to use a light stroke to cover the canvas in a pink sunset. "I'm creating a masterpiece," he stage-whispered.

I snorted and swallowed down the overly-sweet white wine, a Christmas gift from one of the girls at the store last year. "You heard the teacher, we're going to Margaritaville, not the Sistine Chapel."

His bottom lip disappeared between his teeth in concentration as he blended in some orange. "That's what you think."

"I—"

"Shh. I'm trying to listen." He tapped the end of his paintbrush against my lips, gracing me with a hint of an indulgent smile.

Skye picked up a different brush to paint the sand, and Zack followed along, deliberately eyeing my canvas, which still only had a bright pink upper half. I poured myself some more wine. "It's part of my process."

He shook his head and continued to work.

Two hours later, the birthday party had all but given up on painting, as they were busy taking pictures and complaining they didn't bring enough wine. Since Zack didn't drink any, I offered the rest of my bottle to them, and they happily accepted, even placing a cardboard birthday hat on my head. I was buzzed enough to agree to a picture and a hug from the birthday girl.

By the time I sat back down, Zack's canvas had transformed to a beach with a palm tree and margarita glass in the middle. His ocean even sparkled. Compared to mine, with a dark sunset and funny-shaped glass filled with a puke-green margarita, he really did create a masterpiece. "Have you ever painted before?"

"Nope." He dropped his brush into the water can. "That's what they call natural talent."

"What other talents do you have that I don't know about?"

His eyes didn't leave mine as he took my brush from my hand and set it down before dragging the party hat from my head.

"Hey! I—"

He cut my argument off with a kiss, his hands softly cradling my head, fingers winding into my hair. Even with all of his strength, he treated me like delicate crystal, and no one had ever made me so comfortable with my own fragility.

His index finger traced the shell of my ear, and I was glowing again. His tongue swept into my mouth, searching and teasing, silently answering my question from before.

What other talents did he have? I would find out.

Someone wolf whistled, and we broke apart to find the birthday party clapping for us.

"You better take him home to bed or I will," the birthday girl called, and I'd never seen Zack turn that shade of red before. When she started toward him, he tore his apron off, waved to Skye, and snagged his painting in one hand and my waist in the other.

"She scares me," he mumbled, slanting his eyes back in the direction of the birthday girl as we trotted out of the door.

I playfully grabbed a handful of his butt as he bent to put our paintings in a small saddlebag. "Don't worry. I'll protect you. You know I've always wanted to get in a fight."

"Savage." He nipped at my jaw and handed me the helmet I'd started to think of as mine. I snapped the buckle into place under my chin and hopped onto the Harley behind him.

Instead of heading right back to my apartment, Zack wove us outside of town as the sun set into our own pink and orange sky. Riding a motorcycle was a kind of foreplay I'd never experienced before. I didn't know if it was because of the man driving or because of the intimate position required for two riders, but it was impossible to keep my hands from roaming.

The thrum of my pulse was as loud as the vibrations of the engine, echoing through my limbs, settling between my legs. I was desperate and aching, and he'd warned me not to tease him while we were riding, but I couldn't help myself. I dragged my hands down his torso, squeezed the tight sides of his waist, curled my fingers around his thighs, and when he covered my hand at a red light, I thought it was a signal to move them back up, where they were supposed to be.

Instead he brought my hand to the bulge under his denim.

I laughed, the sound lost to the wind as we took off again, but I felt the tremor of his chuckle when I molded myself more firmly against his back, keeping my palm cupped around the growing length of him.

By the time we arrived home, it was dark and my wine buzz had worn off, but when Zack climbed off the bike and slipped his arms around my waist to lift me up, I buzzed in a new way.

My fingers itched to reach under his T-shirt, and I didn't deny myself as he removed my helmet, tunneling his hands through my hair so the nerve-endings on my scalp tingled. I explored the planes of his stomach, the curve along his hip, where the Viking ship was tattooed into his skin. And when I didn't think I could handle waiting any longer, he gripped the nape of my neck, tugging me close enough to kiss but stopped short.

I blinked in confusion.

"I want to make sure you're sure." His lips brushed mine. "Are you sure?"

I answered by skimming my hands from his sides to the front of his jeans, yanking on his belt loops until his hips met mine. "I'm sure."

"Good." He bent down and hauled me over one shoulder. "Come on, Amazon."

I flailed. "Put me down, you're gonna hurt yourself."

He carried me inside the apartment complex. "You went from fantasizing I could build you a house to now assuming I can't carry you?"

When he dropped me down, I opened the door and locked it again after it was closed behind us. He flicked the light on like he knew the place, and I didn't mind. Liked it, actually.

I pitched my purse on the couch before stepping out of my shoes and moving onto my jeans. "Not like that."

"Not like what?" He set our paintings down on my desk and unlaced his boots. As he kicked out of them, he shucked off his shirt.

"I knew you could carry me." I waved down the length of him. "You're built like a bull."

His jeans came off next, and he steadied himself with a hand on the back of the desk chair as he pulled one leg out at a time until he stood in only his black boxer briefs. "I'll take that as a compliment."

"You should." I wrenched my tank top off, leaving me in only my bra and underwear, and pointed toward my door. "I just didn't expect you to pick me up and fling me around like that."

"Yeah? Well..." He licked his lips, his eyes roving down the length of me. "You should get used to it."

And then we collided. He picked me up again, this time from under my butt, his fingers digging into my thighs, forcing me to wrap them around his hips. With his lips and teeth moving from my cheek to my neck, he walked to my bedroom and tossed me down on the bed.

There was no face-to-face longing or mood lighting. In fact, there was almost no light, except for what seeped in from my living room through my open bedroom door. He bent over me, offering a single searing kiss as his hand wrapped around my hip. "Don't move."

He left the room for a minute, and I scooted up the bed to turn on the lamp.

"I told you not to move."

His voice was rough, and I shrugged. "I couldn't see anything."

He huffed in dissent and prowled over to where I sat by the edge of the bed, placing two condoms on the bedside table.

"Ambitious," I said, and he quirked an eyebrow at me, a little daring, a lot dangerous. "What?" I smiled. "Is this where you tie me up because I disobeyed you and moved?"

The lines of taut muscle along his shoulders and stomach rippled as he towered over me. His hands and knees bracketed my head and hips while I laid flat on my back. "You talk an awful lot."

"I thought you liked that about me."

"Sometimes." He slid his fingers over the base of my throat and down, flattening his hand over my breastbone. With the way my heart pounded beneath my ribs, I was sure he could feel it, but his hand didn't stay there long. He ventured his mouth over my chest, pulled the cup of my bra down with his index finger. "And sometimes not."

He bit down, and I hissed. "Right now," he murmured, lowering himself so he fit in the pocket between my legs, "the only words I want to hear are yes and fuck yes."

Without any more warning he sucked my nipple into his mouth and *yes, fuck yes*. He walked a fine line of pleasure and pain, pinching and sucking on the undersides of my breasts. His hands, rough with calluses, were tender but strong, soothing the places he nibbled and bit from neck to navel. He spent time learning the lines of my tattoo and the curve of my belly, nuzzling his beard along my most sensitive place after he slid my panties down my legs.

First, he dropped chaste kisses on the creases of my thighs then licked along the same path, and I dug my fingers into his hair as he spread my entrance wide with his thumbs. He blew a soft stream of air over me, and I shuddered, a ragged moan escaping the back of my throat a moment before his tongue dipped into me, and *yes, fuck yes*.

"Tilly, look at me."

I lifted my head at Zack's smoke-filled direction, needing a moment to focus on him and his eyes, dark and full of even darker promises. Without lifting his mouth from me, he took hold of my hands, removing them from his hair to lace our fingers together on either side of my hips, never losing eye contact.

In the midst of what was one of the most intimate acts two people could do, *this* was even more so. Staring down my quivering stomach at the man drinking from me. I'd never watched someone give me this pleasure. I'd never took notice of how his nostrils flared slightly, how his pupils dilated, how he backed a hair's breadth away to swallow and lick his lips, shining with my arousal, and then dip his chin to continue like he couldn't get enough.

Watching Zack watching me, and how I arched and shivered and gasped, it was the most intimate thing I'd ever experienced.

He released my left hand to push two fingers into me, and I couldn't hold eye contact anymore. I sunk my hand into his hair, giving into a moan that originated from deep inside, where he swirled his tongue until I was wild and breathless, begging for release.

"Look at me," he directed. "Look at me, Tilly. I want you to know *I'm* the one here with you."

I forced my lids open, and when I found him again, staring at me like I was the center of his world, I was set free. Split open. A wave of ecstasy rolled over me, yet I didn't blink. I couldn't. I wouldn't.

He was here with me, and I didn't want to forget even one second of it.

With soft, sweet kisses to my overworked and damp flesh, he gave me time to emotionally put myself back together and sit up. He wiped his beard with his forearm then crawled up my body, but before he could lean down for a kiss, I shoved at his shoulder. It wasn't enough force to flip him to his back, but he relented with a half-smile, making himself at home against my headboard, spreading his legs to make room for me as I kneeled in front of him.

He twirled a lock of my hair around his finger, that indulgent crooked smile growing to a grin. "The one time you're taller than me."

I pointedly dropped my gaze to the solid length of him peeking out from the top of his boxer briefs then arched my brow in his direction. "Good thing too."

He breathed out a laugh and hauled me into him for a kiss, nipping at my lips, but before he could waylay me, I ducked down, kissing along his throat and shoulder. I grazed my fingertips over his biceps, and when he lifted his arms to cradle the back of my head, I bent, licking the barely visible blue line of his vein along his inner elbow. That's how I learned he was ticklish.

I lowered, kissing the bow of the Viking ship pointed to the ridges of his lower abdomen, and I traced them with my tongue so his skin dotted with goosebumps. I finished my exploration by dragging my fingers over his stomach, and he canted his hips, easing my effort to remove his underwear.

Under the dim glow of the bedside lamp, I took in all of him, from the hair on his head to the blunt tips of his toes, and everything in between. Although there was not one part of him that appeared inconsequential, I was drawn back to his eyes. Those unblinking, unnerving eyes that spoke his promise to me in silence.

I'll take care of you.

Now, I wanted to take care of him.

When I sunk down to lick the tip of his cock, I felt him blow out a long breath. Then when I took him in my mouth, licking and sucking, the muscles of his legs clenched under my fingers, and he wrapped my hair up in one of his hands, groaning his appreciation.

He was both hot and hard, soft and sensitive, like his entire essence was wrapped up in this part of him. He tasted faintly of salt, smelled of his soap, clean cotton, and dewy earth—everything I'd become familiar with—and I took him further into my mouth.

"That's it," he said, his voice barely above a gravelly whisper. "That's my girl."

And those were the last words that made sense. The rest was all nonsense, mumbles that made me feel as powerful as the Amazon he teased me to be. With only my fingers and tongue, I could bring him to his knees.

He was succumbing to me.

Like I had succumbed to him.

"Enough," he grated after a few minutes, towing me back up to him. "I can't wait any longer."

He handed me a condom to put on him then brushed my hair back from my face as I rolled it on. It wasn't until now I realized there was nothing in the background, no music or television or anything else to take away from this moment. Only our panted breaths and suctioned kisses.

"Hey," he rasped, gripping the nape of my neck in one hand. "You trust me?"

I smiled against his mouth. "I trust you."

Then he positioned me over his hips, helping to guide me onto him, his firm thickness filling me so agonizingly slow, I had to grip his shoulders, unintentionally creating half-moon divots in his skin from my nails. But he merely pulled me to him, kissing my mouth and jaw and temple.

Once I was fully seated on him, he encouraged me to roll my hips, arch my back, find the pace and angle I needed. He kept one hand on my hip while his other traveled from the crook of my neck to my hair hanging over my shoulder to my breast. But all the time, his eyes never left mine. And if I ever threw my head back or closed my eyes, lost in the moment, his fingers would press into me, wherever they were, drawing my gaze back to his.

It was intense, his unrelenting eye contact. It made me feel like he could see into me, through the bravado, to everything I often tried to hide.

Not with him though. I couldn't hide.

I couldn't hide any of me. My insecurities, my goals and dreams, my secrets and truth. He knew it all. And he held it all in the palms of his hands.

"I can't hold on much longer," he told me, his fingertips *just* this side of bruising.

Exactly what I knew it was going to be like.

"I'm close," I said, tilting backward so he could slip his fingers between us, to the place where we met, where I was slick and swollen, and with one circle of fingers at the cleft of my sex, I was there, falling off the peak.

Zack followed, yanking me to him, scraping his teeth along my collarbone, muttering quiet words about how beautiful I was and how good I felt. But when I came down from my high and I was able to catch my breath, I couldn't look him in the eyes any more.

I tucked my face into his neck, hating myself for thinking of anything other than the perfectness of this night, but I couldn't stop my brain from wandering.

Sarah and her sunshine voice popped in my head, reminding me in her own words that she'd been with Zack before me. Then Tyler appeared too, cementing which of the seven deadly sins would land me in hell.

I envied Sarah because she had been where I was right now, in Zack's arms. I hated that she had known his body like I do now. That she ever had any of his smiles and reluctant laughs. That she—or anyone for that matter—had any piece of him because on top of envy and lust, I was greedy. I wanted him all to myself. I wanted all his *before* and all his *after*.

I wanted only us.

"Tilly." Zack cupped his hands on either side of my face, urging me to raise my gaze, and when I finally did, his eyes drifted between mine as if searching for an answer to a silent question.

Whatever it was, the answer was yes.

Yes, let's do that again.

Yes, let's order pizza.

Yes, you can cut me open and have my heart, but only if you take it with you to your log cabin and keep it in a safe place.

"Lie to me."

He flinched. "What?"

"Lie to me and tell me it's never been like that with anyone before."

"No."

I tried to hide my disappointment with a silly pout, but he held me steady so I couldn't disappear behind the façade. "I won't lie to you, but I'll tell you the truth."

His thumbs stroked my cheekbones, and when I swallowed thickly, he kissed my throat. Even after all our talks and the time we'd spent together, I still feared his truth. It's not like we had known each other that long, but even so, I didn't want to think about losing what we had. I was blindsided by him, completely enamored, and I didn't think I could bear it if he didn't feel the same.

"I'll always tell you the truth," he said. "And it has never been like that with anyone else."

Selfish relief coursed through me, and I sank into him. "For me either. I feel like…"

I didn't have the word.

But I knew *a* word, a four letter, single syllable word, though it was ridiculous to use that particular word after only a few weeks. Especially when I didn't believe Tyler and Sarah should have rushed into anything.

"I know. Me too," he said, filling in my blank with whatever word he had in his head. It might have been the same one as mine, but he didn't seem to be in a hurry to tell me, and that was all right with me. He combed his fingers through my hair, gathering it all over my shoulder, staring at me like I was a precious piece of art.

"Do you want to do it again?" I asked.

"Yes, but I'm hungry."

"Pizza?"

"Yeah." He dropped his legs over the side of the bed and stepped into his boxer briefs before aiming his index finger at me. "No pineapple."

I rolled my eyes petulantly, which earned a playful smack on my hip on his way out to the kitchen.

Good thing he walked away too, because my hands were at my chest, ready to rip my heart out and hand it over.

After a few moments of convincing myself that I was okay and still whole, he poked his head around the doorjamb, startling me.

His gaze floated over me while I was still naked and flushed, gripping the bedsheet like a lifeline, and he smiled. One that crinkled the corners of his eyes and warmed me all over.

"Are we always going to argue about pineapple on pizza?" he asked. "It would get boring after a while, wouldn't it?"

I nodded, my chest rapidly rising and falling. Yes, it probably would get boring, but it didn't worry me. What did was how suspiciously light my chest felt.

Like he'd already taken my heart.

Twenty-Two

Two weeks out from the wedding, I hired a driver and stuffed all seven of us—me, Tyler, Ricky, his brothers, Rob and Freddie, and his friends, Logan and Henry—inside. First up on the bachelor party agenda: indoor sky diving. Tyler had always wanted to go sky diving for real, but I was pretty sure you needed training, and I wasn't about to jump out of a plane.

When we arrived, we were given jumpsuits to wear and met our "flight instructor" for some quick directions before we sat around the wind tunnel in the middle of the room, waiting for our individual turns. Our red and black suits were totally unattractive on everyone except Ricky. Probably because that guy had more confidence coming out of his pinkie than the rest of us combined.

However, once he entered the tunnel, he lost it all, and Tyler and I fell into each other, cracking up. Ricky couldn't pull it together. Even with the instructor's help, he had trouble launching in the air, and once he finally got up there, he was blown all over the place.

"Bro, hold your legs out!" Freddie called, and we all hooted when he somersaulted, most definitely on accident from the way he screeched. The instructor caught him and brought him back down to the ground, helping him step out of the tunnel.

"Nice try, cuz," Tyler taunted, unable to wipe the grin from his face.

Ricky sank down onto one of the open chairs with a pained grunt. "It's fucking harder than it looks, dick."

Tyler put his helmet on and met the instructor at the tunnel, and I handed a bottle of water to Ricky, but he caught my hand before I could walk away.

"Pet my head?"

"What?" I snorted a laugh. "No."

He patted the chair next to him. "Come on. I feel sick."

"Ricky."

"Tilly." He stuck his bottom lip out, all his normal bluster gone. "Please?"

"Fine." He did look a little green. I plunked down so he could rest his head on my shoulder, and we watched Tyler inside the tunnel. He made it into the air without much problem, a big grin on his face. Though it could have been the 120 mile per hour wind that kept his mouth and cheeks locked in a permanently Joker-eqsue smile.

Ricky reached for my hand, lifting it up, hinting at how he wanted me to caress him, but my grip on my cell phone prevented it. He nuzzled his head into my neck like a cat. "Come on, put that down and pet me."

I snatched my hand out of his fingers. "No."

"Why? You got something important to do during Ty's bachelor party?"

I lowered my shoulder so his head rolled off. "No," I said, but at the same time a text message from Zack arrived, and I aimed my gaze right at it.

In the week since our date, things naturally fell into place. Zack came to hang out with me while I closed up at the shop a few times, and I brought him lunch on one of his busier days since he said he'd forgotten to eat. Tomorrow we'd planned to hang out with my parents, and Dad was going to grill.

Every morning we didn't wake up together, he texted me hello, and every night we didn't go to sleep together, I texted him goodnight.

"Who're you talking to?" Ricky asked, his chin back on my shoulder.

I palmed his face. "No one."

"No one? Then why are you all red? Even the tips of your ears."

I covered the screen of my phone, hoping Ricky hadn't seen the last message from Zack about tying me to the bed for hours. He had never specifically said he was uncomfortable with me putting Tyler's bachelor party together, but from the way he'd scratched his beard whenever I had talked about it, I could tell he didn't like it.

And I had no idea how to even begin to have the conversation with Tyler about how Zack and I met. If I had to choose between Zack's affection and Tyler's friendship, I didn't think I could. I wouldn't. There had to be a way to have them both in my life. I just hadn't figured it out yet.

I tugged the hair tie from the bottom of my braid, strategically spreading my hair around my shoulders, hoping it covered my blush.

Ricky offered me his winningest smile. "If it's no one then you're free to go out with me."

I huffed. "You've asked me out at least once every time you see me. What would make you think I'd suddenly say yes when the answer has always been no?"

"You wound me, cariño." He slapped his left hand on his chest, his right arm around my shoulders. "How can I get you to say yes? Promise you strawberries and champagne? Tickets to the Met? Entry into any and all clubs? Home plate seats for the Phillies?"

"None of those things interest me. At all."

He raised a perfectly sculpted dark brow.

"All right the champagne does. But everything else is a no."

"Okay," he purred. "Let me take you to this rooftop bar tomorrow, it's got the best views of center city."

I folded my arms. "I have plans, sorry."

"With your boyfriend?"

"He's not my—"

"Aha!" Ricky sat up tall, snapping like he solved the case, and I inhaled sharply, flushing that he'd caught me. In perfect timing, Tyler exited the tunnel in time to hear his cousin accuse, "It's a he! You *do* have a boyfriend."

"Tilly doesn't have a boyfriend," Tyler said, bumping fists with Freddie when he passed for his flight in the tunnel.

"Yeah, she does. She's sexting and getting all..." Ricky wiggled his fingers in the direction of my face. "Red."

Tyler slanted his attention to the side of my head. "Unless her ears turn red, it's not a big deal."

To hide the evidence, I hunched over with my elbows on my knees, my face in my hands.

"Till, really? You're seeing someone?" Tyler sat on the other side of me, evidently having caught sight of my ears.

I shrugged. I didn't know the answer to the question. Zack and I never labeled what we were doing, but it didn't feel necessary. We'd already had those big conversations about what we wanted. Like the best kind of kisses, our time together wasn't perfect because of what we did—which was boring everyday stuff most of the time—it was perfect because we were together.

"When did it start? Why didn't you tell me?"

"You've had a lot of stuff going on," I said, gesturing to the groomsmen.

A frown marred his features, like I'd kicked a puppy. "Yeah, but you can tell me anything."

"I know but..." I struggled for a defense. This certainly wasn't the place to have the conversation about what I had tried to do.

Or, why even have it at all? Things were going okay. I didn't need to spoil it.

"We haven't really had a lot of time to talk," I said, and Tyler opened his mouth to reply, but Freddie sauntered out of the tunnel.

"Who's up next?"

I tossed my phone in my purse and jumped at the chance. "Me!"

With my helmet on, I climbed in the tunnel. The wind whipped my hair around my head, and the instructor held onto me as I stretched out flat, floating a few feet above the floor. Once I grasped the feel of it, the instructor let go, and I floated higher, bobbing up and down like a balloon floating in the sky.

My body may have been weightless, but my conscience tethered me to earth. If this were an actual skydive, and I had to jump out of a plane, I'd be afraid the weight of my guilt would plummet me straight down into the ground. My best friend was getting married in a matter of days. Sarah was slated to pick her dress up on Tuesday. The Kellys had a week of festivities planned, beginning with brunch next Sunday, including a round of golf for the men and a spa day for the women, before culminating with the wedding the following Saturday.

I'd also begun to write my Best Woman speech. I couldn't tell the truth now. Although not telling the truth left me at odds with what I wanted. Or more accurately, *who* I wanted. It's not like I could bring Zack to the wedding. On top of not being able to explain how we got together, it would be plain weird.

As the instructor clutched my arm and ankle to guide me back to the floor, I decided I would wait until after the wedding, when Tyler and Sarah were blissfully happy...hopefully. Then I would tell a sort of version of the truth, skipping over my tie-the-damsel-down-to-the-tracks plot, and explain to them both that Zack and I were together, and we were all adults. We would be able to work through it.

And in fifty years, maybe we'd all have a good laugh about it.

Until then, I'd continue to weave my web. Too bad I didn't have eight legs. I needed them for all the juggling I'd been doing.

Out of the tunnel, I snatched my phone and made a hasty getaway to the bathroom. Behind the locked door, I did the one thing I could in moments of stress. I micro-managed.

"Hello, this is Michelle's Belle's, Fatima speaking, how can I help you?"

"Hey, it's Tilly," I said, placing the phone on speaker so I could comb my fingers through my hair. The wind had knotted it all up.

"Hey. Aren't you supposed to be off with Tyler for the day?"

I nodded even though she couldn't see. Fatima was a generous employee in her 40s with two children. Since she liked to be home when her kids got off the school bus, I always scheduled her to open the store, so I didn't get to work with her very often, but I often relied on her to fill in for me on special occasions.

"Yeah. I was thinking about a bride who popped in yesterday. She's eloping in Vermont. I left a note about her—"

"Yes, I got it."

"She said she'd be back in today but didn't know when. I set everything aside for her."

Fatima laughed good-naturedly. "Tilly, I got it all. She's buying the Vera off-the-rack."

"Uh huh." I twisted my hair up into a bun, a few unruly curls slipping out at my neck. "The hemline is yellowed slightly, and I tried to—"

"I already spoke to Galina about it. She's taking care of it. I'll have the dress pressed and ready to go as soon as Galina is finished with it. Don't worry."

"I'm not worried."

She hummed sympathetically in her warm Mom tenor she deployed in her sales. Brides loved her. I loved her too. "You go have fun. I'm taking care of the store."

I tapped my fingers on the sink, making a spur of the moment decision. "Fatima, would you ever consider taking on more hours?"

"More hours?"

"Yeah. I could train you on some of the back end stuff. You could take on more responsibility. You already take such good care of the store, and I probably don't tell you enough, but if it weren't for you opening all the time, I'd lose my mind. You're as detail-oriented as I am, and we're really lucky to have you at the store."

"Well, I..." Her voice drifted away as she spoke to someone on her end before coming back to me. "Tilly, my appointment just walked in. Don't worry, I have things covered here. You enjoy yourself, and we'll talk about me working more hours later, all right? I could probably move my schedule around now that the kids are older. Nadia is going to middle school in the fall, and Amir is nine going on nineteen, so I could handle more time here."

"Really? You're an angel."

"Depends on who you talk to." She laughed. "Bye, Tilly."

I hung up and then scrolled back through my text thread with Zack to find his last messages.

When will you be home?

By home, I mean in my bed.

I texted him back with a smile. **Your bed is too lumpy.**

He responded immediately. **Your bed is too small.**

My fingers were bolder than I was because they got away from me, sending out a message before my brain could say no. **Guess you better get going on the log cabin. Make the bedroom big enough to fit a king-sized bed. I'd like a view of the lake when I wake in the morning.**

He texted back, **Working on it.**

My grin stayed on my lips as I changed out of the jumpsuit and made my way out of the bathroom to the lobby, where all the groomsmen were huddled together. "Are we ready for the next stop? I have a whiskey tasting scheduled in thirty minutes."

Twenty-Three

Following the tasting and steak dinner, Tyler and I relaxed at the end of the bar in one of our favorite Philly dives, where the jukebox still took dollars and the drinks were cheap. Most of the guys teetered on the edge of drunk, but I remained sober since my job was to wrangle the men-children all day. Henry had indulged in too much whiskey and barely made it through dinner. Rob and Freddie were currently playing darts, which didn't strike me as the best idea with how many beers they'd consumed, but I didn't have the energy to tell them to stop after having to talk Logan down from fisticuffs after he hit on some guy's girlfriend.

"So, you finally gonna tell me about this guy?" Tyler asked, bumping his knee against mine.

"What guy?"

He eyed me.

I tried a diversion. "Do you want another shot? You're not nearly as drunk as I thought you'd be. Have another, if you want. This is your party." He didn't fall for it, and I slumped back. "It's really new."

"*And?*"

"*And...*" I lifted my shoulders dramatically, buying myself a few seconds of time. "I don't want to jinx it."

"You're not going to tell me anything? Not even his name?"

I twisted the silver ring on my index finger back and forth.

"Since when are you so secretive with me?"

If he only knew. "I really like him. He's not who I pictured myself with, but..."

"Can't force matters of the heart, I suppose," he said in a funny, faraway voice and slid his elbows on the bar, readjusting his glasses.

I leaned in closer to him. "What's wrong?"

"I don't know." He rubbed at the condensation on his beer glass with his thumb. "Sarah's been...off."

The word came out more like a question, and I didn't know if he expected me to have the answer or not. I hoped it wasn't me. "Probably stress."

"Has she said anything to you? About anything that's bothering her?"

I tucked a few wisps of hair away from my face. "You know her better than I do."

"Yeah, but I thought she might confide in you. It's been different between us lately." He sucked down a big gulp of beer. "I don't know if she's getting cold feet or what."

The burden of guilt was heavy on my shoulders. Too heavy to breathe properly, and I had to say something. Anything. "Um, well..."

He shot his dark gaze to me, his eyes a little desperate.

Tyler was my best friend, but I was sure Sarah and I had some kind of girl code to abide by, concerning how much of *her* truth I could reveal. "When she came for her dress fitting, she did mention she was nervous."

"Nervous?" His voice was high, slightly panicked. "About marrying me?"

I held my hand up to calm him. "I don't know if it's about you per se, but more about the whole lot of it, you know? Getting married, settling down. But my mom talked to her, and if anyone can soothe a soul, it's her."

He breathed deeply, staring at the dark wood bar. "You think... Do you think she's still in it with me?"

I gnawed on the inside of my cheek. I prayed to god she was. "She'd have to be stupid not to be in it with you." I rubbed his back. "It's totally normal to be nervous. I know you are, too. I can tell."

"Yeah. Yeah, I am." He gave in with a shake of his head. "I just love her. That's all. I love her and want to be with her."

"I get it," I said, and that was the absolute truth.

He dragged his hand through his hair. It had gotten long recently, below his ear.

"You'll be able to tie your hair back in a man bun soon," I joked, hoping to shake him out of his funk, but it didn't work. "We're supposed to be having fun," I told him. "Weddings are stressful, but they should also be fun. You're getting married." I held jazz hands out by my face. "Come on, don't look like that."

"Like what?"

"All pouty."

"I'm not pouty." He scrunched his nose up at me, the opposite of pouty, I supposed.

"You are, and if you really think something is wrong then ask her. I feel like we're in third grade passing notes back and forth. We're sitting at a bar, and I'm supposed to be getting you drunk and possibly arrested. Instead, you're sulking because you're upset about your fiancée. Talk to *her* about it, not me."

"I know, but—"

"I can't solve this for you," I told him, a little too aggressively, but I'd finally found the end of the rope which had eluded me these past few years, and it all clicked into place in my head.

He wanted me to be his sounding board, the eternal advice giver. I helped solve his problems, but I couldn't do it anymore. I had to start solving my own problems. "You're getting married, Tyler. Sarah is going to be your wife. If you two have an issue, you need to address it with her, not me. I'll still be here for you, always, but I can't be your go-between anymore."

Even as I said the words, my heart hurt to acknowledge the reality of the statement. Things had changed between us. They would continue to. I couldn't make it—us—stay the way we were.

"You're right. As usual."

I knocked my elbow into his ribs. "You'll talk tomorrow with her, okay? Tonight we have fun."

"And possibly get arrested."

"Yes! That's more like it." I clapped once and ordered two shots. We clinked glasses and tossed the whiskey back.

"Is he putting on another Michael Jackson song?" I craned my head around to Ricky, standing at the jukebox in the corner. Indeed, it was another MJ song, the fifth or so he'd played since we'd been here. He kicked his leg out to the side then spun toward the bar. He grinned, pointed a finger at me, and wobbled his head back and forth in an uncanny imitation of the King of Pop.

When I gave into a smile, he eased an elbow on the bar next to me. "Your boyfriend as entertaining as me?"

"I would venture to say no one is as entertaining as you."

He raised his hand for the bartender's attention and

ordered another beer before speaking over my head to Tyler. "Tell her she needs to give me a chance."

I rolled my eyes while Tyler made a game of it. "*Pfft*. No. Can't tell Tilly anything. She does what she wants."

As if I wasn't right next to him, Ricky went on, "Yeah, but she's meant to be part of our family. If not with you then with me."

And, yeah, that one stung. I wasn't meant to be part of their family.

"She has been around a long time," Tyler said, inclining his head to his cousin.

"I hate you," I muttered, and he smirked, knowing exactly how to irk me.

"I honestly don't think you could handle her." Tyler scratched at his chin with the back of his fingers. "She's a little wild."

Still pretending I didn't exist, Ricky lifted his brow lasciviously. "I like a little wild."

"This is really fun, guys." I intentionally moved my head between them and lifted my beer to my lips, blocking them from seeing each other.

Tyler stretched his neck up, talking over me. "You're going to have to try a different angle though. She's not into your whack-ass swagger."

Ricky choked. "Whack-ass? Get the fuck outta here."

"Listen," Tyler said, seriously. "Tilly's ridiculously smart. If you want to be with her, you've got to be able to keep up. She doesn't go for that, like, loud energy. She reads non-fiction books for fun."

Ricky cocked his head back at me. "You serious?"

I nodded, and Tyler continued. "She likes podcasts about stuff you never learned in history class and talks to her plants. She never turns down a dare though."

Ricky liked that. "Yeah?"

"And Van Morrison is her favorite."

"Who's Van Morrison?"

I slapped my hand to my forehead. "Jesus, Ricky. Is it no wonder I turn you down all the time because you know nothing about me? But you don't know who Van Morrison is either?" I sipped my beer. "There's no chance of a future for us."

He pressed his hands to his chest. "No chance?"

Tyler let out a sniffling laugh as he stood from his stool. He inserted a few dollars into the jukebox, and Van Morrison's smooth voice poured over the bar. Ambling over to me, he offered his hand without any words.

"*This* is Van Morrison," I said to Ricky. Even though no one else was dancing and there was hardly any room, I let Tyler tow me out to a tiny open space and hold me close while we swayed to "Crazy Love."

Like always, I rested my hands on his shoulders, my temple against his chin, and he skimmed his fingertips along my spine.

It was perfect.

For a moment, my heart stuttered to a stop before syncing up to a new, more unusual rhythm.

I loved Tyler. More than that, I loved the comfort he provided me. I loved our history. I loved our memories and the safety of what we've always had. But it was over. Like a little girl who had to give up her toys eventually, I had to put away the childish things. I had to give this up. I couldn't grow and move on with Zack while still holding onto the notion that everything would remain the same.

Everything was changing. Tyler was changing. *I* was changing.

And it broke my heart.

I wiped an unexpected tear away, and Tyler bent down, his gaze searching mine. "You okay?"

I nodded and leaned my cheek on his shoulder. "I miss you."

"We're here now." He huffed a laugh. "What's there to miss?"

"I feel like..." I reached for the closest description. "You know when you're going through old photo albums, and you see a picture that's familiar to you, you can almost smell it? You can remember what you experienced in the picture and your heart aches to go back there?"

He nodded.

"You're my album. You contain it all."

He raised his shoulder, urging me to lift my head, and he kissed my cheek. "Yeah," he murmured, his hands gently circling my back. "Too many pictures to count."

"Some pictures we never even got to take. I miss those too."

Even though he held me closer, his eyes drifted above my head, so I couldn't read them to see if he understood my meaning. Not only did I miss what we had, but what we didn't. I missed the future I had dreamed up for us which would never happen. In another universe, in a different world, maybe we would have ended up together, but not in this one. I wasn't angry or upset about it anymore, but I couldn't ignore the wistful melancholy shading the last moments of our time together.

As Tilly and Tyler.

When the song ended, he released me, our pinkies entwining for what felt like the last time, even as he was smiling at his friends at the bar. I let him go.

Rob and Freddie met him with joyful pats on the back. I was the Best Woman and Tyler's best friend, but there was something between brothers I couldn't compete with. He didn't need me anymore tonight.

"I'm going to head home, boys." I hugged each of them. "You make sure he's good and hungover tomorrow."

"Yeah, but no getting naked and dancing in the middle of a football field," Rob warned.

"That was her." Tyler jutted his chin in my direction. "Not me."

"First of all," I started, sticking my finger up in defense, "it was the soccer field. It was the middle of the night, and I only did it because somebody dared me to after prom. Who was it?"

Tyler snapped his fingers in remembrance. "Brian McDermott, I think."

"Right." I grinned. "He didn't think I'd actually do it."

"Well," Tyler said with a one-shoulder shrug. "You never back down from a dare."

Ricky's hand shot in the air. "Tilly, I dare you—"

"No." I cut him off, and the guys all chuckled.

Tyler sulked when I hugged him. "You're really leaving?"

"Yeah." After our dance, I wanted to go home. We had our time together, and now he was going to get married. I was ready to find my own crazy love.

"To your mystery boyfriend?"

"Mm-hmm." I nodded.

Tyler squeezed my shoulder. "He's not good enough for you."

"How do you know?"

"Because no one is." Then he ruffled my hair in a brotherly fashion. "But he better be trying." He chucked me under the chin. "Night, Till." Then he thundered back to the bar. "Shots!"

The boys all roared, wild animals in their natural habitat. "Shots!"

I smiled and tried to brand this feeling to my memory. This carefree harmony, like the world had righted itself. Yes, I was sad, but even more happy now that I could clearly see the path in front of me. It led right to a red-haired shirtless man with glorious tattoos.

"Did I wake you up?" I asked when I finally arrived, well past midnight.

Zack shook his head and opened his door wider for me. "Never went to bed."

"Waiting for me?"

He played it cool, but the blooming red of his cheeks told me the truth. I slid my hands up his bare chest, over his neck to his hair. His lips met me halfway, hungry for mine. Good thing because I'd been starved for him.

His skin was warm, and I couldn't stop touching him. His arms, his back, his shoulders. When I etched my nails down his stomach to the top of his shorts, he grunted and hoisted me up to sit on the counter. I curled my hands around it to keep steady as he unbuttoned my shirt, a plain gray number I tied at my waist which he couldn't seem to get off fast enough.

I gasped when a button popped. "Hey!"

He arched an eyebrow back, schoolboy mischief in his eyes. "Oops."

"I really like this shirt," I whined.

He dove his hands beneath it to my bra. "I like it better off."

I pulled a face and tugged it off, but my irritation faded to a giggle when he moved his hands to my high-waisted sailor inspired shorts. He muttered, "More buttons."

"Don't touch them." I batted his hands away, lest he ruin another piece of clothing. As soon as I had them undone, he scooted me to the edge of the counter, so he could drag them and my underwear off. "In such a rush," I teased, nibbling at his ear.

"I've gotten used to living with fire." He tugged on my

hair to angle my head back, his mouth taking no prisoners. "And I've been cold without you."

I palmed the hard outline of his cock through his shorts. "Then let's warm you up."

And then his mouth was on my collarbone, his fingers unsnapping my bra so it landed on the floor on top of the rest of my clothes. He plumped my breasts, licking the valley between them, and I worked my fingers beneath his underwear, stroking him with tender tugs. Too tender because he growled my name into my skin. A warning to stop teasing him.

"You ready for me?" he asked, trailing his fingertips down my stomach to the throbbing need between my thighs. He sunk his fingers into me, finding me wet and willing. "You missed me, huh?"

"Always," I breathed, inching close enough that the swollen tip of his length rubbed at my entrance.

"Tilly," he ground out, another warning, but I only tangled my fingers in his hair, directing him to suck at my nipple. He complied, and I melted, bringing us in even closer contact, the broad head of him pushing inside.

"Tilly, Tilly, Tilly," he chanted, sounding a little distraught. "Christ... Tilly. You feel..."

"I know." I vaguely gestured behind him to where I'd thrown my purse to the side when I'd first came in. "I... I have a condom..." I panted while he sucked on the skin over the beating pulse in my neck. "But..."

His neck corded for a long moment and then his gaze was on mine, focused and narrowed. "But what?"

"But I'm okay with it if you don't want to use one." The significance of my words hung heavy between us. That I trusted and loved him.

He wrapped his hand around my neck, pressing his forehead to mine. "Are you sure?"

"I'm sure," I said into his mouth.

And then there were no more words. Only heat and fire, devouring kisses, and bursts of so much pleasure, I couldn't conceive of the pain of being without him. Fire needed air to survive, and that's what he gave me.

Air in my lungs.

Air in my hopes and dreams.

Air and space and security to run wild and free.

Twenty-Four

I woke up with the sun streaming through Zack's bedroom window, his broken blinds providing no cover from it. I tucked myself into his side. "I don't want it to be morning."

He cinched his arm around me, and we sunk further into his mattress. Any movement caused a new lump to form. "It doesn't have to be," he said, toying with strands of my hair. "Close your eyes. Go back to sleep."

"What time is it?"

"Almost eleven."

Instead of closing my eyes, I stacked my hands on his chest and propped my chin on them, studying his sleepy, heavy-lidded gaze. He looked drunk, and I told him so.

"I feel a little hungover. We were up almost all night." When he palmed my butt, I squirmed out of his grasp with a laugh, but he squeezed it again. "I love this."

In a moment of weakness, I frowned. "Really?"

It's not like I was fishing for compliments, but I wasn't petite. I was "substantial," as one guy had called me a few years ago. I'd promptly put my shirt back on and marched out of his place, but that didn't mean it didn't stick with me. Just like all the years in school when I'd been taller than most boys, and how I worked in a business that had sample sizes that were the same number of inches around as my thigh. I hated that I let these things chip away at me sometimes, giving me a reason to use Tyler as a crutch yet again.

But I was determined to be different now. Especially with Zack's hand venturing up the line of my back. "There's not one single thing I'd change about you. No freckle, hair, curve, or dimple. Your confidence was the first thing I noticed about you when I walked into your apartment." He traced my tattoo. "You have this quality about you like..." He dragged his index finger down my nose. "You don't care what anybody thinks. You want what you want, and you go after it."

I rolled off him, not bothering to cover up, and he took advantage, palming my breast.

"I'm not that confident, I only hide my insecurities well."

He kissed along my collarbone. "You insecure? I don't believe it."

"Until recently I wasn't secure in anything. I had no idea what I wanted."

After a nip of my shoulder, he tipped his head up, his hair adorably rumpled. "What do you want?"

I didn't hesitate. "You."

He suppressed a smile, allowing only one corner of his lips to tick up. "Tilly Mahoney doesn't rely on a man. What else do you want?"

I fidgeted with the edge of the bed sheet, and he trailed his fingers over my stomach, settling on my belly button, petting me like a house cat. Being Zack's house cat didn't seem so bad. I might want that.

"What else?"

"I know I don't want to keep working at Michelle's. It's my mom's dream, not mine," I said, and he draped one arm over my torso, the other behind my head as if he knew I needed the support. "Before the accident, I knew what I wanted. I was going to get my degree and apply to graduate schools. Live in Ireland for a while and work toward my doctorate. But that life feels so far away now. I'm afraid of having to start all over again."

He nuzzled my temple. "You won't be starting all over again."

"I know but..." I didn't want to confess how scared I was of leaving the shelter I'd built around myself, of trying something new, of leaving my mom. Or to admit how much I cared about him, of what he thought of me, of what would become of us if I dared to step outside of my comfort zone. "I can't just fly off to Ireland now."

"Why not?"

I blinked at him. Wasn't he supposed to be the more pragmatic one? "Since when are you so spontaneous?"

He pushed up on an elbow. "It's not like you're going right this second, but if you want to go to Ireland, go to Ireland."

"What about you?" My eyes darted between his, trying to suss out how he factored himself into all of this. After all, last night *did* happen. I know I didn't imagine it.

"What about me?"

I tugged the sheet up to my shoulder, and he narrowed his gaze, but I wasn't the bold, go-getter he thought I was. I could barely acknowledge my feelings for him without flushing red. "I don't want anything to change between us."

There was no suppressing his smile then. "I don't want anything to change between us either, except for a new bed. I want you to be happy. If it's selling wedding gowns or studying rock carvings or..." He circled his hand in the air. "I don't know, making your own candles. I'll be here either way."

I slid my hand into his hair and kissed my gratitude into

his mouth, as I snaked my other hand under the sheet to find his erection. "Good morning."

He let out a gruff breath when I moved my kisses south. "It's always a good morning with you."

My hair splayed out on either side of me as I licked a line down his chest, but I froze when a phone buzzed. "Is that yours?"

He reached an arm out for his cell, where it was plugged into a charger. "Nope."

I returned to the task at hand, but when I kissed his hip bone, it buzzed again.

"Ignore it," he said, tucking hair behind my ear.

A few more buzzes sounded in quick succession, and I sat up.

On a last ditch effort, Zack grazed his mouth along my jaw, but I was too busy trying to locate my phone under the pillows. When I didn't find it, I got up to search the floor, and he heaved his usual sigh like I exhausted him. It was one of my favorite sounds.

"Don't worry." I glanced over my shoulder to spy him holding his thick length in his hand, plainly waiting for me. I bit back a giggle. "I only want to check who it is. I'll be back."

I unearthed my cell phone from under his bed. The alerts were from the group groomsmen text, reliving the day and comparing hangovers.

"It's the guys." I sat on the edge of the bed and typed out a text that I was happy to hear no one got sick, and Zack flopped back on the mattress behind me. I laughed at a picture of Ricky, still asleep in his boxers on Tyler's couch, a pizza crust next to him as if he'd fallen asleep eating.

"You have fun yesterday?" Zack asked through a yawn.

We'd never gotten around to chatting about the bachelor party last night—or anything else—and I turned to him as he rubbed at his eyes with the heels of his hands. "Yeah. Tyler loved the sky diving."

He stretched before shifting toward me. Ever too perceptive. "You all right?"

I bit the inside of my lip, absently braiding a small section of my hair. "It was fun but a little weird too."

"How come?"

I relayed the conversation I had with Tyler about Sarah, and how it'd been difficult for both of us to navigate our friendship lately. He stilled my hands from playing with my hair and tugged me back down to the bed. "I've never really had a best friend, but I can understand why it's hard for you. For him too." He brushed his lips over mine. "I don't like the guy, but I think I feel worse for him. He never saw what was right in front of him."

To put a finer point on it, he gathered me up, holding my head in his hands, bracketing my shoulders tight with his elbows. As soon as he leaned down to trace my lower lip with his tongue, my phone went off again. I wiggled free of him to read a text from Tyler only to me.

Thanks for last night. And for everything else.

I ignored Zack pawing me and typed a reply. **I'd do anything for you, you know that.**

I'm headed out to talk to Sarah, he said.

I stretched my neck away when Zack tried to kiss me there. **I hope it all works out.**

You don't think it'll work out? Tyler texted back.

I groaned, closed my eyes, and rolled away from Zack's roaming hands.

"What?"

"Nothing. Tyler's going to talk to Sarah, and I told him I hope it works out. I think I freaked him out," I said, retracing our steps from last night to collect my clothes.

By the time Zack met me out in the kitchen, he'd slipped into underwear. "Why would it freak him out?"

"Because..." I finished dressing, buttoning up my shirt, minus one at the bottom. "If he gets an idea in his head, he obsesses over it from all angles. If *he* thinks *I* don't think it'll work out, he'll get it in his head that it won't, and he'll spiral."

Zack flicked the coffee maker on, filled it with water, and dumped the grounds into the filter. "So you *do* want it to work out?"

I finger-combed my hair and tied it back. "I want what he wants, which is to marry Sarah, so, yeah, I want it to work out. Do I think they should get married? No."

He offered me a sardonic headshake as he grabbed two mugs from a cabinet along with milk and sugar for me.

"It's complicated." I sank down into a chair at the kitchen table. "Maybe I should call him."

He drummed his fingers on the counter as the coffee filled the carafe. "You told him yesterday he had to figure it out. Let him figure it out."

"Yeah, but—"

"You say he's over-analytical and obsesses over things, but *you* obsess over *him*." When the coffee finished, he poured it out into the two mugs then set the pot back down with a bit more force than necessary before offering me a cup. Although it felt more like a good-bye send-off than a friendly invitation to stay a while.

"He's my best friend," I said, and Zack rubbed his hands over his face before crossing his arms.

"You keep saying that like you're trying to convince everyone. Including yourself." He stood opposite me, at the corner of the counter, tension rippling off him in waves, threatening to upend me. "We met because you wanted to blow up his wedding? Your *best friend's* wedding."

"I know that." I shoved my coffee mug away, in no need of it anymore. "Are you trying to make me feel bad?"

"No." He tugged at his beard. "I'm not trying to make you feel bad, but I am trying to make sense of all this. You're obsessed with a relationship you have nothing to do with."

"I want—"

"Nothing!" He slammed the cabinet shut. "You have nothing to do with them," he said and spun away from me to grip the counter.

My spine snapped straight as a pin. I wasn't scared of him, or his past, or of the infamous temper I was quickly becoming acquainted with, but I didn't appreciate being yelled at. "Don't shout at me."

"I'm sorry," he mumbled after a while and pushed his clenched fists against the top of the counter. With his elbows locked, his shoulders hunched, he hid his face from me. "Less than an hour ago, I told you I'm all in. You want to go hopping all over different continents? Cool. But you want me to play second to Tyler?" He finally fixed his eyes on me, his expression hard. "Not cool."

I stuttered, confused and taken aback. "I-I-I...never asked you to be second to anyone."

"Not with words, no. But what happened when *we* were in bed together not even twenty minutes ago? *You* put me second for *him*."

I opened my mouth to argue, but he cut me off before I could. Like he knew exactly what I was going to say. "This isn't about me being jealous or me not wanting you to be friends with a guy. This is about you running to him every time he snaps his fingers. No matter what."

Offended and ashamed, I held onto Nellie's necklace for comfort. My eyes burned with tears. "I'm not some kind of lap dog."

"I know you aren't." He pitched forward as if he wanted

to reach for me, but he kept his hands firmly on the counter. He closed his eyes, grimacing beneath his copper brows and beard. "That's why I hate it."

I struggled to get past the word *hate*. "Hate it?"

"I hate that you change yourself for him."

This time my anger got the best of me. "You don't even know me! How can you say I change for him? You don't know me or him."

The way his shoulders curled inward like he was deflated made me deflate too. Like we were the same balloon falling back down to earth, all the air leaching out of it.

After a few moments, his eyes sharpened, his voice prickled. "That's what you think? That I don't know you?"

No. Of course not. He saw me for what I was, but I couldn't back down now. This argument was about more than the secrets we told each other in the dark by the lake or late nights at the shop.

"I'm not going to choose between you and Tyler. Don't make me."

He blew out an acerbic chuckle. "I haven't made you choose anything. You did it all by yourself, sweetheart."

"Don't be condescending."

He folded his arms, the wall back up, and I knew him so well, I knew the exact position of his left arm over the right meant there was no getting through to him now. This arm fold was different than his more relaxed crossed forearms. I even knew his derisive sniff meant I was dismissed.

"So, that's it?" I asked.

He raised one shoulder.

"You're not going to answer?"

Apparently not.

I let my hand drop to my side with a thwack against my leg. "Great. That's great." I looped my purse over my shoulder, heading to the door. "If those are your two speeds, screaming or silence, I guess I understand now how Sarah was under the impression it really was over."

He caught my wrist as I stepped out of the door. "I told you I don't play games. I won't settle for second place, and I don't want to constantly be compared to other people."

With a fleeting, heart-wrenching look, he released me and closed the door. I stared at the door, chafed he would insinuate this was all my fault. I took the steps two at a time, imitating him in a curt voice, "I don't play games." I huffed. "Fuck off."

He couldn't hear me, but it made me feel better to say it anyway. He went hot and cold like a light switch, and what was that, if not a game? And what did it say about our relationship if he so willingly jumped ship at the first speed bump?

And putting him second? I told him I wanted him. He was my future. I wanted his log cabin and a big bed. I wanted midnight motorcycle rides and long, boring days together. If he assumed my feelings about him were associated to the manner in which I responded to text messages, I didn't know how to make him believe otherwise.

I drove home to shower and change before heading to my parents' house. Zack and I were supposed to both go for a picnic. I figured it would be our *hey, Mom and Dad, meet my boyfriend* moment, so when I showed up alone, my dad pulled me into his side to kiss my temple in an unusual demonstration of sentiment. A long joked about trait in the Mahoney clan, which was probably true of most Irish families, was our stunted emotional spectrum. We weren't good at *Big Emotions*.

Maybe Zack was onto something with the whole therapy thing.

"You need a chat?" Dad asked, and when I nodded, he called for Mom. "I'm going to start the grill."

With a sad laugh, I plopped down onto a chair at the kitchen table with a half-completed coral reef puzzle laid out.

"Hey, hon, where's Zack?"

I held a few pieces, not meeting my mother's gaze. "Not coming."

"Oh?" She set herself up next to me. "Everything all right?"

I tapped a piece on the table and forced a smile at her.

"What's wrong?"

Maybe I was losing my touch on the fake smiles. The lying. "Do you think me and Tyler—do you think we have some kind of unhealthy relationship?"

Mom tilted her head. "What do you mean?"

"Zack called me a lapdog."

"He what?" She rolled her chair back in Mama Bear mode, ready to go after him.

"We got into an argument," I said, holding my hand out to stop her. I appreciated that she always sided with me no matter what, but I needed an unbiased ear. "He said I put Tyler first and him second, and I basically run whenever Tyler calls. Is that... Do I do that?"

Mom thought on this, scrutinizing the puzzle for a moment before meeting my eyes. She had always been so tender and affectionate with me, the opposite of my father—and to a certain extent, me—I wondered how hard it must have been for her not to be able to cuddle with me on the couch like we used to.

I never thought a lot about children. Only in the vaguest sense, that I wanted kids eventually. I wanted to someday pass on the love I'd inherited from my mother, to be able to cuddle and give good advice and make cookies together. Not that parenting was easy or all sunshine and rainbows, but I wanted to pass on the gifts given to me. Those small intimate moments when she'd wrap me up from behind and peck kisses all over my face. Even after I'd outgrown her, she'd teasingly haul me down, leaving a smacking kiss on my forehead.

I laid my head on her shoulder now, and she leaned her cheek on me.

"I guess you have to tell me," she said. "Do you put Tyler first?"

I answered honestly. "I don't know. I don't know how to be without him. We've been Tyler and Tilly for so long, I'm not really sure who I am without him."

"You are your own person." She clucked her tongue in reprimand. "Never think twice about that. But you two have been friends for a long time."

I raised my head to face her. "So much of my life has involved him, you know? We're a part of each other, and I don't know what it means to put him first or second or anywhere because to me I'm just living my life. And Tyler's there."

"Yeah, I understand, but is it possible you're confusing your most important relationship with your longest one?" When I furrowed my brows, she smiled. "It's hard to let go of habits and routines. Tyler is your routine, and you probably do things with him out of habit. Do you act like a lapdog with him? I don't think so, and I'm a little mad Zack would ever say that about you."

I dropped my elbows on the table and held my head in my hands. "It's the least of my problems, Mom."

"Well, besides that, if you want this relationship with Zack to work, you need to form new routines. If he's the most important person in your life, it's not enough to say it. You have to show it." Her eyes shifted over to the window, where Dad worked outside. "Priorities change when you're in love." Smiling sweetly back at me, she admitted, "I'd be lying if I said Sylvie and I didn't used to talk about you and Tyler ending up together, and for a while I expected it. He's an amazing person, but, honey, you deserve someone who puts *you* first. You give yourself to everyone."

I waved her off. "No, I don't."

"Yes, you do." She poked my arm with her knuckle. "You never say no to anyone, to Tyler, to me and your dad, to Sarah, to that mom with her kids who broke down that one Christmas."

I shook my head. A few years ago, about a week or so before the holiday, I'd been driving home after closing the store, and a light snow had fallen. A woman had been outside of her broken-down car, so I crammed the mom, her two kids, and all the Christmas presents they'd purchased that day into my tiny car and drove them home. It wasn't because I was nice. The Christmas Spirit had gotten to me, that's all.

"It's a shame you don't see yourself very clearly." Mom skimmed her knuckle down my cheek. "I want you to be happy, and the day Zack was here after our dishwasher exploded—"

"It didn't explode."

"I haven't seen you so relaxed and happy. You were more like yourself with him, and I haven't seen you like that in a while. Not even around Tyler." She patted my leg. "Now come on, let's go outside. I'll take the plates and forks if you can bring out the drinks. A new Hallmark movie is on tonight, and I don't want to miss it."

"God forbid," I mumbled, shadowing her with drinks in hand and lots of thoughts in my head.

Twenty-Five

The days before the Kelly-Rodriguez wedding zipped by in a blur. I hadn't seen hide nor hair of Sarah. Her mom had come in to pick up the dress, and aside from a few texts asking my opinion on finishing touches like when to have the toasts or if they should have First Look photos taken, I hadn't heard from her. Tyler had informed me he'd had a long sit down with Sarah, and she promised to be more open with him about her feelings, which I was happy to hear.

I, on the other hand, had not had the same promise from Zack. We'd barely spoken. I'd left him a voicemail about wanting to talk, and he texted me back with **Yeah me too.** And that was it.

After my chat with Mom, I knew I had to change my routine and let go of my security blanket in Tyler. I was willing to do it. I wanted to. Though, it didn't appear like Zack was ready to work on it with me. Although with the impending nuptials, I put him on the back burner for the time-being. I would be able to get myself sorted after I got Tyler married.

The day before the wedding, we were scheduled to be at the country club by 4pm for the rehearsal. The Kellys had rented out the whole place for the event. As I parked in the lot, men unloaded chairs and tables from a truck on direction from a woman with a clipboard. She seemed important, so I made my way over to her.

"Hi, I'm Tilly Mahoney. I'm here for the wedding rehearsal, part of the bridal party. Do you know where I should be?"

She placed her sunglasses on top of her head and flipped a few pages on the clipboard. "Yes, wonderful. You're Tyler's Best Woman? I'll take you to his dressing room. When you arrive tomorrow, you can head right there. I think most of the other groomsmen are there already."

I followed her through the two-story lobby which had a New England flare with wainscoting and floor to ceiling columns. On the right, a sitting area with a giant gray stone fireplace took up most of the wall, while glass doors opened up to a perfectly manicured lawn to the left. A winding path down a small slope led to the first hole of the golf course, and a swimming pool with an outdoor bar were directly behind the main building. Tucked around the other side, was a small garden and alcove perfect for wedding ceremonies. Workers bustled about, setting up rows of silver Chiavari chairs, tied with white and blush pink tulle. At the end of the aisle, a wooden trellis with a wall of greenery behind it set the scene for the vows.

"Everything is beautiful," I said.

The woman tapped her pen on her clipboard. "Once we're finished, it'll be picture perfect with the rose petals down the aisle and the flowers woven around the lattice. This might be the biggest wedding we've ever done. Okay, here we are." She motioned to a door, and through a small window, I could see a small sitting area. "There are some light refreshments and a bathroom inside. My name is Gretchen, if you need anything."

I nodded my thanks and opened the door.

"There she is!"

"You're late."

"You think we can get more of these Swedish meatballs?"

"Is there alcohol in an Arnold Palmer?"

I stepped into the circle of men, lounged on every couch and chair, and answered each of their statements in turn, starting with Ricky. "Hi. Yes, I'm here." Then to Tyler, "I'm only two minutes late." To Rob, "Gretchen can get you more meatballs." And finally to Henry, "There is no alcohol in an Arnold Palmer."

He sulked and plunked the drink down. "Then why am I drinking it? Can't we get some beer?"

I helped myself to it and drained a few gulps before sitting on the arm rest of the couch next to Tyler. "You look frantic."

"Sarah's not here yet."

I shrugged. "It's rush hour. Give her time."

He hunched over, tossing his cell phone back and forth between his hands. "Her bridesmaids are here."

"I haven't seen her parents yet." I pointed my thumb to the window, hoping it was nothing. "They might all be—"

"I'm going to find Gretchen," Rob said. "I'm starved. I need more meatballs."

Tyler flicked his gaze up at his brother. "My god! Shut up about the goddamn meatballs."

Rob's eyes widened, and he slowly chewed the last meatball as he slunk off toward the door. "No need to yell. Wedding nerves are totally normal."

"I'm not nervous," Tyler grumbled, stalking to the window.

Rob waved Freddie to follow him outside, and when Ricky eyed me, I motioned with my head for him to do the same. With a tap to their shoulders, Logan and Henry were out too, leaving Tyler and me alone.

After a minute of letting him fret silently, I tugged him out the door. "Come on, let's get some fresh air."

He didn't refuse, but his steps were sluggish as we ambled toward the pool. "I can't get rid of this pit in my stomach."

"Did you eat something funny?" I asked, ignoring my own pit forming. Tyler wasn't one for dramatics. If he had a bad feeling, there must have been a reason, and I already knew it before he lifted his phone up to me when it buzzed.

"It's Sarah," he said, pivoting back to the dressing room, his voice trailing off with, "Hey, babe, what's going on?"

I tried to stay positive, mulling over the reasons Sarah might call Tyler instead of showing up to her wedding rehearsal. Maybe she was in a car accident. Maybe she had a spray tan incident. Maybe...

Maybe she was calling it off.

And I was going to puke.

The whole wedding was planned. They were less than twenty-four hours away from becoming Mr. and Mrs. She couldn't call if off now, not after all I'd done to keep them together...after I tried to break them up. Guilt seeped into my bones, turning my stomach, and I tied my hair up as sweat dotted my neck.

Sarah was a well-known runaway bride, and it was possible this was a case of cold feet. It might all be fine. They could very well get married tomorrow. And I might not have had anything to do with it.

After a minute or two, I gathered my nerve and prayed it wasn't what I anticipated as I quietly opened up the door. Tyler had his head in his hands. His phone laid on the table in front of him next to his glasses.

"What happened?" I asked, knowing the answer.

His voice was weak. "I'm not getting married."

I let out a soft curse and momentarily froze in place as a wheezing cry racked his body. I couldn't remember the last time he'd cried. Maybe when his grandmother had died a few years ago. He wiped his face, and it spurred me into action. Crouching down next to him, I rubbed his back. "I'm sorry. I'm so, so sorry."

"It's not your fault." He swiped his hair back— he'd gotten it trimmed for the big day that was now off—and locked his fingers at his neck. "Can you tell them? Gretchen and my parents? I don't think I can right now."

"Yes, of course. Anything you need. I'll do whatever you need me to." I smoothed my hand across his shoulders and swallowed the lump in my throat, adding to the growing pile of rocks inside me. "Did she, um... Did she say why?"

"Only that she couldn't go through with it." He shook his head, blinking rapidly. "I knew she was anxious but..." He slanted his head to me, twin tracks of tears on his cheeks. "Did she say anything to you?"

My heart broke at the crack in his voice. Tyler and I had always been there for each other, and now, on a day when we should be celebrating, he was here crying. And it might have been my fault by putting some ideas into Sarah's head about coincidences with Zack and doubts about Tyler. I didn't think it had actually worked, especially since I'd given up, but now that she really did call it off, I couldn't help but feel like it was my fault.

It was all my fault.

Avoiding his gaze, I focused on the plush carpet.

"Till," he said, pulling me to sit next to him on the couch, lacing his fingers with mine. "What did she say?"

What did she say? The question should have been *What did you say? What did you do?*

I stared at his hand, his knuckles and trimmed nails, the fourth finger which was supposed to wear a platinum wedding band. "She didn't really say anything out of the ordinary to me, but, uh..." I could barely raise my voice above a whisper, the last thing I wanted to do was hurt him. And I was going to do exactly that. "I don't..."

"Just tell me the truth." He urged me to face him, our knees touching.

The truth.

Right.

"The truth is..." I held his hands between mine, maybe a little too tightly from the flash of uncertainty across his face. The movie of our life together played in my mind.

The two of us selling lemonade at a stand.

My 13th birthday, when I had to cancel my party because of a snowstorm, so my mom let Tyler sleepover, and we stayed up all night in the living room watching all the Jurassic Park movies.

The weekend we bought fake IDs with Ricky to go to a club in Manhattan.

Last Valentine's Day when we took a couples' cooking class, and he burnt our heart shaped cheesecake.

"The truth is the guy—" I cleared my throat of the tremor in my voice "—the guy I'm seeing is Zack."

"Zack?" His bloodshot eyes darted around the room before returning to me. "Sarah's ex-boyfriend? What does that have to do with anything?"

"Well, I, um..." I shot up and shook my hands out, pacing the room, unable to look at him as I blurted it out in a rush. Best to rip it off like a Band-Aid. "When you told me you were marrying Sarah, I was upset. Like, really upset. I thought it was a terrible idea, and I didn't understand how you could want to marry her after only knowing her for a few weeks, and I got it in my head that if I could somehow show you how wrong Sarah was for you, maybe you wouldn't go through with it."

I chanced a glance at him. He sat stone faced.

"I love you, Tyler, you're my best friend, and I stupidly thought we could, I guess, you know..."

He didn't move. Didn't blink. I didn't even know if he breathed.

I rambled on, the truth spilling out of me now that I'd turned the faucet. "I didn't understand how you could love her and not me, and I was confused about what I wanted. I'm so sorry," I panted, my chest seizing.

He didn't acknowledge me at all, and I trembled as I confessed the rest in one long breath.

"I tried to get Zack and Sarah back together so you two would break up. I know it's absurd, I know, and somewhere along the line, I realized I only wanted you to be happy. Sarah made you happy, and I gave up on the idea, but Zack and I actually started to see something in each other, and I didn't know if I had anything to do with Sarah's decision, but I'm so sorry. God, Tyler, I wish I could take it back. I wish I could take it all back, but I can't, and I'm so, so sorry."

A beat of silence passed.

My heart thrashed in my chest.

He dropped his head toward the floor, and when he remained silent, I fell to my knees in front of him. "Say something."

He sniffed, shaking his head. "I don't know what to say."

"Please, say something," I begged, my own voice cracking. "Anything. I feel horrible."

"You should." He nodded and then burst out of his seat, knocking my hands from his knees as he shot up. "Why? Why would you do that?"

I dabbed at the tears forming in the corner of my eyes. I needed to lay it all out there and face this head on, but I already felt my grip on him slipping. Sand through my fingers. "I was mad. Jealous and possessive." I stood up and braced my hands on the back of the sofa. "It had always been me and you our whole lives, but the last few years we've been drifting apart. I was uncomfortable and unsure of myself, but knowing I had you made me feel better. When Sarah came into the picture, I didn't know what else to do. I couldn't lose you."

"Lose me?" He threw his arm out, his voice course with tears and anger. "Why would you lose me?"

"I've been losing you, Tyler," I cried. "This whole time." I paused for a moment to catch my breath. "All these years, you've been with so many girls, and each time it's like you forget about me. I'm your wingman, and I'm there for you, but it's only on your terms."

"What are you talking about?" He put his glasses on and stalked to the other end of the room, his volume rising with each new question. "What the fuck are you even talking about?"

I waved my arms in front of me, stomping my foot. I felt like I was sinking into quicksand. Fighting a losing battle. "I'm talking about how you drop and pick me up like a toy. Whenever you want a new girl in your bed, you put me away for a while, and then when you're done with her—no matter if it's one day, one week, or one month—you pick me back up, expecting it to be fine. And I act like it is, but it's not. It's not okay. I think I've been pretending like it is for so long, I don't know how else our relationship is supposed to work."

"Oh, that makes sense!" He pivoted in a tight circle. "Because you're pissed at me for being a bad friend, you think you needed to destroy my wedding?"

"I don't know!" I roared, my vision blurred with tears, my face wet, my palms sweaty. "I know I've loved you for a long time, and I was tired of always coming in second when I put you first."

He lunged one foot forward, his words thrown at me like knives. "Well, congratulations, you did it. You have all my attention now!"

"I'm sorry! I'm sorry. I don't..." I couldn't keep my weight up anymore and sunk to the floor with my back against the wall. "After all these years, of you cuddling with me, and kissing my forehead, and me basically being a part of your family, I thought one day you'd realize you loved me. Not love me, but love *love* me."

His only response was to rub at his temple.

"I know I was wrong." I folded my hands together in front of my chest, praying he might understand. "At first, when you told me you were engaged, I was furious and wanted to break you guys up because it wasn't me you proposed to, but after a while I stopped thinking about me and started thinking you two weren't right for each other. I'm sorry if anything I did caused you to break up. It was stupid and awful and the worst thing I've ever done in my life. But it doesn't change the fact that you guys barely know one another."

I don't know if he was listening to me anymore, but I kept on with my explanation. "I don't think marriages are supposed to be easy, but I think both parties should be willing to at least try. You guys don't even—"

He threw a small vase against the wall, smashing it to pieces. I recoiled, goosebumps racing up my arms.

His jaw set in an unforgiving line. "Get out."

I scrambled to stand up. "I thought you wanted me to tell—"

"Get out," he seethed, his back to me. "I can't even look at you right now."

My legs shook as I stepped toward him. "Tyler, I think—"

"You thought you could break me and Sarah up?" He whirled on me. "Well, I'm breaking up with you." He swiped a hand under his eyes.

I didn't bother to wipe at my face. The tears wouldn't stop.

"You flushed twenty years of friendship down the drain. I hope you're happy. You got what you wanted."

I reached for him. "Of course not. I'm not happy, I'm—"

"Leave me alone!"

I flinched and dropped my arm.

"I'm done with you," he said, effectively cutting me in two. He strode by me, not sparing a glance in my direction as he made his way out of the door and toward the gazebo. I watched through the window until he found his mom, and then I couldn't bear to look anymore.

I did it. I ruined my best friend's wedding.

Twenty-Six

I drove away from the country club as fast and far as possible until I couldn't see anymore and parked on the side of the road, letting the sobs take over. I cried out of guilt for what I had done, pain for what I'd lost, and relief it was finally over. The truth was out, the reckoning over.

I never meant to hurt Tyler, although I don't know how I ever thought I wouldn't with my ridiculous plan. I simply wanted him for myself, but even thinking that now, it all sounded so silly and childish. And maybe deep down, I did want to hurt him a little. To make him feel how he'd made me feel. One thousand tiny cuts for all the times he left me at a bar, or rescheduled a hang out, or blatantly ignored me for another girl, in exchange for one big tear right through his wedding, leaving both our hearts broken.

Tyler didn't deserve what I did to him.

I also didn't deserve to be treated so transactionally by my best friend.

Although none of it meant anything now. I'd lost Tyler. Maybe forever.

And for what?

I found an old receipt on the floor of my car and blew my nose. If I truly did lose my best friend, there was only one person who could make me feel like I didn't lose everything.

I drove to Zack's house, still wiping away the last of my tears, trying and failing to clean my streaked make-up, but when I pulled up, an unfamiliar car was parked in the drive. An open tool box and random tools laid strewn about on the small platform outside of his door like he had been in the middle of working with them.

I fixed my hair and smoothed out my dress before heading to the lion's den. The storm door was completely removed, so I knocked once on the metal door then opened it to step out of the sunlight and into the dim trailer.

Zack and Sarah both spun to me, deer in headlights.

"Tilly," he said, bare-chested with a dirty towel in his hands, his hair all askew and sweaty.

For her part, Sarah appeared surprised to see me here.

"Wh-why?" I blinked between them. "What?"

This was, literally, the worst thing I could have imagined. Which was utterly fucking bizarre because it was what I had planned all along. There he was, tattoos out, big arms frozen toward me. And there she was, with perfect make-up, not one eyelash out of place as if she hadn't shed any tears about her canceled wedding.

I pointed at Sarah. "What are you doing here?"

Her jaw flapped up and down, but no words came out. I held my hand up anyway to stop any answer she might produce. I didn't want to know what she was doing here.

"You're supposed to be marrying Tyler," I snapped, then faced Zack, who didn't appear to know what to do with himself. His teal athletic shorts hung low on his hips and his shoulders were red with sunburn.

"I was working on my door," he said by way of explanation, and I huffed out a hysterical laugh. Maybe I had finally gone insane. I'd destroyed my friendship with Tyler, I'd succeeded in stopping the wedding, and I'd reunited these two lovebirds.

"Go to hell," I hissed at Sarah, still in defense of Tyler. "You too," I whimpered to Zack before showing myself out.

After a short commotion behind me, Zack bounded down the three steps and grabbed my forearm, spinning me to him.

"Let me go."

Under the sunshine, his skin glistened with sweat, and I tried to twist away from him, but he held me tighter, wrapping his other arm around me. "No."

"Ugh! I hate you," I said, so broken down I couldn't communicate in anything other than primal grunts and juvenile retorts.

"Why are you so upset? This is what you wanted, isn't it?"

This is what you wanted, isn't it?

I hated it.

I hated everything.

I met his deep-sea eyes for only a second, too fearful of drowning. It already felt like the end of everything; I didn't want to lose my breath too. My lungs burned, and when I shuddered in his grasp, he brought my wrists together, holding my hands between us. I let my head fall to his shoulder one last time, hiding a sob.

"Tilly."

I refused to look at him, so he cupped my chin with one hand, forcing my gaze to his. I'd be lying if I didn't want to spend our last moments close like this. If I could, I would dig open his chest and make a room inside his ribcage. Maybe then I'd find my heart next to his.

Smoldering tears fell from my eyes, and he stopped one in its path, kissing my cheek. I let out a very unladylike snuffle and pressed my fingers to the hollow in his throat. "I didn't mean it."

"Didn't mean what?" He loosened his hold on me, gently caressing my cheek with his work-rough fingertips.

"I don't hate you." I blinked up at him, indulging in one last stroke of his beard. I had nothing to lose anymore, so might as well let it all go. "I love you."

He inhaled audibly and released me completely as if I'd burned him.

I certainly felt incinerated, my heart crumbling to ash when he let go. "Goodbye, Zack."

For the second time in a matter of hours, I got in my car, speeding away.

At my apartment, I took off my sundress and hid the new black tuxedo jumpsuit I'd special ordered in the back of my closet. I didn't wait for the water to warm up in the shower and curled up into a ball on the floor. Memories slammed into me—Zack and me in the lake, the way he came to rescue my parents and fixed the leak, and the daydream I had of getting married in front of the ocean had become more reality than fantasy lately.

From his eyes to his deeply protective and compassionate soul, he *was* water. No match for the wildfire I'd let loose though.

Thoroughly drenched and cold, there was nothing left inside me to burn, and I crawled out of the shower. After wrapping a towel around me, I confronted myself in the mirror. I noted my puffy eyes and sallow skin, and I fingered the pendant around my neck. It had become a worry stone for me over the years, a nervous tick that I didn't notice most of the time. Now though, I closed my eyes, wondering what Nellie might say to me.

Jaysus, Mary, and Joseph.

Despite myself, I smiled, hearing her sing-song voice.

Mo stoirín, she would say to me when I was little and point to the floor at her feet. *Teacht suí*.

Nellie, in her hatred of the English, had tried to speak Gaelic as often as possible, though once she came to America, she had stopped almost completely, so I only knew the most basic words. *My little darling, come sit.*

She would braid my hair and let me learn the tiny grooves on her rough-hewed mother of pearl necklace. She'd worn it every day, the one piece of jewelry which had been passed down in her family.

When she had gifted it to me, shortly before she died, she had given me more than a necklace. She'd given me a piece of herself. A piece of all the strong and sturdy—and most likely belligerent—women who had come before her.

She would sing to me about ancient chiefs and clans, ballads of sons lost to war and rebellions, and my favorite, *The Song of the Seal*. She had sung it in Gaelic, so I hadn't understood any of it other than the beauty of her voice and the basic story of it being about a selkie who would not relent to the fear of being hunted by humans.

What I wouldn't give to have her with me now, if only to smooth my hair and tell me *Never be afraid of the wind or snow, the sun will always rise and you will always be loved.*

The wind and the snow had knocked me down, and, right now, I couldn't see the rising of the sun. But like Nellie had always said, *There's nothing a good whiskey can't cure.*

I found a dust-covered bottle of Redbreast at the back of my cabinet and sat at the kitchen table. The couch and my bed held too many memories I didn't want to encounter.

So, I did the next best thing.

And got black-out drunk.

Sláinte.

Twenty-Seven

They were dropping bowling balls on the floor. It was the only possible explanation for the noise coming from the upstairs neighbors. I cracked my eyelid open, realizing maybe those bowling balls were in my head.

I didn't know when or how I'd made it to the floor, but I rolled to my back, pulling the bath towel over me. I'd never bothered to dress or even comb my hair last night, and it stuck to my face and shoulders in knotted clumps. I gave myself a minute for the nausea to pass, but when it didn't I ran into the bathroom, smacking into the doorjamb on my way, and barely made it to the toilet before throwing up I didn't know how many ounces of whiskey.

When I finished gagging, I wiped my mouth with toilet paper and somehow found the handle to flush through blurry eyes. I crawled to the sink and hung my arms over the sides, splashing water into my mouth but mostly hitting my face until I couldn't handle being upright anymore. Then I fell back to the floor and closed my eyes.

I woke up, I don't know how many minutes or hours later, and forced myself onto my feet. I wrapped the towel around me once again and brushed my teeth, refusing to look at my reflection in the mirror.

In relatively better condition though still completely unsteady, I searched for my phone and found it near the couch. I had multiple missed calls, mostly from my mother, but two from Zack mixed in there, and like I'd summoned her, Mom called again.

"Finally," she said when I answered. "Where have you been?"

"Uh…" I blinked around my apartment. "At home."

"I've been calling you since yesterday. What happened? Why was the wedding called off? Sylvia sent me a text. She said Tyler's heartbroken."

I rubbed at the burn in my chest and pushed myself to sit on the sofa. "Yeah. I'm not really feeling good."

"No?" She went from frantic to concerned immediately. "What is it? Stress? I know you sometimes get a pain in your stomach when you're stressed."

"Uh huh." I dropped my head between my knees.

"Is there anything I can do? I feel so bad for Tyler, I'm sure you were a big help to him yesterday."

I grimaced in pain. "Mom, please, stop."

"What? Honey, what's wrong? You sound terrible."

"I…" The weight of Nellie's pendant dropped, hitting me square on the chin in my inverted position, and I held onto it as I slowly rolled my spine back up straight. If Nellie had the courage to face down English soldiers and brave a trip across the ocean to a new country, I could certainly stare down the mess I'd made and clean it up. "Actually, could I come over?"

"Yes. Yes, of course. I don't even know why you're asking."

"Because you won't like what I have to tell you."

My mother remained silent for a few seconds and then, "Come over. Your father and I are here for you no matter what."

SOPHIE ANDREWS

I hung up and chugged water straight from the tap then slipped into the comfiest clothes I owned, sweats and a well-worn Olsen Heating & Plumbing T-shirt Zack had left on accident that I'd never bothered to give back. I lifted the collar to my nose, but it didn't smell like him anymore.

My chest caved in a little bit further. I supposed I didn't need my ribcage anymore. There was nothing left inside me to protect.

With an exhausted whimper, I got into my car to drive to my parents' house. When Dad saw me, his brow scrunched so deep with concern, his eyebrows had become one. He escorted me to the kitchen table, bare of any puzzle pieces, but with three cups of tea waiting. Mom's smile wobbled to a frown. "You look a wreck."

"I feel a wreck."

"What's going on?" Dad asked, taking a seat across from me.

"A lot," I said, my eyes already wet with tears. I didn't think I had any left, but I couldn't turn them off, as if all my take-it-on-the-chin Irish bluster had vanished. Or it just all caught up to me at once.

Mom handed me a napkin, and I blotted my face. "Remember when we talked the other week about me and Tyler?"

She nodded.

"Well, not only did I screw things up with Zack but with Tyler too."

Dad cleared his throat and repeatedly tapped his finger on the table.

"You might want to grab a cigarette for this one," I told him, and he played at horror before giving into a laugh. I supposed my life had become tragedy enough that we didn't need to pretend he wasn't smoking.

"I'm trying to quit. I swear."

"Sure," Mom agreed with a smile.

Calmed from the familiar teasing, it was easier to tell them the whole sordid tale. I started at the beginning with brunch when Tyler and Sarah broke the news of their engagement, and I didn't skip any details of how I planned to break them up, using Zack.

Mom stayed silent while Dad muttered the occasional, "Jesus, Mary, and Joseph."

I explained how I'd fallen in love with Zack and gave up on my plan to destroy the wedding, albeit a little too late. I recounted my fight with Tyler, and how I found Sarah at Zack's house, and that I wasn't sure how or if I could fix any of it.

By the time I finished, Dad had drunk all of his tea and did, in fact, grab a cigarette. He had them hidden at the bottom of the big jar filled with loose pens and pencils. Opening the backdoor, he stood half-in, half-out. "You know what you did was..."

"Crazy?" I offered.

Mom nodded in agreement.

"Wrong," he corrected then took a puff, exhaling the smoke through his nose. "There is no need to keep beating yourself up about it. Like my grandmother would say, when a bomb goes off, people will get hurt. It's only a matter of how many."

"Oh, John," Mom muttered with a shake of her head, and I snickered. Dad tried to be helpful but pulled from the wrong Irish proverb. Nellie would definitely have said that, but probably only in the instance of exacting revenge during the war. Although Nellie had never confessed to it, the rumor was she'd run messages for the Fenians, never one to shy away from a fight.

"I'm trying to fix this," I said, "not maim more people."

"Well, yeah." He circled his hand, the smoke trailing after. "I meant it in the terms of keeping casualties to a minimum."

"The damage is done already," I told him, and he stubbed his cigarette out. After throwing it in the trash, he sat back down at the table and held my hand.

"You know I'm not good at this, but I love you, and if Zack and Tyler love you, it will work out."

"That's what I'm afraid of. That they don't love me anymore...if they ever did."

"Oh, sweetie," Mom tutted, rubbing the back of her hand along my arm. "The best you can do is apologize and tell them the truth, that you love them and you'll do better. You did one very stupid thing, but your friendship with Tyler is based on years of stupid things. I remember you guys got into a fight over those concert tickets—"

"We were, like, fifteen, Mom. It's not the same."

"No, but you've been friends for so long, he knows the real you, and I know it's hard now, but he'll come around eventually."

I dropped my chin to my chest. "What about Zack?"

"You said he called. Why haven't you called him back?"

"Because I'm afraid," I said, slow to meet my mom's eyes.

"Tilly." My name carried an admonishment.

"Mahoney women aren't afraid of anything," Dad piped up, and I laughed through my tears.

I have been afraid of everything. I've been afraid of change, of leaving my home and something happening to Dad or Mom again, of losing the things I loved most. It's why I wanted to break-up Sarah and Tyler, because I didn't want Tyler and me to change. It's why I was afraid to leave the boutique, because trying something else would bring new and more difficult challenges.

But if I was going to follow Nellie's advice, I couldn't fear the wind and snow. If I wanted to be alive like fire, I needed to be more like it. Fire changed and moved, sometimes growing, sometimes fading, but always glowing.

"There's something else, too." I shifted in my chair. "I'm not happy managing Michelle's."

"You aren't?" Dad asked.

Mom waited, listening.

"I'm not sure what exactly I want to do, but I know I don't want to work at the store for the rest of my life. And I can't figure out what I want if I'm there." Before Mom could say anything, I charged on. "I talked to Fatima. She said she might be interested in taking on more responsibility. Maybe we could promote her and hire another person or two? I'll train them myself. I promise I won't leave you without help, I just need—"

"Honey." Mom shushed me. "It's all right."

I froze. "It is?"

"Yes." Her brown eyes welled up. "I want you to be happy. You volunteered to help out all those years ago, and you're so good at it, I didn't hesitate. But don't think you *have* to be there."

Liberated of some of the tension that I'd been holding all the years, I sagged into her. All these years I'd convinced myself it was fine, that I was fine, but it was a lie. Finally, the truth.

"I love you, no matter what, sweetheart," she said.

Dad agreed, sneaking around to our side of the table to wrap an arm around me. "What would be the point of my grandparents coming here all those years ago if their family couldn't find a way to be happy?"

I heard Nellie's voice once again. *Mo ghrá thú. You are my love.*

Twenty-Eight

I may have been on a new path, a more adult-ier, honest way of living, but I was still a kid enough to know when I needed my mom and dad. I stayed with them all day, letting them fuss over me, feeding me my favorite grilled ham and cheese sandwich, and putting a new puzzle together. This one of an illustrated *New Yorker* cover of people on a beach. After dinner, we watched the History Channel because they were finally playing "something other than that stupid ancient aliens show," and I stayed until my parents went to bed. They invited me to sleep over, but I returned home to listen to Zack's voicemail in the solitude of my own apartment.

He had called twice, and left one short message.

"Hey, it's me. We have to talk. I know I was an asshole before by ignoring you. I'm sorry. We need to talk. Whenever. Call me. Please."

I waited, wondering what we would say to each other that wouldn't break my heart even further. But when I reminded myself I needed to be more like Nellie—or like Zack to run toward the roar—I finally called, and he picked up immediately.

"Tilly."

My chin trembled at the sound of my name coming from his mouth.

"I'm glad you called."

"Hi," I said after a while.

"You ran away so fast yesterday. I didn't know what to do or say."

I pressed my thumb and index finger into my eyes, maybe I could jab my brain into working again. "Yeah."

"Can we talk?"

"About what?" I rubbed at the burning in my nose. "I got what I wanted and you got Sarah. Everything went according to plan."

"No, it didn't. I'm not with Sarah."

I closed my eyes, releasing a watery, relieved breath.

"Tilly, we need to talk."

I opened my eyes and glanced around my dark apartment. "Right now?"

"Yeah. You could come here or I could come to you?"

"Oh." I tugged on his shirt that I wore. "I haven't even showered today."

"You don't need to. I don't care."

"It's ten o'clock." The excuse sounded weak even to my ears.

"I'm coming over," he snapped, and before I could say otherwise he hung up on me.

Despite Zack saying he didn't care, I did, and I showered and changed into fresh clothes. If I was going to face down the damage of the bomb I threw, I wanted to at least appear somewhat respectable.

My door buzzed, and I took a breath before answering. Though I didn't need to. Because as soon as I opened the door, all the air I'd lost since yesterday came rushing back into me. My heart beat wildly beneath my ribs, which was weird. I hadn't felt it in so long. As his eyes swept over me, my skin tingled, my embers were brightening, warming with every passing second.

Until I couldn't stand it anymore. Neither could he.

We reached for each other at the same time, his hands in my hair, mine at his sides, our lips meeting in the middle with a force of nature. Wind swept around us, fire built between us, and without any words, I knew I was home.

Everything we needed to talk about would have to wait.

Gently, more gentle than he'd ever been with me, he lifted me off my feet, one arm around my back with the other under my thighs. He carried me to the couch and settled me on his lap, wasting no time in removing my shirt. His mouth set course over my neck and shoulder as he stroked my sides, squeezed my breasts.

It hadn't been that long since we'd been together, but after yesterday, the energy between us was different. We were on a new track after making a slight stop.

I kissed my apologies into the sensitive part of his throat, below his ear, into the palm of his hand, and then after I lifted his T-shirt off of him, into the middle of his chest. He seemed to accept them as he laid me on my back, stretching out on the couch. Braced on his forearm, he drew his palm down the length of me, taking his time at my shoulder, my waist, and my hip. His teeth nipped at my lower lip, pushing my leggings down and off, followed by his jeans and underwear.

He paused fleetingly for a nod from me before I yanked him back down to me. I didn't need sweet words, or face-to-face longing, or his playful smacks to my thighs.

I needed his heart.

I needed his love.

I needed him.

When he finally pushed inside of me, I gasped. Oh, how I had missed him.

Wrapping my arms and legs as tight as I could around him, his kisses turned impatient and sloppy, his lips merely next to mine. Every one of his exhales became my inhales. Every one of his sighs became my own. Even every heartbeat, we shared those too. Until it was too much, and we both found release, finally collapsing in complete bliss.

He laid a track of kisses along my jaw as I traced the ridges of his spine. He shifted over me, skimming the tip of his nose along my cheek until he whispered in my ear, "Hi."

I let out a drowsy giggle. "Hi."

"Didn't mean for it to go down this way."

"Oh." I moved underneath him, pushing his weight off of me, suddenly unsure if I had fever-dreamed what we'd done. The last 48 hours had been the worst of my life, and I hoped to find the light at the end of the tunnel. Here, I thought we were right again, but to him, maybe this was a final good-bye.

"I missed you so much, Tilly," he said, clutching my hand, keeping me from putting on my shirt. "I wanted to talk first." The corner of his mouth kicked up, amusement in his eyes. "But when I saw you... That was good, too."

Allayed this wasn't good-bye, I quirked a smile. "Good?"

"More than good, but I don't know if there's a word for it." He rolled a lock of my hair between his fingers. "For when everything inside me feels like it's trying to get to you, and it's so painful the only thing that helps is for you to touch me. Then, at least, all my blood and muscles and bones don't feel so out of place inside me. Is there a word for that?"

I didn't know the word, but it was exactly how I felt, too. So I kissed him instead.

He held my face in his hands, his thumbs smoothing over my cheeks, as he hummed in pleasure. "Ah. See? Everything in me knows it's home."

I threw my arms around his neck. "I don't know how

anyone would ever think you're not the most romantic person on this earth."

"It's only the truth." He held me tighter, carrying me from the couch. "Let's get cleaned up."

We showered together in my tiny stall, laughing at how the two of us could barely raise our arms without bumping into each other or a wall, but we figured it out. After, we dried off and climbed into my bed. *Now* we could talk.

He tucked me into his side, and I rested my head on his shoulder.

"What happened last night?" he asked, drawing aimless shapes on my back.

"I got plastered."

"Yeah? Did it help?"

"No."

He glided his fingertips back and forth over my tattoo. "Usually doesn't."

"I didn't want to feel anything. Or remember anything, for that matter."

"The look in your eyes when you walked in yesterday, I won't forget it. It was...you looked broken."

I curled closer to him, burrowing into his skin as a shield. "I felt—feel broken. And then when you said 'Isn't this what you wanted?' I thought you meant you and Sarah."

"I meant the wedding. You didn't want it to happen," he said, his voice walking the thin line of a mild reprimand.

"But that's the thing." I moved over so I could see him better. "After I realized me and you had something, I didn't care anymore. I wanted to be happy, as happy as Tyler was, and if it meant he was going to marry someone even though they clearly had stuff to figure out, it wasn't up to me to do anything about it."

His chest rose on a deep breath, and I placed my palm over his heart. "What did Sarah want? Why was she there?"

His attention drifted to the ceiling, but I shook him so it came back to me. "She wanted me to give her another chance. She said she couldn't marry Tyler when things were unfinished between us." When I cringed, he brushed his finger over my forehead and down my nose until I relaxed. "I told her no. I'm in love with someone else."

There it was again. The glow. "Yeah?"

"I was caught off guard yesterday when you told me, and I should have reacted better. Everything that happened, it was a…a lot, but I should have told you then. I love you, Tilly."

I smiled and folded into him, kissing him until the words burst out of me. "*Mo ghrá thú.*"

He squinted at me. "What's that mean?"

"You are my love. I love you. You're mine. Take your pick."

His grin grew slowly, tenderly, his eyes alight like the sun's reflection on the ocean. "All of them." He urged my head back down to the crook of his neck. "I pick all of them." He toyed with strands of my hair, allowing our mutual declaration to settle between us.

Then he took a big inhale and asked, "What happened with Tyler?"

"Besides the fact that I smashed our friendship to bits, nothing much. He wouldn't even—" I stopped, waiting for the tears which had gathered in my eyes to dry. I rubbed at my forehead. "He told me I'd flushed twenty years of friendship away."

"I'm sorry." Zack wrapped me up more firmly in his arms, and I was grateful to have this. Him. After all I'd done, I didn't merit anything, and yet I had him. And he was everything.

"I deserve his anger. I let my emotions get the better of me. Instead of dealing with my problems, I let them fester and build up inside of me so when they exploded, I took him out. And—" I kissed Zack's chest, right over the teeth of the lion "—almost you too."

"But you didn't. I'm still here. I'll always be here."

I slid over to lay on my stomach, with my chin in his hands, meeting his gaze. "I talked to my parents. I told my mom I want to leave the boutique."

His copper eyebrows shot up. "You did?"

When I nodded, he brushed his hand up and down my back, soothing me.

"It won't be anytime soon," I said, "because I need to figure out what I'm going to do, and I'll have to find a replacement. But I think I want to finish my degree."

"Okay." He smiled my favorite half smile. "If that's what you want, do it."

I bit the inside of my lip.

"What?"

I told him the truth. "I'm scared."

"That's all right." He draped his arm around me and kissed my temple. "I'm here. We can run toward the roar together."

"What about us?"

"What about us?" He pushed his head back into the pillow, confusion crossing his features. "I told you. I'm here."

"I know," I said, beating back the last dregs of fear. "But... I mean, for good?"

He let out a mocking snort. "You think I'm going to let you get away? No. No way. I'm building you a log cabin and locking you inside."

I nibbled his bicep. "You know that won't contain me."

He rolled us, so he was on top of me. "Yeah, but it'll be fun to try. Mogra...who."

I cackled. "What?"

"My love. How do you say it?"

"*Mo ghrá thú.*"

He tried again, and I shook my head. "It's throatier." I repeated it. "*Mo. Ghrá. Thú.*"

"Mo grrrahu."

"We'll work on it." I laughed, and he playfully smothered it with his hand. I snipped at the pads of his fingers until he released me with a kiss.

"You're mine, you little savage."

"Little?" I stretched out beneath him.

He huffed. "We're getting out my tape measure tomorrow to settle this once and for all about who's taller."

"Tomorrow?" I raised my brow in question. "Why not right now?"

I stirred, meaning to get up, but he trapped me. "No. Tonight, you're not leaving this bed."

Then he sucked on my neck. And, yeah, okay. Tomorrow.

Twenty-Nine

Two whole months had come and gone. October and November had brought shorter days and grayer skies. Fatima had transitioned into my managerial position, and while I'd still worked at the shop, the shifts were fewer and farther between as I prepared for school in January. I was able to transfer my credits to Villanova University, where I'd be commuting for the next year and a half. After that, I'd see about graduate programs, but for now I was content to train the new sales consultants and spend as much time as I could with Zack before my semester started.

I had called Tyler every day for the first week after the canceled wedding. The second week it fell to every other day, the third week even fewer, and since the beginning of this month, it'd been one text once a week.

I'd come to accept he might never respond, but I had to try. He had to know I would never stop being his friend. The more Zack had learned of my history with Tyler and how close our families were, the more he'd softened on his dislike of him. Although he still said I was too harsh on myself by taking all the blame. On more than one occasion, he'd made it clear

Tyler had apologies to make, too. Relationships, he reminded me, were two-way streets.

It's why on the last day of November, I gasped at an incoming text. **Hey. Want to meet up?**

My fingers were so shaky, it took me multiple times to get the one word reply typed out. **Brunch?**

How about Starbucks? he responded, and the slight was obvious. We had never gone to Starbucks. Neither one of us liked big chain places, especially being from a small-town. We only ever went to Mom and Pop shops. Starbucks was impersonal.

I supposed it fit us now.

Ok. Tomorrow? I typed.

Noon, he said

And that was it.

I proceeded to open all the window's in Zack's trailer—our trailer. We had decided—since he owned it outright—I should move into it with him and save my rent money. It was much smaller than I was used to, but with our combined savings we would be able to put a down payment on the land to build our log cabin soon. A small price to pay, I thought, for the man and house of my dreams.

But with how my anxiety had me sweating, I needed more windows than we currently had now. I ended up on the steps outside, airing out my sweater, as Zack pulled up. He tilted his head to the side in question as he hopped out of his truck. All I had to do was show him the text messages for him to understand.

"I'm freaking out," I said, and he kissed my forehead before tugging me inside and shutting the door.

"I know, but you're letting a lot of cold air in."

"Don't be rational with me right now."

He stifled a smile with his bottom lip between his teeth as

he hung up his coat and tossed his keys and wallet on the counter next to Bambi, our thriving succulent.

"My best friend who broke up with me wants to talk. I can't worry about things like heating and air conditioning."

With an amused shake of his head, he towed me to one of the chairs in the living room and sat me on his lap. "Try not to get so worked up about it."

"How can I not?"

"Because you stressing about it won't change the outcome."

"I don't even know what the outcome will be, which is why I'm stressing."

He played with the tips of my middle and ring fingers. "You two need to talk, and I know it's scary, but you'll be fine. It's not going to be any worse than it is right now, right?"

I nodded, my eyes off in the distance.

He tucked a loose strand of hair from my braid behind my ear. "Do you want me to come with you?"

"No." I swiveled my head to him, changing my mind. "Yes. Is that awkward?"

"No."

I scratched at the O in Olsen on his work shirt. "It'll be like you're my chaperone."

He stilled my finger and kissed it, drawing my attention up to him. "If you want me to come, I will. We'll run toward the roar together, remember?"

When I nodded, he tucked my head under his chin. "That's my girl."

Then he kept me occupied for the rest of the night with more kisses and a short break for pizza. I tried not to watch the clock, a countdown until I met with the lion.

We arrived at Starbucks early, and I bought a drink for myself and Tyler then found a seat by the window. Zack lounged in a chair at the other end, busying himself with a magazine someone else had left, but by the time Tyler arrived, I had myself worked up into a ball of nerves so as soon as I saw him, my lips trembled with unshed tears.

He wore a long pea coat and new glasses. They had rounder edges, different than the sharp rectangular ones I'd been used to. He'd also gotten a haircut. When he removed his droopy wool cap, his curls were short and only on the top of his head, the sides faded. He looked really handsome.

"Hi." I stood with his coffee in my hand. "Cream, two sugars."

He took it, careful not to touch my fingers, and when he sat, one tear fell before I could stop it.

"Don't cry," he said, a little perturbed. "You know I hate it."

"I know." I dabbed at my eyes with a napkin.

Tyler's gaze worked over me. "You cut your hair."

"So did you."

"Makes you look older," he noted. "Not like the forest fairy I'm used to."

"Yours makes you look younger."

"I feel one hundred." As if to demonstrate, he rubbed the back of his neck before cracking it.

A long silence descended, and I didn't know what to say. We'd never had this tongue-tied tension between us before.

"Are you still traveling a lot?" I tried.

"Yep." He sipped his coffee. He had planned to stop, but that was *before*. His focus lazily drifted to the side, catching on something—someone—who made him sit up. "You're with him then?"

I didn't need to follow his glare to know who he referred to. "Yes," I said, more confident about that than about anything else in my life. "I love him. We're looking for contractors to build a house."

Tyler fiddled with his glasses, his eyes downcast. "That's good."

But his voice was flat and devoid of emotion. I couldn't stand it. "I'm sorry. You have to know that. I'm so, *so* sorry."

He nodded and scooted his coffee away.

I did the same. I hadn't even taken a sip of mine. I couldn't with the way my stomach flip-flopped.

I cleared my throat. "I heard you went to Costa Rica."

"Yeah," he said, gaze still down. "At first I felt like a fool, staying in a honeymoon suite on the water by myself, but after the first couple of days I didn't mind. Pretty nice, actually." His honey brown eyes met mine. "I'd never really been alone by myself before. No one to talk to, only me and my thoughts."

My insides unraveled and recoiled like a yo-yo. I knew everything about him, and yet nothing at all. "Yeah. You were never big on isolation. Always needed something or someone."

He brought his hands up, one covering the other in a fist. "Exactly." He shrugged. "I guess that's one positive."

More silence.

"How're your parents?" he asked.

"You know them. Dad's back at school, complaining about kids on their cell phones." I forced a smile. "Mom's hired more workers since I'll be leaving the store."

That caught him off guard. "Really?"

"I'm going to Villanova to finish up my degree."

"That's..." The first hint of a smile graced his face. "That's great to hear, Till. I'm proud of you."

My heart buoyed. "Thank you."

More silence.

"It's weird, huh?" I started, tugging at the ends of my hair. "We know each other so well, and playing catch up is strange. It's all, yeah, *I* know, or yeah, *you* know."

"I know," he said, and we both smiled, but his quickly

dropped. "But it's different now. What happened... I don't know if it'll ever be the same."

I swallowed past the sandpaper of my throat. "I don't know what else to say besides I'm sorry."

"You've said it enough." He shook his head. "I'm sorry, too. When you were saying all those things about how I had treated you..." He wiped his palm over his mouth, nodding to himself before he continued. "You were right, and I did take advantage of our friendship. I was really, really angry at you. I think I still am, but you have a right to be angry with me. I took you for granted, and I am sorry for that."

I couldn't speak through my tears.

"I, uh..." He scratched his eyebrow with his thumb. "I talked to Sarah a couple weeks ago, and she said she'd been having doubts for a while. What you did was—" he briefly met my eyes "—hurtful, but Sarah calling it off wasn't your fault. You were right. She does jump into things too quickly, and I was too blinded by her..." He held his hands up, gesturing for the right word.

"Her shine?"

"Yeah." He took his glasses off and wiped at his face, the telltale sign of exhaustion. I hoped it wasn't this conversation that made him so tired. Although, the other option—being tired from the whole of his life—didn't make me feel any better either.

"You're a Libra. You like shiny things," I said, hoping to earn a laugh.

I did.

"I did want it to work out for you, Tyler," I told him. "That day, when we were in your apartment, and you were describing how much you loved her and didn't want to waste any more time without her because you had already missed out on jokes and smiles and ugly Christmas sweaters, that struck a chord in me. I'm sorry I ever wished you wouldn't have it all because I didn't."

He clucked his tongue and inclined his chin over me. "You have it with him?"

"You can say his name, you know. Zack."

He rolled his eyes. "You have it with Zack?"

"Yes, I do, and I hope one day, you can forgive me and get to know him. The real him." I smiled even as I wiped wet cheeks. "The real me too."

Behind his glasses, his eyes watered, and he stared at the wall. "I don't know how to make it better between you and me."

"Me either."

"It might never be," he said, his voice cracking, and I nodded. I had already accepted that.

"But I would like to try." I said, my own voice like it had gone through a shredder. "You're a part of me."

He licked his lips and cleared his throat after a sniffle. Then he turned back to me to say, "I know. Crazy love."

He smudged a tear on my cheek with his thumb and rested his hand over mine on the table. An unspoken conversation had with only smiles.

I love you.

I love you too.

I sensed his presence behind me as Tyler leaned back in his chair, removing his hand from mine. Zack gave my shoulder a squeeze. "Everything okay?"

I nodded, crumbling my wet napkin in my hand.

Tyler assessed him for a long time before finally saying, "I hope you like Van Morrison."

I heard the grin in Zack's voice. "*Moondance* is all right."

"All right?" I rolled my eyes. "Just all right?"

Tyler reluctantly smiled at the two of us.

"I'm glad you agreed to meet up," I said.

"Yeah." He skated his coffee back in front of him.

I scratched at my nose. "I hope...we can do it again."

"Me, too," he said tightly, and I stood up, knowing this was as far as we would go today. I would have to accept it as enough for now.

"Bye, Tyler."

"Bye, Tilly."

When he didn't stand, only offering a wave instead of a hug, my stomach dropped a little, but Zack was there to catch me. He nodded an acknowledgement to Tyler then laced his fingers with mine, kissing the back of my hand as he led me out of the door, into the chilly fall air.

"I love you," he said. "Forever."

I closed my eyes, remembering the words which had gotten me through the dark moments these past few weeks.

The sun will always rise and you will always be loved.

Epilogue

A YEAR AND A HALF LATER...

"I'm hungry," I whined, traipsing down the terminal toward our gate at the Philadelphia Airport.

"Hungry?" Zack checked the time on his cell phone. "We ate before we left."

"Yeah, but you know I'm a stress eater, and I'm stressed about the flight."

"Yeah, and if you eat, you'll get that pain in your stomach, and you'll be miserable the whole time."

He was right, but I was nervous about flying to Ireland again. Nervous excited. Not nervous anxious.

My parents, along with some help from my aunts and uncles, had graciously gifted me the trip for my graduation present. With Olsen Heating & Plumbing expanding, Zack had taken on a managerial position, and the construction on our house was almost complete. We had a lot to celebrate.

Michelle's was doing great, Dad was set to retire next year, and I was starting grad school in the fall. Ahead of us, Zack and I had ten days on the Emerald Isle. I couldn't wait.

"Just a snack." I motioned to the gift shop on the corner. "I need something salty."

He grinned lasciviously over at me. "I got something salty for ya."

I refused to give in to a laugh. "Don't be gross."

He tossed his arm over my shoulders, guiding me to the snacks. "You love me."

I browsed the food selection and snagged a bag of pretzels and a cheese stick before eyeing the books and magazines.

Zack held up a sweatshirt with the Philly Phanatic on it. "Who would see this at an airport and think I need to buy it?"

"I don't know, but that reminds me, I promised Tyler I'd bring back Jameson. Can I pack it in my suitcase?"

He hung the sweatshirt back on the rack. "You know you can get Jameson here, right?"

"Yeah, but it's better from there."

He eyed me. "Is it?"

I shrugged. "It's right from the source. I'd assume so."

He grabbed a bag of gummy bears and a big bottle of water. "But he won't know. We could buy a bottle here when we get back and call it a day."

"I promised him." I poked my boyfriend's side, and he acquiesced with a kiss to my temple.

My friendship with Tyler had never fully mended to what it was before, but I thought this patched up version might have been better. I'd learned to appreciate Tyler as my sibling and playmate. The bond we shared was too strong to throw away, but we really didn't *need* each other anymore.

After paying for our snacks, we ambled to our gate, and I unscrewed the cap of the water, spilling it on myself. I grumbled and handed Zack the bottle to rummage through his backpack. "You have tissues or something in here?"

"I think so. In the front pocket," he said, and I unzipped it, sticking my hand in. "Oh, shit. No, wait," he nearly shouted and seized my arm, but it was too late.

My jaw dropped to the floor as I withdrew the small box.

His face flushed. "I didn't mean...I...that was..."

I gawked at the velvet jewelry case in the palm of my hand. "Is this...?"

He took it from me, turning it over between his fingers, a low chuckle escaping as his normally cool demeanor returned. "Nothing with you is ever as it's supposed to be." His ocean eyes met mine, and he grinned. "I meant to do this after we found an old castle at the foot of a cliff overlooking the water."

"Do what?" I asked unnecessarily.

He skimmed his fingertips down my cheek then sunk down on one knee in front of me. People around us murmured and giggled in delight.

"Tilly, I can't wait to marry you. Not because it will be any different than it's been, but because it'll be more of the perfect, content, and safe life we've built together. I want you and your kisses and your hair that won't stay in place and your knowing, wild eyes and your history lessons and your insistence that you're taller than me."

"But I am."

He opened the box, revealing an intricately woven band of gold around a small ruby. "It's vintage. Reminded me of you."

I pressed my hand to my mouth. "It's gorgeous."

"*Mo ghrá thú*," he said flawlessly, and I threw my head back to laugh.

"You've been practicing."

He held my left hand, placing the ring above my fingertip. "I want all your yesterdays and tomorrows. You're already mine, my heart, my love, so will you marry me?"

"Yes," I cried, and he slid the ring on my finger to a smattering of applause. He lifted me up off the chair, spinning me in a circle, both of us glowing. We kissed and laughed and kissed some more, in our perfect, content, and safe life. I couldn't wait to call him my husband, but, yeah, he'd been mine for a long time.

I'd secretly made plans to elope in Ireland ages ago. I already had the castle on the edge of the cliff overlooking the water picked out.

And that was the truth.

Acknowledgments

Indie publishing is a wild ride. Thank you, reader, for coming along with me.

I wouldn't have published this book if not for the the encouragement of the diamond dogs of writing. Otherwise, it would still be languishing on my computer and collecting digital dust. I'd also like to thank Despina Karras for being an authenticity reader and for being one of the first people to tell me this story was special. Thanks to my original beta reads: Laura Adams, Esher Hogan, and J.R. Yates. Big shout out to my ARC team and those wonderful readers who DM or text me their thoughts on my books while reading. It never fails to pick me up.

If you'd like more information about me, you can find it at https://sophieandrewsauthor.com/

About the Author

Sophie Andrews is a contemporary romance author who writes steamy books that will leave you smiling. As a millennial, she's obsessed with boybands, late 90s rom-coms, and will always be team Pacey. When she's not writing, she's most likely trying to wrangle her children or drinking red wine. Or both at the same time.

Also by Sophie Andrews

Tangled Series

Tangled Up

Tangled Want

Tanged Hearts

Tangled Beginning

Tangled Expectations

Tangled Chances

Tangled Ambition

Stand-Alones

How to Ruin a Wedding

Love at a Funeral and Other Awkward Conversations

Made in United States
North Haven, CT
29 August 2023

40880219R00174